# Abducted

## Mihwa Lee

Copyright © 2024 by Mihwa Lee

All rights reserved.

No part of this publication may be reproduced, distributed, or transmitted in any form or by any means, including photocopying, recording, or other electronic or mechanical methods, without the prior written permission of the publisher, except as permitted by Canadian and U.S. copyright law. For permission requests, contact mihwawrites@gmail.com.

The story, all names, characters, and incidents portrayed in this production are fictitious. No identification with actual persons (living or deceased), places, buildings, and products is intended or should be inferred.

1st edition 2024.

No portion of this book may be reproduced in any form without written permission from the publisher or author, except as permitted by Canadian and U.S. copyright law.

# Contents

Trigger Warning — v

1. Day One: 1 March 1833 - seven in the evening — 1
2. Day One: 1 March 1833 - nine in the evening — 8
3. Day Two: 2 March 1833 – Past midnight — 13
4. Day Two: 2 March 1833 - one in the morning — 19
5. Day Two: 2 March 1833 - two in the morning — 30
6. Day Two: 2 March 1833 – three in the morning — 36
7. Day Two: 2 March 1833 - Noon — 45
8. Day Two: 2 March 1833 – half past noon — 49
9. Day Three: 3 March 1833 – one in the morning — 57
10. Day Three: 3 March 1833 - four in the morning — 61
11. Day: 3 March 1833 – five in the morning — 66
12. Day Three - 3 March 1833 – six in the morning — 70
13. Day Three - 3 March 1833 – half past seven in the morning — 74
14. 3 March 1833 – five in the evening — 79
15. 6 March 1833 – seven in the morning — 86

| | | |
|---|---|---|
| 16. | 8 March 1833 – six in the morning | 98 |
| 17. | 8 March 1833 – eleven in the evening | 106 |
| 18. | 9 March 1833 – seven in the morning | 113 |
| 19. | 9 March 1833 – quarter of one in the afternoon | 124 |
| 20. | 9 March 1833 – ten in the evening | 133 |
| 21. | 10 March 1833 – two in the morning | 138 |
| 22. | 10 March 1833 – seven in the morning | 141 |
| 23. | 10 March 1833 – four in the afternoon | 152 |
| 24. | 11 March 1833 – past midnight | 156 |
| 25. | 11 March 1833 – two in the morning | 163 |
| 26. | 11 March 1833 – nine in the morning | 173 |
| 27. | 11 March 1833 – ten in the evening | 181 |
| 28. | 12 March 1833 – ten in the morning | 184 |
| 29. | 17 March 1833 – six in the evening | 186 |
| 30. | 20 March 1833 – three in the afternoon | 192 |
| 31. | 29 March 1833 – nine in the evening | 195 |
| 32. | 1 April 1833 – half past six in the evening | 198 |
| 33. | 2 April 1833 – eight in the morning | 207 |
| 34. | 3 April 1833 – quarter of eleven in the morning | 217 |
| 35. | 6 April 1833 – midnight | 224 |
| 36. | 7 April 1833 – half of ten in the morning | 231 |
| Epilogue | | 238 |
| More Spicy Stories by Mihwa Lee | | 244 |

# Trigger Warning

Abduction (off page), voyeurism (light on page), forced intimacy (light on page, consensual), violence (light on page), mature content, explicit language

Steam level – 8

# Chapter One

# Day One: 1 March 1833 – seven in the evening

Having a manure sack over her head was like being plunged into the bowels of a donkey. At least that's how Elara imagined it would be while she squinted desperately for a hint of light. She had been tossed into a room by the blackguards who had carried her like a sack of dirt. Using her bound hands behind her back for support, she scooted on her backside towards the sound of fire crackling. She welcomed the heat and the smell of burning wood to cut through the stink of the sack. Grimacing at the raw pain on her ankles, she leaned against the warm wall near the fire.

"Hahh... Hahh... Hahh..." Elara could not stop the shallow breaths despite sharp fibres filling her mouth and smothering her lungs. The sound of her panting echoed in her ears as she tried again to see through the burlap. The flame must be bright, but she saw naught.

Elara shook and scraped her head against the wall but failed to get the sack off. A tight knot kept it secure, and the coarse rope grazed against the tender skin under her chin.

She ought never to have ventured unchaperoned to the music hall in the dodgy quarter of London. Due to her foolishness, she was missing the welcome celebration for the king and queen of Bavaria at the Acton Manor. Instead of dancing in her new gowns, she was awaiting a fate of absolute ruination and slaughter.

Hot tears soaked into the burlap as she pondered her fate, with the scent of manure filling her nostrils. If only she could rip the stifling sack from her head, she might find some means of escape. Elara strained against the chains, attempting to slip her small hands through the manacles.

The door burst open, jolting her from her effort. She heard a thud and a man's grunt as something slammed onto the floor. The fast thump of boots receded after the door banged closed, and the entire room seemed to shake.

"Look me in the eye, you cowards!" The man's deep voice echoed in the room.

Another crash and another rattle followed. Was he throwing himself at the door? The darkness of not knowing carved a sour pit in her stomach. After one final crash against the door that shook the very walls, silence ensued. Then stumbling footsteps and... She screamed as a large and heavy body landed on top of her, throwing her off-balance. The man quickly rolled away. Elara toppled over sideways, helpless to break her fall.

"What the devil?" The man's baritone boomed.

Elara screamed, her breath coming in short, ragged spurts. Though all signs indicated he was a fellow captive, her terror only escalated at being locked in a room with an unknown man. Panic clawed at her chest, squeezing the very air from her lungs.

"S-stay away! Do not touch me!"

Screaming, Elara strained and used her hands and the wall behind her to sit up.

"Cease your shrieking, woman!" the man barked, as if her cries were unfounded. "Your wailing is intolerable atop the headache I'm suffering! I couldn't tup you even if I wished!"

His manner of speaking might have appalled her before, but she hardly noticed now.

"I shall swoon. I cannot draw breath," she choked out. The sack's knot dug cruelly into her throat, tightening with each panicked word. "I beseech you. Lift this wretched sack."

The man sighed impatiently but surprised her with a gentler, cultured tone. "My hands are bound as steadfast as a curing ham. I've a foul bag over my own head and itching fierce as the devil. I'm as helpless here as you are."

Elara detected a polished accent underneath his street cadence, but this was not the time to dwell on superficialities.

"Then we are both at their mercy," she choked out despairingly. "Do you know who has done this to us?"

"Not a bleedin' clue," he muttered. "I reckon we'll find out soon enough."

Who was this disreputable man? Gentlemen never uttered such vulgarities in front of delicately bred ladies. The thought flung her into panic once more.

"I shall faint dead away if you do not remove this accursed sack at once!" Elara cried shrilly.

"What did I say about that banshee wailing?" the man grumbled with a sigh. "It is nerves, not cloth, choking that neck of yours." He then muttered under his breath, "Heaven help me. I'm trapped here with a hysterical chit."

At this callous dismissal of her distress, hot rage momentarily stalled Elara's frenzy. "You reprehensible brute! I pray to heaven that I don't kill you myself before we escape this nightmare! Without a doubt, you are the most vexing, callous, rude scoundrel I have ever had the misfortune to meet!"

Frustrated tears poured forth anew, though she thought herself drained dry. The stale air beneath the sack grew hot and moist.

After some minutes, the man exhaled heavily. "Forgive me," he rumbled, his tone gentling. "This is my fourth kidnapping. I sometimes forget such things are more than a trifling annoyance to some folk."

"Fourth?" Elara blurted out incredulously, her suffocation briefly forgotten. "Is this some fool's prank at your expense, where I am but accidental collateral?" She inhaled the musty scent of old straw as she shook her head in bafflement. "What manner of man is abducted four times and speaks so casually of it?"

"A man who has escaped kidnappers thrice and irate husbands too oft to count," he replied casually. "And that is where my skills shall prove handy. I know the layout of these cottages built for stuffy fools swimming in lard. I can tell by the quality and design of the wood. That's a mighty sturdy door I've no chance of busting down."

Elara gasped in disbelief that he had escaped his captors thrice. And she was trapped with a man who shamelessly admitted being a rogue. Was this a blessing or a curse? Only time would tell.

"Then this whole sorry mess could be entirely your fault," she said.

"Now, now, let us not cast blame before we're acquainted," he replied. "I think we have not met before, seeing as you're a lady. Unless you frequent gambling dens or brothels?"

Amusement coloured his tone. She could not help but huff a laugh despite the shock of his ludicrous suggestion. She had to admit his teasing had created a welcome distraction, if only briefly.

"Certainly not! You, sir, are incorrigible." Her voice came out hoarse, her throat raw from screaming.

"Perhaps we've been intimate. Could this be retaliation from a jealous husband, betrothed, or a scorned beau?"

Mortification and indignation heated Elara's face despite his obvious attempt to fluster her. She realised then it was not his words that had warmed her. However cheeky his meaning, his voice had cascaded over her from head to toe in a hypnotic baritone rhythm. She was both soothed by its calming ripples and unnerved by its appeal.

"H-how could you propose such an indecent suggestion to a lady? I am utterly unattached."

"So, you and I have never been intimate?" he persisted, a grin evident in his tone.

She supposed there was a modicum of decency in him for swallowing the chuckle lodged in his throat.

"I assure you we have never met! I would remember an exasperating man like you."

He shuffled closer, only the clink of chains ruining the brief silence. Elara started and drew her knees into her chest. After some moments, he thudded down before her with a rattle of iron. Though muffled by the sacks between them, the melodious baritone washed over her frayed nerves, draining all thoughts.

"Are you certain the sack needs to come off just yet? You've managed admirably thus far," he said gently.

His velvety timbre reverberated along her skin, which caused goose flesh. Elara shivered at his nearness and shut her eyes. How was it that the words exchanged between them felt more intimate than if they had been staring into each other's eyes?

"I... suppose not," she conceded as her breathing hitched.

"There's a good girl," he murmured in that low tone of his.

Annoyance snapped her eyes open and straightened her spine. "You take shocking liberties, sir! I am not your girl!"

"Well..." His voice was smoky now and lingered in the air, causing a seesaw in Elara's stomach. "As you depend on me for survival, you shall be whatever I wish you to be, darling."

One minute his voice offered nothing but solace, the next his words threw her into a fit of exasperation.

Elara bristled. "You presume too much. I insist you address me properly!"

# ABDUCTED

The man chuckled low, both thawing and torching her temper. "This is no gilded palace for spoiled debutantes. No one gives a whit about your lofty station now. Unless you can take a blow or kill a man, you've more need of me than I have of you." His blunt words brooked no argument. "Now, are your hands bound in front or back?"

"Clearly at the back, else I'd have no need of your assistance," she said testily.

"I meant no offence. I could not measure your obtuseness while you were squawking, fit to wake the dead."

"Why you, you reprehensible scoundrel!"

"A fair point," he agreed, skilfully placating her. When only her breathing filled the silence, he said, "Come now, let us have a truce. We must work together if we're to escape this accursed place. What say you?"

Elara weighed her options before grunting in grudging agreement. Insufferable he may be, but the man was right. For now, he was her only hope. She must swallow her pride and cooperate whether she be his lass or lady.

"Good," he said cheerfully when she didn't object. "Seems we're in the same fix. I take it your feet are chained too. Can you see anything?"

"No, it is utter darkness."

"Nor can I. Tell me, what events led to your capture?"

"I was set upon returning home from a theatre performance."

"Are you an actress?"

"No. I was a spectator."

"Judging by your speech, I'd say you're not a common wench."

Elara hesitated, wondering how much to reveal. "I had snuck out of my home to watch an afternoon performance. I was on my way to get a hackney when... You know what happened."

"And where were your companions when these blackguards came upon you?"

"I was alone. My maid had gone home to visit her mother."

"That is a coincidence," he murmured. "You ventured to the theatre unchaperoned?" he asked, a note of censure entering his tone.

"I did." Her tone was too timid and sheepish for her liking.

"No need to feel ashamed. I'm not your father," he assured her. "Now, where was this den of iniquity located?"

"Bankside," she mumbled.

He gave a low whistle and said, "Blimey, you are a brazen hussy, aren't you?"

"No! I only—"

"As I said, not your father. What name do you go by?"

"Why ever do you ask for my name?"

"I don't ask out of idle curiosity. I ask only to discern if there is a link between us."

"I see." She hesitated, unsure if she should entrust this stranger with her identity. "Perhaps you might tell me your name first, sir?"

She heard the metallic slither of chains as he shifted position.

"You've no need to fret. I'm no kidnapper, nor a wicked man," he assured, reading her thoughts. "I may make a rotten son and worse beau, but I'll prove to be a fine jailbreak accomplice."

Elara pondered her hesitation and reminded herself her captors already knew her identity. "I am Lady Elara Frances. My father is the Earl of Stamford."

"Deuce take it! Stamford's daughter? They've hooked quite the prize!" He paused before asking, "Any chance they mistook your identity? You're wearing a woollen dress of cheap quality. I assume that was for a disguise."

She was surprised by his astute observation. "I think not. They called me by name before seizing me."

"What name did they call you?"

"Lady Elara Frances."

"That leaves no doubt, then. Have you enemies perchance? Or your father?"

"I don't know. My family shares little of such matters with me."

"The daughter of a wealthy earl, free as a bird without protection..." he tsked.

"Father has been ill of late, and as I am not an heir, I suppose such precautions were deemed unnecessary."

The man scoffed. "Foolish notion. The value of the ransom coins remains the same, regardless. I wonder if they've issued their demands yet... though that still doesn't explain why I was ensnared in this plot."

Elara knew her curiosity would be considered distasteful, but whose judgment was she afraid of?

"I take it fortune has not been overly kind to you, then?"

"I'm but a humble solicitor and barrister, which has earned me a few enemies amongst the privileged sorts," he replied with a hint of pride in his tone.

Elara's stomach sank in disappointment. He was not a man of physical strength or an experienced brawler, then. His weapon of choice was words not fists. He would stand no chance against the brutes who had carried her.

She gathered her nerves and asked, "How have you earned the wrath of the privileged?"

"I make a habit of defending the poor and prosecuting the wealthy and wicked. As you can imagine, it breeds considerable resentment."

"Could one of those privileged foes be behind this, then?"

"Mayhap, though I suspect jealousy was the true motivator. I confess I am overly blessed with intelligence and charm, beyond what lesser men can endure."

Elara rolled her eyes impatiently underneath the sack. She found boastful men tiresome as they often did not live up to their arrogance.

She heard the grin in his voice as he continued, "Having said that, Mrs Smythe at the market is forever rapping my knuckles, worried I might bruise her fruits and vegetables. But in truth, the list of those wishing me harm is endless. I've not the faintest idea which blackguard we face this time."

"I begin to comprehend their grievances. Having just met you, even I feel inclined to stuff you in a sack of manure."

His rich laughter filled the space between them, surprising and delighting her.

"Come now, my lady. Cease your attempts at seduction," he teased, mirth still warm in his voice and draping over her like honey.

## Chapter Two

# Day One: 1 March 1833 – nine in the evening

This evening was turning out to be more enjoyable than Preston had expected. As far as being a captive, it was splendid to be imprisoned with a lady who was both entertaining and radiated a delicate fragrance.

The sack over his head reeked of earth and faint manure, but he caught a whiff of something citrus when she moved, a faint scent of mint and orange. It was a bastion of civility, a welcome respite. From experience, he knew such reminders were crucial for maintaining one's sanity. He didn't know how long they would depend on their captors' hospitality after all.

After Lady Elara stopped crying, she was proving to be sharp and witty beneath her gentle breeding. Her laughter was like the tinkling of fine crystal on a summer day. He sensed she was a tender but tenacious soul. Being a scoundrel, he took amusement in listening to her flustered responses to his lewd remarks.

"Mister! Have you no shame?" Lady Elara exclaimed in response to his suggestion that she was seducing him.

"None whatsoever. Whose scorn should I fear out here?" he replied blithely.

"It seems we shall never agree. Let us focus our energies on escaping this dreadful place."

The determination in the lady's voice made him smile. He had been attempting to distract her from the horrors of the situation, but it seemed he may benefit from her courage as well.

"Your gallantry is admirable, my lady. However, escape is quite impossible now. We are on the fourth floor, surrounded by open fields. There appears to be no viable egress through the window, even if I could remove the planks and bars. Five men guard us, two at the door and three below, armed with pistols, rifles, and knives. And we are at least a few days' ride from London."

Her muffled gasp was followed by a light cough. "Could that be true? It felt scarcely an hour had passed since I was taken."

"They likely administered a sleeping draught of some kind," he deduced thoughtfully.

"Heavens... Did they render you unconscious as well?"

"Aye, though they had not used sufficient dosage in my case."

"However did you determine all else?"

"Just attentiveness to sundry details," he replied modestly.

"But how could you identify their weapons?"

"I smelled the gunpowder and recognised the sounds of cleaning pistols, having cleaned them too numerous times to count. Getting walloped with a knife handle also helped me distinguish them." He hesitated before adding lightly, "It would be most helpful if you could charm one of the louts into relinquishing a pistol."

"I... I cannot imagine how I would manage such a thing." Her voice emerged strained and hurried, like a sparrow fluttering in alarm.

"Hm, am I truly trapped with the sole English female unversed in the womanly arts?" he asked with humour and challenge in his voice.

It would simplify matters if she were *une femme fatale* who could seduce and distract the villains. She was not Lady Hertford, to be sure. It was unfortunate for more reasons than one.

"I have not been out in society much lately," she said, as if that explained her reluctance to charm a fiend.

"Are ladies taught how to seduce blackguards into surrendering their weapons in society?"

His pretended bemusement brought about a pretty chuckle from her. Her sweet voice soothed his tightly coiled nerves. Upon her shifting, he closed his eyes and breathed in her scent.

Her soft voice asked tentatively, "Will you tell me your name now?"

Preston hesitated. He could give her one of his two aliases. She'd be none the wiser. But something about this woman and their shared fate demanded honesty and honour.

"Preston at your service," he said.

"Mr Preston, barrister and solicitor," she repeated slowly as if committing to her memory. He quickly guided the conversation away from himself.

"How many rogues accosted you?"

"Three, I think."

"Did you note anything particular about them?"

"All had the Yorkshire burr. I could not grasp their full meaning."

"Were they violent with you?" he asked delicately, concern tingeing his voice.

"No. No more than tying me up and throwing me onto a carriage."

Preston exhaled in relief. At that moment, heavy bootfalls outside interrupted their hushed conversation.

"That's a fair number of guards for just us two," he murmured. He held his breath, listening intently until the footsteps faded into the distance.

"If I may ask, how were you taken, Mr Preston?" Lady Elara inquired politely once silence fell outside.

"I was ambushed outside the Inner Temple shortly after dusk."

"Were you able to glimpse any part of their faces?"

"Nay, the villains were masked... Did you catch sight of your captors?"

"I did not. They too had obscured their faces."

Preston sighed thoughtfully. "There is little we can do presently. But we shall seize an opportunity to escape."

"What conditions would be ideal for such an attempt?"

"I must procure a weapon of some kind. The leader ought to be on hand, so we've leverage for bartering. Also, there can't be too many louts lurking about, else we've no way to account for them all. I've no wish to be surprised."

After a pause, Lady Elara inquired softly, "How did you manage to escape your previous captures successfully?"

"Befriending my jailers helped considerably. They're but human too and inevitably revealed some weakness or lapse in due time. It takes time and patience."

At this statement, soft sniffles came from the woman. "I am sorry, Mr Preston." A faint quaver in her voice confirmed the fear churning inside her.

Preston deduced he had been sitting across from the lady. He turned and backed up against the wall as metal slithered alongside him. He shifted closer until his body nudged against her right side, his arm brushing hers. The slimness of her arm hinted at her dainty size, and the position of her shoulder suggested she was of average height.

He turned his head toward her voice, injecting as much kindness and confidence as he could muster. "I know you're frightened, but truthfully, this is an ideal situation if one is to be kidnapped."

"Ideal?" Lady Elara blurted. "How can being shackled and imprisoned with no escape be ideal?"

"Well for one, they've shown no particular tendency for violence thus far. And we were clearly targeted not randomly seized."

"And why is that promising?" Her bafflement was clear in her voice.

"It means this isn't some senseless, violent kidnapping. Having an objective suggests there's a leader at work. Organised criminals tend to be more careful about rash actions that could jeopardise the group. Unless they're Muns, of course."

"I'm afraid I am unfamiliar with these 'Muns'."

With disgust plain in his voice, Preston explained, "They're degenerate sons of aristocratic men who amuse themselves by accosting and debauching women. And anyone else they please."

"How perfectly horrid!"

"Aye, they're a despicable lot. My point is you've the good fortune to be trapped with an experienced escapee."

To his delight, the woman chuckled.

"I suppose it is better than being trapped with another helpless, frightened woman like myself."

He nudged her playfully with his arm. "Given the circumstances, you're comporting yourself remarkably well. You've stopped weeping, you're pleasant company, and you smell quite lovely."

Her ladyship laughed, and he felt the tension recede a little.

"Do you have a family who might be searching for you as we speak, Mr Preston?"

"Nay. I have no one. I'm hoping to benefit from your father's search for your whereabouts."

"I pray that he does. Your friends would wonder about you. Would they not?"

"My secretary might look for me and may alert the few friends I have, but they're also accustomed to my vanishing without forewarning."

"What circumstances have led you to disappear so?"

"I quite enjoy spending time in the woods to clear my head. It started with patrolling in the military."

As he shifted, Preston's knee accidentally brushed against the lady's over the thick fabric of her frock. She withdrew quickly as a cat pawing blindly would if met with a foreign creature. Preston estimated the woman had never been in such improper proximity to a man or spent so much time with one.

To sit sprawled thusly on the floor with a stranger and receive his flirtations was unthinkable in polite company. Judging by her voice and timid innocence, he bet his money she was barely out of finishing school.

They lapsed into tense silence as the rough and muted speech of men approached from outside. Preston felt the lady lean into his side. However improper, he was grateful to be a comfort to her. He was not as confident about survival as he had made it seem. Escape would be more difficult with a woman in voluminous skirts. But a false hope was kinder than the bleak reality.

It was unlikely this abduction was related to his past covert missions. He had lived a civilian life for seven years now. Hopefully, it was as simple as a jealous husband seeking revenge, and the woman was detained for a different reason. One matter was certain. Considerable wealth lurked behind this scheme, judging by the lavish accommodation.

Based on their Yorkshire dialect, Preston was relatively certain their captors were the Scuttlers, renowned for their violence in northern England. They were likely taking orders from the Muns or some wealthy individual.

The day he discovered who was behind this infernal plot would be the day Hades broke loose. He prayed he might save the woman from this dreadful predicament.

## Chapter Three

# Day Two: 2 March 1833 – Past midnight

Lady Elara's slender figure leaned against him, her head resting on his chest while she dosed. If he were free to do so, he would have held her and kissed her temple. As it was, not only his hands and feet, but his heart was bound.

The years of military service taught him what this overfamiliarity and affection was. The shared hardship, the trust they required from each other to survive, had bonded them beyond their imagination. This woman, so vulnerable without him, might easily mistake the bond to mean something other than human connection. But in her time of mental anguish, he couldn't bring himself to pull away. He would be what she needed him to be until she was safe again.

Their captors had not sought their company thus far, but Preston predicted it would not be long now. He strained to listen to the voices approaching closer from outside.

"*Der Anführer des Rudels ist endlich da,*" he murmured.

Lady Elara surprised him by asking softly, "What does that mean?"

"The leader of the pack has deigned to grace us with his presence," he said.

"How do you know?"

"By the tone of their voices, footsteps." Sensing her distress, he quickly distracted her with, "Do you speak any other language?"

"I spoke French with my governess growing up," she said as chains jangled, and her skirts rustled.

"*Vous vous souvenez encore?*"

"*Oui, je me souviens des bases. Ou avais vous appris le français?*"

"I lived in France for five years," he replied.

The lady was momentarily distracted by a set of heavy footfalls, followed by several lighter steps, approaching closer. She inhaled sharply next to him, pressing her body against his side.

"This is good. We may have some answers, finally," he said evenly.

He felt the woman turn toward him and nestle her head against him.

"All will be well, my lady," he whispered.

The key in the lock clanked noisily and the door burst open. Preston cradled her with his body in whatever way he could as she flinched at the abrupt assault on their senses. Multiple heavy boots and the fetid stench of unwashed bodies tromped through the doorway.

He inhaled slowly as his mind rapidly calculated the number of men. He approximated four men, including the leader. Lady Elara trembled against him but kept silent, placing her faith in him.

"Good day gentlemen. To what do we owe the honour?" Preston asked cheerily.

"I'll do the talkin' here. Thee keep thy trap shut," a rough voice growled back.

"Right," Preston drawled.

The man barked abruptly, "Thee's gotta get up the duff, lass. I need me a bairn!"

The full impact of the words did not register at first. Preston simply stared into the darkness, noticing only the icy chill spreading to every muscle in his body. Then the awful meaning sunk in, oozing through his mind like a poison that paralysed his very thoughts.

His eyes widened in disbelief as outrage and dismay warred within him. He opened his mouth, but the words died on his tongue. He sank back against the wall as if the devil's hand itself had plunged into his chest and stopped his heart. Finally, revulsion washed over him in waves as the appalling truth slowly crushed his soul.

"What did he say, Mr Preston?" the lady asked, her harsh breaths sawing through the rough-spun material. He yearned to take her away from this hellhole, but what could a blind and lame man do except urge death? His despair notwithstanding, his horror would be nothing compared to hers.

"I shall tell you in a moment, my lady. I need to clarify a few things first," Preston said softly. He was loath to distress her further until the ghastly edict was fully revealed.

As he had suspected, this abduction was not related to his past spy mission or legal affairs. He could not fathom why these scoundrels demanded such a heinous act. These were seasoned professionals not mere foot soldiers. Escape would prove difficult unless drastic measures were taken.

"Is that the only objective for this capture?" Preston's muscles were as taut as a bowstring, and his mind raced furiously.

"Aye, that be all," the gruff voice confirmed.

Preston adopted a perplexed tone. "Must it be this lady? I assure you I could charm a lady to volunteer."

"It got to be her," the man said impatiently. "Just get her bred quick. Soon as she's expectin', thee both can toddle off home."

Preston exhaled slowly, fists clenched. "And what happens if we fail to complete the deed?"

The lout grunted out, "Thee has to try for one year."

"Twelve whole months? Bloody hell!"

"Mr Preston, would you kindly apprise me of the situation?" Elara implored, her voice trembling. Rather than answer, he discreetly nudged her ankle with his toes to reassure her.

Adopting a cooperative tone, Preston asked, "If we succeed, can the lady go free?"

"Aye, quick as ye like."

"And what if we plain refuse your request?"

"Then we take her for ourselves, nice and slow," the blackguard sniggered.

Preston swallowed the bile in his throat. He vowed that this beast, more worthless than an incestuous dog, would die at his hand at the first opportunity.

"I must speak to the lady and explain," he said through gritted teeth.

"Get on with it, then!"

Preston pressed his body against Lady Elara and rested his knees over hers in an attempt to cocoon and soothe her. He then leaned close and whispered, "Do not fret, my lady. All will be well. I swear it."

"Yes," Lady Elara whispered shakily.

Speaking in a mellifluous baritone timbre, he began gently, "My lady, this will shock and appal you terribly, but we shall find a way through this trial together. This fiend demands that I... impregnate you before we may go free."

He omitted further details, judging she was nearing the limits of what her mind could endure. She was silent for a long moment.

"I d-do not understand," she said finally.

With a heavy heart, he said, "You grasp his vile meaning perfectly well. He aims to force a child between us."

As if in a daze, she mumbled, "This must be some monstrous jape. I have never heard more senseless words."

The villain spoke up impatiently. "No jest, lass. Thee heard true."

The lady's spine stiffened. With a small tremor, her voice rang out in breathless, frantic tones. "I refuse, utterly and completely. I shall not be forced so!"

The fiend leered. "I can take his place instead, girly."

"I could find another woman who would gladly volunteer," Preston offered once more.

"Nah, must be her."

"Why me? Why us? Do you know the reason behind this madness?" Lady Elara asked, urgency colouring her voice.

"Thee no need to know why." The fiend added impatiently, "Get crackin'. Now. The sooner thee does, the sooner thee both can bolt."

"We only just met! We need time to prepare," Preston insisted firmly.

The fiend considered before yielding. "Tomorrow, then. We'll be watchin' ye close to make sure it gets done."

Fury suffused Preston's insides as the lady whimpered and shook beside him. He tried to stand but was promptly pushed back down by one of the blackguards.

"Absolutely not. I will not allow it! Why the hell is that necessary?" he shouted hotly.

"'Cause we aims to see thee finish the job, and not slackin'," the villain chortled.

"No! I would rather perish!" Lady Elara cried wildly. "I cannot—"

Preston addressed her calmly. "Hush now. Let me do the talking."

As she muffled her sobs, he tried reasoning with their captor again.

"Release us and we shall make you a rich man."

The lout laughed mockingly. "No amount be enough. Lettin' thee go will have us killed."

"You can be on a ship before anyone finds out."

"A young one from here could get word to them in two or three hours. I'd be done for, I would."

Preston dropped his head, trying to think. "The lady shall be traumatised, as you can see. The condition needs to be right or we cannot perform properly."

The villain grunted reluctantly but Preston pressed his point. "Our sacks need to come off and hands and feet unshackled.

The man scoffed. "Can't be untyin' the wench. Your hands'll be free."

"We'd fare better with no cuffs. You've men guarding the doors. There's no escaping this place," Preston reasoned.

"Nah. I knows who ye are, guv. Your tricks won't work here."

"And who am I?"

"Ye're a spy."

"I was. Not for seven years now. How did you learn that about me?"

"Thee no need to know that."

"What else did you learn about me?"

"Naught."

Preston prayed that whoever orchestrated this did so without the knowledge of his real identity. If not, he and the lady might eventually pay with their lives.

"And your name?"

Preston doubted the leader would reveal his name. Hence, he was surprised when the lout replied, "Dauid."

"All right, Dauid. These blasted sacks must come off."

"Yours can be off when ye eats and when ye tumble with her," came the reply.

"The lady needs it off now, lest she swoons dead away," Preston insisted.

"When she conks out, we wakes her back up," Dauid sneered cruelly.

Nasty bastard, Preston thought darkly.

"We'll be needing hearty meals and drink," he said. There was a pause before the man replied, "Aye."

"And only you can stay. We will not cooperate if there are other blokes about."

"Can't be promisin' that. The other lads'll stay or leave as they fancy."

Suddenly, Lady Elara loosed a blood-curdling scream. She screamed until the room echoed with the shrill sound. Preston simply waited while other men barked orders and complaints.

"Allreet, allreet!" Dauid shouted over the din. "No one but meself! Now quit that horrible screechin'!"

## Chapter Four

# *Day Two: 2 March 1833 – one in the morning*

"I ought to have remained at home. Surely, this nightmare is a punishment for my recklessness," Lady Elara exclaimed after the louts quit the room.

Her head was still resting on Preston's chest. She had remained attached to him like a barnacle, using his body as a shield and armour since he first sat down beside her. She seemed to fear he might vanish and leave her to endure the terror alone if she detached herself from him.

"You have done nothing to merit such draconian treatment. It was but ill fortune that landed you in the villain's snare," Preston soothed.

She shook her head woefully. "There must be another way other than succumbing to their demands..." Her voice trailed off in despair.

"I shall closely observe the fiends tonight and tomorrow. Some chance of escape may yet present itself," he said.

He felt her raise her head. Soft flesh pressed against his arm. Preston closed his eyes and relished the contact with a silent moan. He imagined the softness must be her breasts, glorious breasts. He has not seen breasts for so bloody long unless he counted the bosom of his clients who nursed their babes. Hell... nipples... tits... he hasn't sucked on them for years. Years! What had he been doing that he couldn't find the time for tits?

His lustful thoughts were soon intercepted by the guilt of desiring a woman who relied on his protection. He wasn't desiring her exactly. He would have been happy with any woman who smelled fresh provided he remained blind. He really shouldn't lust after Lady Elara who was likely too young, too innocent, and the situation was entirely too inappropriate for him to covet her.

He cleared his throat and redirected his attention to his stomach. "If they don't feed me soon, I shall break out tonight."

Though his quip drew a faint chuckle, melancholy seemed to reclaim its grip on her. They sat in heavy silence until the sharp clank of the heavy door made her recoil as if struck.

"It is a lady delivering our meal," Preston said quietly. "The softer footfalls and the clank of earthenware tell me so."

She relaxed at his intonement, her body slackening against him. Light footsteps entered the room accompanied by a strong odour of meat. Lady Elara jumped against him at the harsh clatter of a tray crashing to the floor.

Unperturbed, Preston called in a friendly tone. "Pardon me, miss."

"What is it ye be wanting?" a woman's sharp voice replied.

"You hail from London too, I'd wager. Same as me," Preston remarked brightly with a stronger street cadence.

"Aye, lived there twenty years afore me scoundrel husband drank hisself to death on gin."

He clucked sympathetically. "You have my condolences, miss. My own father died just the same, crushed beneath wagon wheels."

"Aye, demon drink ruins all," the woman said darkly.

"Name's Preston. Might I ask yours, miss?"

"Martha."

"Martha, dear, would you be a love and free my hands?"

"Not me place to decide. Oi, Charlie!" the woman yelled towards the door and waited. She then bellowed at the approaching footsteps, "E needs 'is irons off!"

The man freed Preston's hands from behind his back and cuffed them in front. Preston gratefully stretched his neck and rolled his stiff shoulders.

"I shall stand and stretch my back, miss," he informed Martha before rising slowly.

"Ye great lump, he needs the sack off to eat, don't he!" Martha scolded the man.

Charlie protested nervously. "But then he'll see us plain!"

"Then fetch yer masks, ye gormless git!"

Preston listened to the footsteps retreat, then return. The man pulled off his sack and he took a deep, welcome breath. Running his palms over his face, he spied two figures wearing sacks over their heads standing before him, one a slight woman with an apron and the other a short, thin man.

Three men sat outside the door playing cards, each with a pistol and a knife. By the fireplace's ruddy light, Preston scanned the room quickly for anything of use. The room was bare except for a bed.

"You have my thanks, love."

Boldly, he raised Martha's wrinkled hand and brushed his lips softly against her cracked knuckles. She giggled, clearly delighted.

"A handsome one ye are," Martha remarked, her tone softening. "Why, back in me day, I'd have tumbled with ye right quick."

Sensing an advantage, he returned smoothly, "Help the lady escape, and we'll get our chance to lie together soon enough, darling." He winked roguishly.

Martha cackled, tapping his shoulder coquettishly before Charlie prodded her impatiently. As she turned to follow Charlie who was already out the door, Preston snatched her hand again, trailing teasing kisses up her arm and cheek. She giggled coyly before taking her leave and slamming the door shut behind her.

"Can you see, Mr Preston?" Lady Elara asked.

"Aye."

Preston surveyed the space more closely. An iron bed stood some ten feet away. Next to him, a slender figure sat on the floor, bound in shackles—his mysterious lady companion. His traitorous brain took notice of her round breasts, tiny waist, and the curvy bottom. She was petite but possessed a perfect hourglass figure. This somehow thrust him into a gloomy mood.

"*Womit habe ich diese süße Folter verdient?*" he mumbled under his breath.

"Is everything as you have predicted?"

"Yes, unfortunately," he grumbled before scrutinising the windows.

Tempting as it was to unmask the lady, more urgent matters pressed. Moving farther away from the door, Preston reached into his collar and removed a tiny metal hook, small enough to fit within the keyhole of the handcuffs. From his rolled-up shirtsleeve, he removed Martha's hairpin.

"Was that German you were speaking?" she asked.

Keeping his eyes on the door, he expertly freed his hands, then placed the hook into the keyhole.

"Aye."

He refastened the manacles on his wrists, creating an illusion they remained locked. He tucked the hairpin in the shirt collar.

"What caused you to learn German?" she asked.

"I grew up speaking it with my father."

"I see. And your mother?"

"English," Preston replied while examining the woman for injuries. He scowled at the sight of her bloody ankles, the silk stockings torn in places. He turned to the lady whose conversation he'd been relishing. "Might I adjust your sack, my lady?"

"Yes, please."

Preston knelt before her, feeling like an oversized ogre. He loosed the harsh knot at her slender throat, noticing the abrasions where the knot rubbed her tender skin. He observed the graceful arch of her neck and swore under his breath. His pulse raced at the sight of her skin, as smooth and flawless as cream. Though he forced himself to avert his gaze swiftly, Preston noted the alluring cleavage beneath her gown. Her proportions were perfect for fitting within his hands.

Dash it. If he were to die tonight, he'd like to die with his face buried between her mounds. He chided himself again for such roguish thoughts. Two years of celibacy had clearly corrupted his mind.

A part of him wished for her to remain just as she was in his mind's eye. But the roguish part of him longed to briefly remove her sack and satisfy his curiosity. He sighed and thought better of it. He needed to consume his meal before they returned and grew suspicious.

"Feeling better?" he asked.

"Yes. You have my gratitude, Mr Preston," came the muffled reply.

# ABDUCTED

Preston's eyes dropped to her ankles once more, and black fury surged in his core. He shuffled to the door and banged on it with his fist, shouting, "We need wine!"

Hearing only silence, he pounded again, adding loudly, "The lady is bleeding! Fetch me wine or spirit!"

A gruff voice barked, "What thee be wantin' then?"

"The swell wants his wine!" one of the guards replied to the gruff voice.

A masked man entered a few minutes later while muttering foul oaths under his breath. A bottle was irritably tossed to Preston before the door clanked shut.

As the lock turned, Preston called out, "Unchain the lady's feet! She's bleeding!"

"Not happenin'!" came the indifferent reply.

Ever persistent, Preston tried again. "And fetch me a glass for the wine, by Jove!"

"Drink straight from the bottle!" the unseen guard snapped.

"I'm a gentleman!" Preston replied indignantly.

"If that be your idea of a gentleman, then I am the bleedin' king!" came the muffled shout.

"Quit your endless bellyachin' afore I shut that gob of yours permanent!" another voice hollered.

Preston persisted loudly, demanding pillows and various comforts until Lady Elara anxiously whispered, "Do you have a death wish, sir?"

"Quite the opposite," he murmured back cryptically. At her puzzled silence, he explained, "I shall prove such an infernal nuisance, they will draw straws on who might enter to silence me. It shall give me more time for my true purpose."

"Which is what, precisely?"

Preston gave an enigmatic smile she could not see. "I've not worked out all the details yet. But it shall come to me."

Settling cross-legged on the floor, Preston drank the thin soup straight from the bowl. Soon the lock rattled loudly again, and a burly guard entered, thudding over to deposit a grimy glass. Before departing, he dealt Preston's temple a vicious smack that briefly blurred his vision. Blinking to clear it, Preston watched the door slam shut once more.

"Are you injured? What transpired just now?" Lady Elara asked, concern tingeing her soft voice.

"A mere trifle. Nothing I cannot endure. As intended, I succeeded in vexing them most thoroughly." He chuckled, though it made his head pound anew. "Straighten your legs if you will," he said as he scooted over to her feet with the wine bottle.

"Are you bleeding? You may tear some of my petticoat to bind it," she offered kindly while doing his bidding.

Preston paused as his thoughts wandered to what lay beneath her billowing skirts. On the morrow, they were expected to have intimate relations. The notion left him unbothered for himself. He was worldly enough. But for a gently bred lady, especially one innocent and untouched, it would prove to be a hellish ordeal. He prayed it would not leave permanent scars upon her soul.

The thought of being the instrument of her anguish churned his gut. There must be some way to spare her, though the blackguards seemed determined.

"Ah, most thoughtful of you," Preston replied hastily when he remembered she had asked him a question. "But I am all right. I should wrap your wounds so they don't worsen. I shall rip some strips if you are amenable."

"Yes, please."

Preston peeled back each layer until he found linen. Bending down, he easily tore two strips with his teeth and set them aside. Uncorking the bottle, he warned, "I'm going to pour some wine on your ankle wounds. It will sting."

"All right. Thank you."

"Where were you raised?" he asked to distract her while tending to her wound.

"Stamford. I have not been outside of the county other than London. You seem quite skilled at adopting various dialects," she remarked, flinching at the pain. "I confess I struggle to place your origin."

"In my work, I have travelled the breadth of the country many a time," he explained, wrapping her wound with the fabric.

"As a solicitor or a spy?"

"Both," he said, tying the two ends of the fabric. He then took large gulps of the wine.

"So, you've lived in France for five years, you were a spy, and you still had time to earn two degrees and work in two professions. Judging by your exploits, you must be forty or fifty."

Preston rubbed the stubble forming around his jaw. "I feel sixty at the moment."

"You must have been everywhere in the world."

"Aye, all over Europe, Africa, America, New South Wales."

"Oh my. I am envious."

"I thought you might be the daring sort despite your shy demeanour," he said.

"Is your name truly Preston?"

"Of course not. I wouldn't want you seeking my company when we're free," he teased.

The woman mumbled indignantly. "You are certainly no gentleman. That much is plain."

"I never claimed to be, darling. It is time to bother them anew," Preston said before he began pounding on the door with his stockinged feet. The bastards took all his possessions including his new boots. They'd steal his teeth too were he to become a corpse.

"Wha does thee want?" a man finally bellowed from outside the door.

"What is the date and time?"

"Thee's no need to know the date or the time!" the man bellowed.

"I am finished with my meal. When will the tray arrive for the lady?"

"It'll come when it comes! Pipe down lest I throttle thee!"

"It seems I am not the only one who finds you intolerable," the woman commented wryly.

"I'm delighted to see your fighting spirit return, sweetheart," he replied knowing she'd disapprove of the endearment.

She pushed her shoulders back in a battle pose when soft footsteps approached again. Martha entered the room, bringing strong floral fragrance with her.

"Did thee enjoy me soup, handsome?" Martha asked shyly.

"Aye, it was as lovely as you, my dearest," Preston replied in his best velvety voice. Martha clasped her hands together and swayed like a shy young woman.

"Would thee fancy more?" she tittered conspiratorially.

"Aye, more for myself if it won't delay the lady's grub. She's growing rather ornery on an empty stomach, that wench," he said, pointing his chin toward his indignant companion.

"Aye, me girl's the same. Turns right foul when hungry," Martha agreed.

"Is that a fact? Is there a cure? No? Blast it. Looks like I'm stuck with this hellcat."

Martha cackled and slapped him on his arm playfully. He looked over at Lady Elara who was sitting unnaturally erect. He was certain her slap would not be so gentle.

"I'll fetch the lass her meal now, save thee the torment."

"You're a gem, Martha, dearie."

The door shut quietly on Martha's giggle.

Before Lady Elara could utter a word, a man promptly returned to shackle and hood Preston. Darkness descended once more. When Martha finally reappeared, the men guarding the door exchanged a few words before letting her enter. He was certain she was reprimanded for speaking to him. Martha set Lady Elara's meal tray down gently and left without a word.

---

Elara thanked Martha for the meal but her voice was drowned out by the door opening loudly. A man roughly unbound her hands from the back and cuffed them in front of her. He pulled off her sack without care and swiftly left the room.

Elara blinked several times and brushed her hair away from her face. Her eyes quickly adjusted to the dim light, the fireplace casting a shadow over the room. The intricate pattern of golden wallpaper glinted in the light.

The windows were boarded and shrouded the room in deeper darkness. She looked around the sparse room furnished with only a bed. It was likely that she would be required to lie with Mr Preston on this bed. Apprehension threatened to engulf her as her eyes snapped to the man sitting on the floor.

Her gaze washed over the tall man with his long legs outstretched in front of him. He was leaning against the wall, his stockinged feet revealing his bulging calves. The light-coloured buckskin breeches stretched over his thick thighs. He was wearing a white shirt and was missing a coat and a neckcloth.

Her eyes drifted to his rolled-up sleeves, the thickly muscled and veined forearm making her pulse race. His large hands belonged to a labourer not a solicitor. They promised brute strength and competence.

"Have you seen enough?" the man asked, his voice melting and pouring over her like liquid heat.

Elara startled, her face flushing from getting caught. "Don't be ludicrous. I was not looking at you," she snapped.

"I didn't say you were." His voice was full of mirth.

"You tricked me!"

"You were tricked because you were guilty," he drawled.

"I—"

"No matter, love. Come closer, if you would, and do something for me."

Without a sack, she suddenly felt shy and cautious. She approached him timidly and knelt before him.

"Loose the knot on my sack, if you will, so I may remove it if the opportunity to escape rises. Take care not to make it obvious."

"As you wish."

Elara reached for the knot, then withdrew hastily when she noticed her hands trembling. Up close, his size overwhelmed her. His shoulders and chest were expansive enough to swallow her whole. She watched frozen as his long and heavily muscled legs flexed and bulged under his breeches. She was expected to be intimate with this man. She would be lucky if she weren't smothered to death by his weight.

Strangely, the man sat wordlessly, as if he was giving her an opportunity to observe and familiarise herself with him.

She took a deep breath and tried again, registering his muskiness and grass scent. Leaning closer, she sniffed him again and again. His scent made her skin tingle.

Pushing herself back up and sitting back on her heels, she pulled on the rope under his chin. Once loose, she raised the sack a little, her fingers scraping against his light stubble. He swallowed, and she became hypnotised by his Adam's apple bobbing in the thick column of his neck. Suddenly panicked by her impropriety, she retied the sack with quavering fingers, faintly registering his warm breath on her skin.

Turning to her neglected repast, she rushed to occupy her flustered self with rapid mouthfuls of bread. She waited for him to tease or mock her girlish behaviour, but he never did.

"We shall chance nothing tonight," Mr Preston said. "There are too many men about. We shall look for an opportunity to escape tomorrow."

Her stomach sank.

She looked at the large bed and wondered how she was to spend the night with a man. And tomorrow, she might die of mortification before she could complete the act they demanded. Elara was unsure if she ought to be thankful or resentful of her married cousins who had informed her about the marriage bed. They had described in detail the pleasures and pains she could expect from joining with a man. Her stomach cramped and nausea suddenly overwhelmed her.

Noticing the wine bottle by her companion's side, Elara reached across his lap, her thighs resting lightly against his, and took a deep draught from it. The wine's ripe, earthy taste bloomed on her tongue.

Feeling her weight on his lap, he spoke to her in feigned astonishment.

"My lady! Are you stealing my wine?"

"It is not yours! I took what rightfully belongs to me as well."

"You audacious thief!" he exclaimed, though his tone held more amusement than pique at her fire. "I would appreciate a basic courtesy of asking me, 'Could you share the wine, my good sir?' It's quite simple to have good manners."

Elara took another long draught. "Manners are reserved for civilisation. In this dire circumstance, self-preservation reigns," she said.

"Is that your stance then? Let me assure you. You will lose."

Her answering rejoinder went unheard, interrupted by the sudden entrance of a figure who roughly blinded her once more. She yelped as he forcefully pulled her arms behind her.

"You wretched oaf!" Elara cried out as pain lanced through her shoulders. "Have a care!"

Her protests went unheeded, his rough hands seizing and lifting her from the floor, carrying her aloft. Overcome with frenzy, Elara screeched as she struggled against his grip. But escape remained beyond her strength to extract from his iron grasp.

"Stop movin', thee wench!" the man shouted. "I'm takin' thee to bed!"

"You, rascal! You will not touch me!"

"Stay your assault or rue this day!" Mr Preston shouted followed by grunts and thuds. He was presumably charging forth blindly to grapple her assailant.

The lout lurched, hurling Elara hard upon the quilt.

"I dun't wanna touch her! She's much trouble!" the villain shouted.

Elara's breath left in a rush as she sank deep into the mattress. Before she could brace herself, the turnkey grasped her wrists and fettered them fast to the headboard with a rattle of chains. Immediately after, Mr Preston, too, was flung and shackled upon the bed.

# ABDUCTED

The blackguard swiftly vacated the room, muttering vulgarities and slamming the door behind him. Silence descended once more, save their panting.

"Are you well, darling?" her companion inquired, breathing heavily from the exertion.

Though shaken, her relief from the fiend's departure and gratitude toward the man she came to rely upon made her elated. She assured him, "Aye, although I did not get to finish my wine. If you had not argued with me…"

"If you hadn't pinched it…"

They relished the easy silence blanketing the swift bond forming between them. Once their breaths softened, Elara broke the silence.

"It was gallant of you to come to my aid. Thank you."

"It was courageous of you to fight the rogue," he said.

Their soft discourse went on, its gentle tenor belying all ordeals yet to come.

## Chapter Five

# Day Two: 2 March 1833 – two in the morning

Preston listened intently for the blackguards to make their ruckus while his head spun with stratagems he could employ to free the lady and himself. As soon as the scoundrels began their spirit-soaked festivities outside the bolted door, he would explore the room for a means of escape.

Next to him, Lady Elara stirred, nodding off briefly only to startle awake again. No doubt she was having nightmares. Soft whimpers escaped her that wrenched Preston's heart. He longed to comfort her yet could not even brush the tears he felt sure wet her cheeks.

If he died now, defending this woman, he would exit this world, having served a worthy cause. His only regret in life was that he had not found a lady to love, or been the recipient of such affections himself, at his ripe age of five and thirty. But that was immaterial in this moment. He had a more urgent duty to concern himself with presently.

When the scoundrels began their singing and laughing over cards and booze, Preston freed his hands and removed the sack.

Then he saw her.

His accursed instincts as a man immediately took in the female form next to him, her chest rising and falling.

Confound it all! She was distracting him.

Preston forced his gaze away and surveyed the room. Naught had changed except for the abandoned wine bottle and Lady Elara's supper tray on the floor.

Swinging his legs off the bed, he shuffled over to the windows. He tugged on the wooden boards, but thick iron nails secured them onto the window frames. He may be able to break them using the handcuffs as a bludgeon but not without alerting the whole house. Nay, the best route of escape was through the door.

He looked under the canopied bed, opened the water closet and the dressing room closets. They were bare save for a chamber pot and an ewer of water. He returned to the bed and inspected the iron bed frame for any gap or corrosion. Naught. The craftsmanship of welding was flawless.

The lady startled awake upon hearing his movements and called his name in panic.

"It's all right. It's me moving about," he said.

She exhaled deeply. "You gave me such a fright. How are you walking about unfettered?"

"I picked the lock with Martha's hairpin."

"You did? Is that why you were flirting with her?"

"Aye."

"I thought your flirtations were solely for amusement."

"That too. Please accept my apologies for disturbing your slumber."

"Think nothing of it. I find sleep eludes me in this place."

Preston lay upon the silken coverlet and refastened the iron cuffs.

"I feel rather like the roast awaiting spit and fire," he quipped lightly, though unease gnawed at him. It was tempting to unshackle them both for comfort, but the risk was too great. He did not yet know enough of the blackguards' routines to anticipate their movements with certainty.

Her laugh was appeasing to his nerves.

"I must say, I prefer having hands bound to a bed than being shackled at the back," she said.

Unchaste imaginings rushed into his mind unbidden, and he chided himself yet again. All that freedom in the past two years, and he had not visited a woman's bed, not once. But now that he is chained to the bed, he decides to lust after a fellow captive? Had he known he would be imprisoned with likely an innocent gentlewoman, he would have taken a respite from his work to release his baser passions.

"Indeed. I concur it is preferable," he responded then asked, "Pray, might I inquire when you made your debut into society?"

"About nine years ago, at eighteen. Why do you wish to know?" She adjusted her position atop the embroidered counterpane, shaking the mattress.

"Idle curiosity, nothing more," he said feeling relieved. Her mature years made him feel marginally less ashamed for the lewd fancies involving her.

Their exchange stumbled briefly into awkward silence until her honeyed voice gently filled the space between them.

"I admit, I would have been quivering with dread were I imprisoned alone in this dreary place. I am eternally grateful you are here," she said.

He tapped her foot gently with his own in a gesture of camaraderie. Smiling behind the burlap sack, he said, "And I must thank you for your company. You are preferable to a burly man."

She laughed, but it sounded sorrowful to Preston's ears. Further lengthy silence reigned before she gave a timorous voice to a private sentiment.

"I confess myself consumed by fear, imagining the morrow's dawn."

"It is only natural to feel frightened. You are enduring superbly, even in this plight." His voice was rough and soft as raw silk.

Swallowing tremulously, her quavering tones gave wings to private terror. "Will they truly insist we... we seal this unblessed union?"

"They seem resolved. Gold must exchange hands for certain, else why such unyielding resolve? I confess I cannot fathom what might sway them otherwise."

She shifted closer atop the coverlet until their knees touched in the gloom. He caressed her foot tenderly with a brush of his toes, fain to impart what poor comfort was possible.

"Mr Preston." Her voice was thin and vulnerable.

"Call me Nicholas. I shall call you Elara, if you'd permit it."

"All right... Nicholas... I..." She took a deep breath.

Preston waited patiently.

"I have never been... with a man."

Dash it all. A virgin. He had expected as much, as most well-bred ladies were, but she was seven and twenty, by Jove. He suppressed a deep sigh. The silence was broken only by the occasional voices coming from outside.

The lady had placed her trust in him. He must handle the matter with utmost care and delicacy. Perhaps if he could reassure her with comforting words... But anything he uttered would seem a hollow platitude under the circumstances.

The thought of despoiling her virtue weighed heavily on his conscience. Being her first under these abhorrent conditions turned his stomach. He tried to make his voice even and unaffected when he spoke. "I am grateful for your trust. If you'd rather attempt an escape—"

"No... not unless the circumstances are ideal. What I'm trying to say is... I am glad you shall be my first."

With a mix of guilt and tenderness he has never felt before, he replied, "It would be my greatest honour."

This exchange brought Preston no joy, as rendering the situation less distressing for the lady remained beyond his power. The best he could do was afford her every due respect and relinquish some control in the affair, deferring to her wishes whenever possible.

Preston adjusted his handcuffs and inched closer until his hip met hers, praying she found solace in his closeness. With a voice as warm as the summer breeze, he said, "My lady, the act of joining can be profoundly pleasurable between sympathetic partners. I care about your well-being most earnestly. I shall do my utmost to protect you from any unpleasantness."

Though circumstances conspired against them, he vowed to make this trial as bearable for her as a gentleman could. Her courage and grace had stirred his admiration along with a protectiveness he had never known. Come what may, he resolved that her gentleness would not be met with callousness, but rather with all the tenderness and care within his power to bestow.

In the profound silence that had befallen them, Preston stroked her foot with tender familiarity as if he had performed this movement for her a thousand times before. Elara found it most comforting, a wordless pledge that in her trials, she had a friend.

He broke the silence most delicately. "I assume you know the... mechanics involved?"

"Yes," she whispered, heat rising to her cheeks. She turned her head towards him, imagining a handsome man with locks of light brown hair and eyes alike in shade. Wonder overcame her at the ease of reclining near this man, as though Fate herself decreed they lie entwined.

"Good. Are you aware it may be painful for inexperienced women or even unprepared women."

"Unprepared?"

"It is important for the lady to enjoy the encounter. If she does not, her discomfort may be intensified."

"Truly?"

"Aye. My question is... if we must do this, would you rather we accomplish it post-haste at the risk of pain, or would you prefer it to be more tolerable despite the extra time required?"

"I, um, I would like my first time to be more tolerable, if possible," she said in a voice hardly audible.

"Very well. I shall do my utmost."

She found solace in his conviction and concern for her comfort. If she was being truthful with herself, she wished he would draw nearer still. This longing was something she had not yearned for since her former betrothed abandoned her. Even with him, she had not felt it this acutely.

She harboured no illusions about the cause of this intense yearning. It had little to do with affection and more to do with the man being her only shelter now. She craved, desperately, for his embrace.

"I wish..." she began, but maidenly shyness overcame her.

"You wish?" he gently prodded.

"Nothing. I had a momentary lapse of judgment."

"Elara, speak your mind. Social mores need not constrain us here. If within my power, I shall grant you your wish."

"Very well... I wish... you could hold me..." Her voice trailed away, her face flaming with distress at giving voice to such longing.

"Then you shall have it. Brace yourself. I must shout."

As she pondered his meaning, he called aloud, "Oi! Gentlemen! We must discuss a matter of great importance!"

In the stillness, they awaited a reply, but none was forthcoming. Preston tried once more, louder. From outside the door came a wrathful bellow, "Shut thee gob!"

When he was certain they would not be disturbed soon, Preston informed her he would release his wrists from the headboard. She assumed he was sitting up when the rope beneath the feather mattress dipped. Then she heard him take a deep breath.

## Chapter Six

# Day Two: 2 March 1833 — three in the morning

Unmasked, Preston turned towards the woman who lay adjacent upon the bed. With care, he unshackled her wrists and untied the knot around her neck. He then waited for her to reveal herself when she felt ready.

Elara rose slowly to her knees, sat back on her heels, and pulled off the sack cautiously. Tousled locks of bright amber tumbled forth across her visage like flames pouring from a dragon's mouth. Sitting back against the headboard, Preston was arrested by the stunning cascade of red across her porcelain skin. With delicate fingers, she brushed the hair back from her face. Eyelashes fluttering open like tender new leaves, piercing green eyes traced his features and marked each line and plane.

As he met the endless green depths of her gaze, the instant connection he felt broke open the dam to his heart, leaving him disoriented. Surprise caused her eyes to widen as she beheld his icy blue eyes in return. Ever so slowly, her attention strayed, following the curve of his smile and the line of his neck glimpsed through his open shirt.

The surge of awe remained in his chest as he sat transfixed by the contrasting hues that made her impossibly vibrant. Her flaming red hair and alabaster pale skin made everything else pale and dull in comparison. The background disappeared around her as Preston studied intently a bloom that lay upon her cheeks like the first tint upon a newly sprung camellia.

Hesitantly, he reached out and brushed away a lone strand of hair atop her nose.

"So..." he breathed, "this is what beauty looks like..."

Her lips parted, but no reply came as her eyes darted shyly hither and yon about his person.

"It is an honour to finally make your acquaintance. I am Nicholas, at your service," he said with a bow.

"Nicholas..."

"Aye."

Bewilderment clouded her eyes. "I am surprised you are revealing your visage to me given how secretive you were initially."

"Well, I have concluded you are neither an assassin nor a spy."

"Alas, no. I have no such intriguing occupations," she returned, a hint of smile touching her lips.

He studied her intently. "In truth, I've met no lady more bewitching."

A blush bloomed from her cheeks down to her neck. Preston averted his gaze, uncertain what to do about the surging longing inside him.

He busied himself propping some pillows against the headboard and subdued his astonishment of seeing a creature so enchanting. He swore under his breath at the daunting task of muzzling his heart before extending his palm in invitation. He waited as she eyed his hand uncertainly.

"Do you still wish to take refuge in my arms?" he asked gently.

She hesitated, seeming to reconsider her earlier entreaty. She finally drew near but remained stiff with her knees a few inches from his side.

With one arm draped over his knee, Preston smiled warmly. "Fortune has smiled upon you, if I may say so," he said in a hushed voice.

Her thick lashes fluttered upward, puzzlement writ across her features. "Whatever can you mean, Mr Preston?"

"Please call me Nicholas." His voice reverberated low with affection and self-assurance. "What I mean is as captivities go, I am the finest companion you could've hoped for."

Elara arched a brow, her expression playful. "Pray tell, what renders you so ideal for this situation?"

Preston's smile broadened. "Well, I have strength enough to carry you, should the need arise. I've been told I make decent company. Above all, I'm still in possession of all my teeth, luckily for you."

Both of her brows lifted now, frowning dubiously.

"Come now, love. You must agree." Preston flashed his teeth with exaggerated arrogance.

She gave him a sly glance. "While I have no doubt of those qualities, I should have thought your talent for locks the more useful skill here."

"Ah, vanity shall prove my undoing. I confess I take more pride in these teeth than in my modest abilities at unclasping locks."

Her countenance gave him pause, as it was brightened by a smile, open and sincere. The green pools of her eyes bore into him with the look of a wide-eyed innocent, possessed of wonder. Relaxing her posture, Elara sat back against the pillows. Preston encircled her shoulders cautiously with one arm and gently stroked her arm with his thumb.

She studied his thumb caressing her arm, then raised her mournful eyes to meet his. He became spellbound by flickering firelight dancing along the ivory skin of her face and graceful neck.

"Exquisite," he murmured. A fiery blush suffused her cheeks as she turned her face away.

Compelled by some primal urge to feel her form, Preston drew her firmly against him. She gave a soft gasp but offered no protest, then soon conformed to him. With delight, he noted how pliantly she curved into his embrace. Lost in her softness and warmth, it was some time before Preston noted the silence between them.

"Your thoughts seem to wander, pet."

"I did but ponder... how strange to imagine surrendering my body to a stranger. If we had been betrothed, we would have become acquainted before the wedding night, strolling in the garden, taking champagne, dancing... Never did I dream my first encounter would be so... abrupt."

At her wavering syllables, Preston covered the back of her hand with his palm, interlacing their fingers. With a whispered caress, he said, "Come now. Surely you have not forgotten, my love? Why, we have enjoyed many a soirees and dances together. So often, in fact, we took a country holiday just last summer. Do you recall the day we first met?" He lowered his voice to a tender murmur. Her ear gradually tinged pink. "You tumbled straight from a cherry blossom, as though Heaven itself had delivered you, a pretty pink parcel, just for me."

Comprehension lit her features, and she joined. "Oh yes. I was quite certain I should break my neck in the fall. But you appeared as if from nowhere to catch me unawares."

"Nay, you landed atop and nearly shattered every bone in me," Preston returned, tone wry. "I have endured persistent pains in my back ever since, thanks to you, poppet."

Elara chuckled gaily. "Mayhap a bit of exercise would mend matters quicker than lazing about like a proper gentleman," she rallied. "We were naught but a tangle of arms and legs! And you quite ruined my coiffure."

Preston clicked his tongue. "Ruined chignon was your chief concern? Ungrateful wench. I have half a mind to take you across my knee, if you were not the most precious creature I have beheld." His smile turned wicked as her face flamed red at his remark.

"The most precious? Am I truly?" she asked, playful scepticism entering her voice.

"Quite so," Preston affirmed with unmistakable sincerity. "I could admire no one as I do you."

---

Between tender caresses and earnest tones, Elara believed him just for a moment.

She watched Preston lean his head back against the wall and close his eyes. His light brown hair with flecks of gold was trimmed short except the strands that fell over his forehead. He was much more attractive than she could have imagined. He possessed a touch of wickedness that had her heart racing. But even before she saw his face, his rich voice and tenderness had warmed her like hot tea in a snowstorm.

Soon, he would bind her again. She would miss the feel of his body against her. She was quite stunned to gaze into the azure eyes crackling with smoky sultriness. There was a glimpse of cool detachment, however, that had given her a pause before she decided to trust him and reveal herself.

Elara rotated slightly to face him, his long fingers bronzed by the sun, still cradling her pale ones. The golden light from the hearth flickered along his chiselled features.

"Nicholas..." she uttered his name, soft and shy. Her eyes met not his own but considered their linked hands instead.

"Hm?" He turned his head and regarded her.

Still gazing down, she queried, "Have you kissed many women?"

"Aye."

"What makes a kiss either sublime or lacklustre?"

Elara waited, feeling the heat spread from her cheeks to her neck.

Just when she thought he would not be answering her bold question, Preston released her hand and traced one finger along her arm. Even with the thick wool as a barrier, she shuddered as though kissed by ice. Upward his fingers roamed, kneading gently at the tight muscles of her shoulders, wringing a low moan as she rolled her head from side to side. His palm came to rest, cradling her jaws. His thumb stroked lightly over the marbled skin made pink.

"How lovely you are, Elara... my pink Blossom," he whispered. "Come here," he bade, desire palpable in each hushed syllable, brooking no denial.

When she didn't move, Preston's hands slipped beneath her rear, then drew her astride him. Every inch of visible flesh now glowing crimson, her shocked and round eyes avoided his gaze. With his hand clasped on her nape, he pressed a tender kiss on the translucent sheen of her neck.

Preston trailed his lips across her neck's sensitive hollows, dusting her collar bone with kisses before meandering to her chin. She inclined her head as though guided by invisible strings tied to his very fingers. Reaching the far side of that elegant arch, he nipped her earlobe lightly with his teeth, causing another shiver within his embrace as slim arms twined about his shoulders.

Unhurried, he continued to bestow feather-light kisses on her lids, the tip of her nose, her rosy cheeks, and her dainty chin. With exquisite patience, Preston brushed his lips along her jaw until his mouth found hers. He laid a loving brush of his lips upon hers, sweeping her lips with petal softness from one corner to the other. Her insides quaked when he nibbled and tugged lightly on her lower lip.

As he pulled back, her sigh filled the scant space still lingering between them. Within his snug buckskin breeches, his arousal grew prominent and strained. Her eyes widened as she noticed the hard ridge between her thighs.

His eyes half-hooded, Preston spoke softly, holding her gaze, then dropping to her mouth.

"How your skin glows in the moonlight, my love. It is wholly beguiling," he murmured with a trace of awe in his voice. "And those eyes, how they sparkle thus. The very stars themselves must envy their radiance."

"How is it that you have not kissed me in all our years of courtship?" she asked accusingly.

"Kissing a woman like you is not for the fainthearted."

"Whatever do you mean?"

"A man must prepare to lose himself in your scent, the taste of you, your plump, honey-glazed mouth... He must prepare to crave you for eternity, for he would never get enough."

His whispers surprised her and stoked her desire for an intimacy she did not yet know. She struggled to tame the ragged gasps escaping her lips, air catching within her throat as her heartbeat pounded in her ears. His mouth was so close but did not close the distance. His eyes, however, blazed and pierced into her. In perfect synchrony, they shared one heated breath before their lips met in sweet communion. A spark ignited within her core, setting every nerve alight.

Parting her lips, she inhaled his breath, commencing an unfamiliar waltz with unsure steps but trusting him. Seeking more of him, her tongue darted forth to taste his lips. They were hot and tasted of wine. As though this was the awaited signal, his large hand shifted to cradle her head. He then claimed her mouth in a searing kiss. His tongue made a subtle entry into her cavity, caressing the silky inner flesh of her bottom lip. It swiped the even row of her bottom teeth before swirling and undulating against her tongue. His wide mouth engulfed hers while his body enclosed her completely.

"Christ, you're sweet," he breathed against her open mouth before sucking the sweetness out of her tongue. His hands roamed confidently along her back, his thumbs grazing the tender side of her breasts. With a moan, he cupped her backside with both hands and pressed firmly onto his hard ridge. He ground her bottom against his engorged shaft as he deepened the kiss and swallowed her breaths.

In the melding of their lips, she sensed the depth of his yearning to safeguard the moment, to sate a gnawing need for intimacy akin to her own, to beautify this moment with equal passion and reverence. Enfolding her in his unwavering embrace, he became a shelter from the tempest that has yet to ravage her.

Leaving her with remnants of their passion, her lips swollen and chafed, Preston eased the kiss to tender licks and brushes.

"So…" she began slyly. "Was that lacklustre or sublime?"

Preston burst out laughing, a rich, warm sound that caused his shoulders to heave. Keeping his volume in check, he shook his head in gleeful disbelief as he looked into her eyes.

"Are you telling me you've had better, Blossom?" he asked, his shapely mouth still curved into a grin. "If you had," he groaned as she shifted her bottom against his generous length, "I'd be extremely jealous."

Feeling more audacious than before, she asked, "Of me or him?"
"Of you, obviously," he replied and took her laughing mouth in his again.

Her mind more relaxed, she wrapped her arms around his head, clasping his thick chestnut curls between her fingers. She rocked back and forth on his lap as he had done, relishing the groan scraping out of his throat. Just as she thought the forced copulation with him might not be as horrendous as she had expected, Preston pulled back and laid feather-light kisses over her cheeks and below the ears.

"Best to resume our former places before the blackguards return," he said hoarsely as they breathed as one.

Her stomach twisted itself in knots at the thought of passing the long night bereft of his warmth. She peered into his eyes, rendered near black by consuming hunger. She watched with satisfaction when he briefly closed his eyes with a groan upon her legs spreading wider over his lap, the steely ridge settling beneath her heat.

"Hell… What you do to me," he muttered. "The things I shall do to you…"

His gaze lowered to her mouth, and she was unsure what for. She felt a sudden surge of need for him and a strong impulse to belong to him. Was it the power of the kiss? Or was it his protection she found irresistible?

Holding his gaze, Elara began to move her hips in a circular motion. He groaned with approval, throwing his head back against the wall and closing his eyes. It felt different for her too this time. His hardness was digging into her crotch beneath her petticoats and massaging the place that ached. She pulled the layers of wool from underneath, leaving only layers of linen and buckskin between their swollen flesh. She moved more rigorously, placing both palms on the wall beside his head and rubbing her heat along the full length of him. He was long and thick like the rest of him. She had never known eroticism like this.

She had, however, reached orgasm alone by massaging herself against various surfaces. When she had found the lewd sketches in her father's study, for example, she had ridden the arm of a chair and had experienced the most pleasant sensation she later learned was orgasm.

Now, every time Preston's thick shaft pressed against her clitoris, she felt the familiar sensation heat her core. Except this was better. Much better.

His firm hands held her steady at the hips, and his half-hooded eyes met hers. "You better stop, Elara, or I shall come in my leather," he rasped.

"Please..." she breathed.

"Please what?"

"Please don't make me stop..." she moaned, rocking faster on his lap.

"Damn it, Elara."

His hands moved quickly to unfasten his breeches. Her eyes stared over the layers of fabric, anticipating seeing a male member for the first time, but her thick skirts obstructed the view.

When he pulled her closer, she felt the sharp contrast of his flower petal smoothness and steely firmness between her thighs. Her slick arousal slathered him in her juice.

"Bloody hell," he hissed before angling her so his shaft rubbed against her clitoris. Holding her firmly at the hips, he began to rock her over his cock. Her hands still against the wall, Elara rested her forehead against his, relishing his moans and pants.

"Nicholas," she whispered when an intense sensation gathered and threatened to overwhelm her. All words were lost and only sensation remained.

"That's it, darling. Come on my cock," he rasped.

As he rocked her against his rod with a fierce speed, Elara fell silent as pleasure took flight and lifted her to the peak. Preston muted her scream with his mouth as the orgasm broke inside her. Soon, his muffled scream was swallowed by Elara as every fibre of his muscle hardened and hot liquid soaked them between their thighs.

Preston released a satisfied exhale.

Feeling embarrassed by such a display of wantonness, Elara moved to slip off his lap. He tightened his arms around her waist and placed a gentle finger under her chin.

"Look at me, Elara. You have no reason to be ashamed or embarrassed," he said.

She nodded, dropping her eyes. He brought her eyes back to him again. Then, without a word, he kissed her long and hard on the mouth, leaving nothing behind. When he withdrew from her, his eyes were filled with tenderness and something else... ferocity. Smiling crookedly, as if he just heard a joke, he began to fix his breeches.

Embarrassed and confused about her boldness, Elara sat in pensive silence while Preston lifted her off his lap and headed to the water closet. He returned with a wet cloth for her and turned away while she cleaned herself.

"Elara," he called tenderly, with his back to her.

"Yes?"

"You are resplendent, Blossom."

## Chapter Seven

# Day Two: 2 March 1833 – Noon

Preston opened his eyes from a fretful slumber. Time had no meaning for a blind man in a windowless room. The activities from the lower floors told him it was the afternoon. Men came and went, more staying than leaving. He heard new voices today, and this did not bode well for an escape. He counted eleven men and two women at the moment, undoubtedly waiting for their performance. Nausea spread through him at the thought.

A gentle prod of toes alerted him to Elara's wakefulness.

"How fare your arms?" he asked.

"Most disagreeably numb and sore. And yours?"

"Alike, numb. Shall I petition those knaves to unbind you awhile?"

"No, I would rather suffer the ache than hasten their company."

"I could unbind you myself for a moment."

"The risk would outweigh any relief, would it not?"

"Aye. You're right." He deftly gathered up her feet with his own and tucked them snugly between his knees.

"What are you doing?"

"Distracting you whilst restoring warmth to your frozen toes. Have I your approval for this service?"

"You do, although I was expecting more from you." Her cunning tone and brazen comment drew a smile from Preston. She was a special woman for jesting whilst wearing shackles and a sack.

"Do you speak of my toe-warming service or something else?"

"Please do not say you are insecure about your... performance."

"You impugn my skills? Given the opportunity, none shall find me lacking in my duties. However, I'm afraid I may execute pitifully under this pressure."

"Please forgive me. I did not mean to add pressure." She sounded sincere enough, but he was no longer certain of her true character. She was all nerves and timidity before their kiss, but now, she was turning into an unabashed fox.

"Tell me. Have you kissed any others before me?" Discussing sensitive subjects seemed to come easier in the dark.

"Yes. I had one other."

Jealousy and possessiveness lurked somewhere deep within, which surprised him. He had only just met this woman, and their intimacy had more to do with survival than attraction. Didn't it? Surely, it was impossible to feel ownership over the lady after only two days of acquaintance. Not after closing his heart to all women for six years and his body for two.

If he had met her within the conventional bounds of society, would he have been stirred by such tender feelings? His resounding certainty upon reflection rather took him back.

"Nicholas? Are you well?"

He cleared his throat to gather his thoughts. "Aye. May I inquire who the first man was that is crippling me in comparison?"

Her pretty laughter embedded somewhere in his gut. Not in his stomach but somewhere deeper. Blast it! This was highly inconvenient.

Elara's voice was timid. "I was betrothed to my cousin, James. I know some people frown upon such an arrangement, but we had grown up together. He had always been kind to me. That's why it was so shocking to learn that he ruined an innocent woman after our engagement. He had kept it a secret from me, biding his time until we wed. I realised then what kind of man he had become. When the poor girl came to see me, I broke off the engagement."

The melancholic tone in her voice disturbed his instinct to protect her.

"Is he the reason you didn't marry?"

"No. It just happened. I was heartbroken and distrusting of men for a while. I had lost a friend, family, and a fiancé all at once. I declined all invitations for social engagements and soon, the invitations stopped coming. Shortly after, I overheard someone refer to me as the heartbroken spinster. Being shy does not help matters."

His chest tightened once again. It was as if his heart finally had time to ponder issues beyond survival. How ironic. He had been immersed in work and scarcely had time for eating. But now, his need for a woman to love was becoming just as acute as his need for survival.

He squeezed his eyes shut and allowed himself to feel the sharp pain penetrating his heart. What did it matter? He could not have her.

With a subtle shift of his legs, he secured her cold feet more comfortably between his thighs. "Does this improve matters for your feet?" he asked.

"Indeed, thank you."

"I live to serve you. Is there anything else I can provide, sweetheart?" he purred lightly, fighting the heaviness in his chest.

"My options seem lamentably limited at present," she said.

"We shall simply need to be creative. I can be anything you desire—a prince with a wooden leg, a pirate with polished teeth, an albino with a perfect tan..."

Her warm, throaty laughter muffled by the sack sent a thrill coursing down his spine. Whilst he was distracted by the pretty sound, he felt her toes curl, gently massaging his thighs. He froze as they came dangerously close to his groin. On the contrary, his clueless appendage went into a frenzy, fondly remembering her pliant form.

It was mortifyingly brief before his erection stretched down his thigh and presented itself under her feet. Raising her curious toes, she traced the prominent ridge, investigating the mysterious bulge. A groan wrenched itself from his throat unbidden.

She gasped and pulled back.

Then the door burst open, and Elara shrieked. Her voice came in gasping, staccato bursts as panic gripped her chest, strangling the breath from her lungs. Preston longed to hold her, but he could only use his voice to comfort her.

"'Tis time," a deep voice said.

"Nicholas! I cannot. I shall die of shame!"

"Fear not, sweet Blossom. All shall be well. Calm yourself, darling. I'm here with you."

Preston tugged on his handcuffs imperceptibly to ensure he could break free any moment if necessary.

"Surely you aren't serious?" Preston said to the lout. "We haven't broken fast yet!"

"'Tis time," Dauid's voice said.

At Preston's side, Elara trembled uncontrollably, coming quite undone.

"Unbind me, you bloody beasts! Can't you see the lady is distressed? Have you got no decency?"

"Gerron with it!" the brute bellowed at the presumably motionless guards.

"Someone is coming closer, Elara. Do not be alarmed. They come to free my hands."

"I... will... not..." she stammered piteously, rendered quite insensible. Anguish wrenched his gut to hear her thus.

He turned upon their tormentor. "Free the lady's hands, you swine! Are you blind or ignorant? She shall swoon at this rate!"

"Nay, it canna be done."

The very moment Preston was free, he cast off his sack and hugged her quaking form fiercely. He could make out near two dozen figures lingering outside the room, two at their posts upon the threshold. Dauid approached the bed with a chair, but Preston settled his cold stare upon him. "Come closer, and you shall have a bloodbath. Do you wish to complicate matters?"

The rascal retraced his steps and settled beside the door while two knaves stood beside him.

"Only you stay." Preston pointed to the leader.

"Aye."

"Not a peep until I allow it!"

"Aye."

"We'll keep hidden beneath the linens."

At this, the villain grinned. "Allreet. I take her fer meself."

Preston saw red with barely leashed rage, noting that his fury had escalated not only by his sense of duty but possessiveness.

## Chapter Eight

# *Day Two: 2 March 1833 – half past noon*

Preston took a few deep shaky breaths, his fists clenched. Lying on his side next to Elara, he shielded her view with his body. He gently removed her sack, untangling the tear-soaked strands from her face. He wiped her tears with his hands and watched her lashes flutter open.

"All will be well, my sweet," he whispered, gazing into her dewy greens. "No harm shall befall my beloved Cherry Blossom."

He placed his forehead on hers and stroked her hair until she stopped trembling and her sniffles diminished.

She gave a delicate snort and mumbled, "Thank you, my bonnie Shattered Bones."

He chuckled, her jest easing his mind somewhat. What a brave and selfless woman she was. She was joking to comfort him, so he'd know she was strong. A man could fall in love with a woman like this.

"Relax and place your trust in me, love." He shifted some of his weight onto her so his entire right side was pressing the full length of her. She stilled beneath his steady weight and fond gaze.

"Elara, you are beauty itself," he pronounced, veneration naked upon his face. His heart clenched painfully because every word rang true.

"Nicholas..." Her eyes gleamed wet but were no longer fearful. Her smile dawned like the sun.

Just then, their tormentor heaved an impatient sigh, blasting through the safe harbour he was trying to create. As Elara flinched, Preston gentled her with a touch. "Keep your eyes on me, darling heart. I assure you, I'm more pleasant to look at."

She smiled, apprehension knitting her brow.

"Look only at me now... think of us and the moment we first met," Preston whispered. She nodded slowly.

"Try anything funny and thee'll pay fer it," the brute snarled, spittle foaming on his bearded chin.

Though fury all but choked him, Preston forced it down for Elara's sake. He lifted her delicate chin and gazed deep into her eyes.

"My love... would you allow me to express my heart's desires?"

She bit down hard upon her lip, then gave a solemn nod.

Drawing back, his eyes bore into hers as if by will alone he might absorb her suffering. His six-year-old barricade against women shattering, he reminded himself he had one day, perhaps two, to love her. Despite his conscience's protests, she had ensnared his soul completely. Somehow, he knew she was fire and ice and everything his battered spirit craved.

Reverently, Preston dipped his head. With a butterfly's deftness, his lips grazed hers, each brush imparting profound adoration. Gently he paid homage to her soft lips, his tongue but a fleeting supplicant at her altar. A sigh escaped into his welcoming mouth as she lost herself in his worshipful embrace.

He held her captive to his reverence with his large hands cradling both cheeks. He kissed each eyelid with fervent blessing before a ragged breath drew him irresistibly back to her sweet lips. Now uncontrolled, the hunger of his yearning suffused each probing stroke of his tongue. His embrace conveyed his need to shelter her. Each breath murmured his need to harmonise the discord in his heart.

He coaxed her to love him, unveil her hidden passion in the cocoon created for her, and take what she needed from him. And by God, she indulged him. She met his every stroke and nip, panting and moaning into his mouth. She kissed him like it was the last thing she would ever do.

His cock was so hard it hurt.

He shoved aside the grim foreboding that warned if he did not rein in this illusion of affection, recovery might prove impossible. This was but pretence, a ploy for survival. His heart whispered otherwise.

He drew back, his gaze no longer gentle but dark and feral with unhindered need. He was a man possessed, prepared to abandon himself to this sweet oblivion.

"Elara, love. Listen to me," he whispered, his voice raw and guttural.

"Yes," came her hushed reply.

"I have searched in vain for some means of escape, but none presents itself. Nor have I secured a weapon as yet. Once so equipped, we shall flee this cursed place."

She nodded grimly, her eyes wide with trepidation.

"You have only to speak it, love, if you wish to stop this... Give word and we shall face our enemies together even at the risk of death."

Then Elara gifted him with an unexpected smile, and in her eyes, he found the only answer needed.

---

Elara searched Preston's countenance, bewildered by her own startling passion, no longer certain what part was true sentiment and what was a mere fancy.

All she knew with certainty was that he anchored her to solid ground amidst this storm. He ensured her survival and kindled a tenderness that both melted her defences and robbed her of reason. He brought peace and assurance she might emerge unscathed from this ordeal. Strange new bonds had taken seed and sprouted, fogging thoughts of propriety once held dear. She felt the urge to declare him as her sanctum.

Eyes locked, he drew her into a searing kiss, teasing and tempting until she was completely lost in his musky and masculine scent, his firm touch, and burning heat.

As though to commit each facet to memory, his hand traced the tender flesh on the back of her knee and her inner thigh. Keeping her covered and shielding her from the blackguards' view, he reached boldly beneath her skirts, seeking silken flesh. Gently yet assuredly, his fingers worshipped all they uncovered, staking claim to some small part of her. He pressed the prominent ridge of his arousal to her hip with primal urgency.

"Had your betrothed touched you here?" His hand paused between her thighs and cupped her heat possessively. He breathed hoarsely.

"No." She was dizzy with sensation.

"Good." His lips brushed her ear. Holding her gaze, he traced the outline of her wet folds, stroking each delicate layer as if they were spring buds. Then he split the folds and revealed her entrance, dipping his finger in her moisture. She gasped at the intrusion and met his eyes, wild with worry and need. "This belongs to me," he rasped.

A smile touched her swollen lips. "Yes," she whispered.

"When we're apart, Blossom, I want you to touch yourself here and think of me."

"Yes." Her reply was air and heat.

All talk ceased as the sweet caress stoked waves of sensation through her body.

"Mm..." She squirmed and arched against his hand.

With his fingers stroking her rhythmically, he ground his hard rod against her hip. He kissed her hard, closing his mouth tightly around her tongue and draining the sweetness.

The grim reality disappeared and only the man she wanted hovered over her. Somewhere between his gentle revelation of their plight and selflessly shielding her from their captors, she had fallen for this man. With their eyes locked, Elara only felt what he was doing to her, both mind and body. His strong hand was invading her most intimate places, stroking her clitoris and...

"Nicholas!" she cried out in a surprised whisper as he inserted a finger inside her sleek flesh. He stroked inside her core, a place she didn't even know existed. It was novel, invasive, and different from anything she'd experienced. It tamed the ache inside her.

With his eager coaxing, her clitoris awakened and pleaded for more. She strained against his thumb that was stirring a delicious sensation. The notion of joining with Preston thrilled her.

"Nicholas..." she whispered feverishly.

"Hell... the way you breathe my name..."

Her body purred each time he stroked with his thumb and finger. His dark gaze, his desire for her, excited her and made her feel beautiful. He could not truly want her that much, could he? His eyes were near black, his needs infinite, and he seemed crazed with possessiveness. A wicked smile touched his eyes as he slid another finger inside her.

Pressure was building in her essence with a faint fluttering. It felt as though she was being tickled and soothed from inside out, and her soul floated. Except there was something else more powerful building, like a storm.

"Nicholas!" she cried out in a hushed tone, her puzzled eyes wide open. She strained against the shackles and stiffened instinctively, the pleasure between her thighs intensifying but not quite reaching the threshold.

"Christ, you're beautiful," he groaned against her open mouth, his voice straining. "I must have you now."

He embraced her tighter, his one hand clutching a fist full of her hair and the other squeezing her bottom under the skirts.

---

Preston looked over at the rogue and suppressed the murderous ire in his stomach. The scoundrel was stroking himself, his eyes fixed on Elara and bleary with lust. So were the five other men in the doorway. He turned back to Elara wordlessly, not wanting to alarm her. There was no point in disturbing her further when the reality was already a nightmare.

Tamping down the nauseating fury mingling with the tormenting lust of his own, he worshipped her with sweet, unhurried strokes of his finger inside her. He didn't expect her to climax given the ghastly situation, but he hoped the manoeuvres would lessen her discomfort.

He prayed that one day he would taste every inch of her with his loving mouth and devour her whole with his loving heart. He yearned to feel her pussy inch by inch as much as he longed to take her savagely, lose himself inside her, and forget all that exists beyond their union.

Despite his need to bury himself inside her, she was still too tight for him. With the strength of restraint rarely exercised before, he placed another finger at her entrance.

"Take what I give you. You're too fucking tight."

The words tumbled out of his mouth–his passion too acute to care.

At her tentative nod, he kissed her deeply and inserted a third finger while rubbing the hardened clitoris.

She gasped. "It hurts," she whimpered.

"I know, my heart. You're doing so well opening for me, taking me in. Just breathe."

Gently, he stroked her clitoris and moved his fingers against her plump inner flesh. He caressed, stretched, retracted, and burrowed into her womanly core. Soon, her sound changed to moans of pleasure, and she began to buck against him. The way she moved, her sensuous sounds, and her expressions even in this ghastly situation, created a surge of arousal and something profound he did not wish to dwell on.

"I can't wait. Will you take me now?"

"Yes," she said as she turned toward the sound by the door. Quickly, he distracted her by kissing her mouth and began to unfasten the fall front.

Away from the blackguards' view, he turned her onto her side. Bending over her and blanketing her body with his, he folded her knees to her chest.

"Since you can't spread your legs, I shall enter you this way."

She nodded, uncertainty crossing her face. He pushed up her skirts a little higher, resisting the temptation to hike it up so his eyes could feast on her pussy. He could imagine her labia being as pristine as the skin of her breasts and the centre as pink as her lips. He groaned low at the image. Keeping her covered, he gripped his cock and positioned the head at her entrance.

"Elara…"

Her green eyes pierced his, and her ripened lips parted as her name passed his lips as an ardent benediction. "I love you, my Blossom."

Her eyes opened wide at his declaration, then wider still when his cockhead nudged at her entrance. Locking his eyes with hers, he pushed his tip into her opening with some force. A primal grunt left his mouth as her soft and sleek flesh sucked him in. His breath lodged in his throat from the overwhelming pleasure.

"So good… so bloody good…"

His words were slurred and airy. His eyes glazed with desire, he pushed gently, but the tightness of her maidenhead resisted his entry.

"Sweetheart, this will hurt."

Before Elara understood his meaning, he drove into her and felt her maidenhead give. He swallowed her scream with his mouth as her virgin tunnel made way for him. He almost lost control when her inner flesh smothered his cock and drew him in deeper.

"Fuck..." he groaned.

Not wanting to cause her further discomfort, he stopped, only partially embedded inside her. Then he embraced her tighter in his arms and buried his face in her nape.

Speech left him. She was unbelievably snug, soft and wet, shooting pleasure from his cock to his toes then to his chest. He raised his head to meet her green flames burning brightly. Her bosom heaved with excited pants. Under different circumstances, he would have taken her nipples in his mouth, but he would not undress her in front of these louts.

Preston moved slowly with a steady rhythm, her panting becoming a sensual harmony with his own breaths. As he withdrew and slid inside her again and again, he sank himself another inch but did not dare breach her all the way. The last thing he wanted was for her to associate her first lovemaking only with physical pain. She had endured enough already.

He took her mouth in his again to express what words could not. Then the inevitable climax arrived with an overwhelming sense of ownership and ecstasy.

*Mine. Mine.*

Pleasure came in waves, re-surging just when he thought all had left him. Eventually, the incredible pressure eased with his body on top of her, breathless from the whirling emotions inside of him.

Spoken in the throes of passion, did he love her? Or was he swept away by her beauty, their unusual fate? Either way, they had weaved pleasure from pain, and this had to be a good thing.

Raising his head and shrouding their bodies head to toe in the blanket, Preston cradled her face against his chest. Then, poking his head out from the cover, he bellowed, "Get out!"

The men smirked, one of them still pumping his cock. He seethed. Preston laid his murderous gaze on Dauid and growled, "Get. Out. Now."

The blackguard sneered as he fixed his trousers. Ignoring Preston's look of warning, he stepped closer.

"Get out before I do you in!" he roared.

Dauid halted. "I'll return to bind thee," he said.

Preston frowned with confusion. Why would the man obey? Surely no one knew his identity in these parts. His thoughts were interrupted by his need to tend to Elara.

Once alone, Preston set about soaking a cloth in warm water and tended to her with the utmost care while preserving her modesty. Elara's flesh turned crimson at his servitude and deepened upon seeing the pink hue on the cloth.

Preston buttoned the fall front and straightened out her dress before lying beside her. He embraced her tightly from behind, his heart full of sorrow and concern for her. Elara linked her fingers with his and burrowed into him.

"Are you all right?" he asked.

"Yes."

"I'm sorry to have caused you pain."

"No… it was fine."

"I know this is not how you wished your first time to be."

She was silent as was understandable. While he relished holding her, a soft voice muttered, "I felt cherished."

Awash with relief and gratitude, he enclosed her in his arms more securely. He pressed a kiss on her temple, the tenderness concealing his inner turmoil.

From the depths of his being, guilt gnawed at him, but he could not stop their hearts kindling from spark to flame.

## Chapter Nine

# *Day Three: 3 March 1833 — one in the morning*

Sleep had failed him in the wake of joining with Elara. Preston's instinct had left him watching for a threat entering the room. Then the moment he had tensely awaited came late at night.

He heard the stealthy click before the door swung open. Dauid crept in, stumbling as he walked. His gin-sodden reek mingled with the acrid tang of smoke, turning Preston's stomach. He had no doubt about the scoundrel's vile purpose in invading the dark chamber. His blood boiled at the thought, but his fury was tempered by the visions of spilling the miscreant's blood.

Preston had loosed both Elara and his hands from manacles in anticipation of something like this occurring. Unfortunately, the pin had not been long enough to free their ankles. Feigning the rhythms of slumber, he forced his breath even and deep. The fetid stench drew closer and the ropes beneath the mattress dipped under the added weight.

With viper speed, Preston ripped his sack off, halting Elara's scream at the sight of her assailant. Long adjusted to absolute blackness, he snatched the pistol and dagger from the villain's holsters. Preston's arm, reinforced by the iron shackle on one wrist, encircled the rogue's throat whilst he jammed the pistol's muzzle to his back.

"Not a motion now," Preston commanded steadily. "Free our ankles without delay."

Beneath the unwavering threat, Dauid reluctantly loosed the shackles. Catching Elara's eyes, wide with shock, Preston flashed a roguish grin. Her countenance relaxed a little.

With the knave divested of coat and boots at Preston's bidding, he drew Elara close behind him. Donning the rough-hewn footwear, he draped the coat across her trembling shoulders.

"Stay behind me, Blossom."

Gathering her hands, he placed them firmly against his back.

They strode past the brute's stunned companions. The guards threw up their hands, acknowledging defeat by tacit consensus and averted gazes. Some awoke from their slumber on the floor and looked dazed.

"I'll kill thee," Dauid threatened through gritted teeth.

"Not if I kill you first," Preston replied coolly.

Three armed knaves blocked progress down the dim corridor. Without hesitance, Preston propelled his human shield into their line of fire.

"Stay close at my heel, sweetheart," he said softly to Elara. Addressing the fiend, he said, "Should shots fly, you'll meet death first whilst I might take mere grazes. Instruct your rogues to lay down their arms this instant."

The blackheart replied solemnly, "I'm dead anyhow if thee flee this place."

"A fine point," Preston allowed. "You may have some time before they learn of the incident and chase after you. Hide until the first sail and journey to the colony. You may die of old age yet."

Beads of sweat formed on the blackguard's brow whilst calculating his options.

When no answer came, Preston repeated his demand.

"Direct your men to permit our passage unharmed or face the consequences."

"Put down yer guns!" Dauid finally shouted.

Sullenly, the guards obeyed, raising their hands.

"The lady requires suitable boots and coat. Fetch them for her."

A lackey swiftly returned with a worn coat and sturdy ladies' boots for Elara. Martha followed on his heels with scathing words about thievery until the unfolding standoff gave her pause. Preston stood vigilant guard whilst Elara hastily donned the ill-fitting footwear and coat.

"Thank you for your contribution, dear Martha. Would you like to come along?" Preston asked as he took Dauid's coat from Elara and slipped it on.

The woman giggled, her anger diffused.

"Will you open the door for us, love?" he asked with a wink.

Martha hastily did his bidding. As they passed through the door, Preston kissed her on her crimson cheek.

"Stay away from the door, love," he said tenderly to the blushing woman.

Once outside, Preston ordered Dauid to bar the entrance. The fiend retrieved his key chain and locked the door.

Spying mounts nearby, Preston queried, "Can you ride astride, Blossom?"

"Yes," Elara assured eagerly, anticipation of freedom seemingly lending wings to her spirit.

"Excellent. Here, stand against this wall." He pointed at the wall near the door. "Get the reins and hold on tight. I'd hate to scare them off," he said whilst training the flintlock pistol upon their captive's crown. The moment she had the reins in her hands, he kicked the fiend away from them. Dauid fell onto the ground but stumbled back on his feet with a sway. Shouts came from inside the house.

Taking swift aim upon the rogue, Preston bade, "Who hired you?"

"I dun't know."

"Who gave the order?"

"Me chief."

"Who is your commander?"

"I dun't know."

"Tell me your leader's name if you wish to live."

The man shrugged, anxiously looking at the door.

"Why did they choose us?" Preston pressed.

"I dun't know."

"What was their aim in taking us captive?"

"I dun't know."

"You dress like a tramp for a Mun."

The villain flinched, wide-eyed, just before Preston's knife pierced the devil's heart.

*Bang!*

A shot fired inside the house onto the door handle.

"Mount!" Preston shouted, hoisting Elara onto the saddle and nimbly mounting the other horse.

The door burst open just as Preston bellowed, "*Hyah!*" This spurred the beast into motion. Elara clung to the rein, her hair whipping behind her as the horse reared and then lurched forward. Leading their headlong charge through the cottage's courtyard, Preston heard shouts and curses erupt behind them as they turned the corner sharply.

"Dun't shoot!" a man yelled from the cottage. "Us needs him breathin'!"

Beneath the watchful moon, Preston and Elara rode briskly into the night's sweet freedom, the cool wind rushing past their flushed faces. But new uncertainties lie ahead.

## Chapter Ten

# *Day Three: 3 March 1833 – four in the morning*

Preston and Elara rode through the bright, chilly morning at a breakneck speed to evade the blackguards. They alternated between ambling and trotting, looking behind them for any signs of horsemen giving them chase.

The chill morning air bit at Elara's cheeks as she rode, but warmth infused her heart. Preston's tender care had made their intimacy profoundly moving, even lovely. She still felt the reverent touch of his hands, the husky sound of his whispered affections—he had even professed his love. His tender "I love you" still echoed in her heart and filled her with joy.

Though her fingers were numb from the cold and body ached from riding astride for hours, the memory of his fervent caresses kindled an irrepressible flush. She now knew the life-changing passion of a good man's love. Though they were not yet out of the woods, she felt safe in Preston's capable hands. And in his arms, she had found a sense of belonging beyond anything she had ever known. However uncertain their future path, she trusted fully in the man who rode ahead of her.

But even the newly blazing flame of love could not shield her from the snow and squall buffeting them relentlessly. Elara's insides leapt with elation when Falcon Inn finally emerged through the storm's white fury. Keeping hidden from view once dismounted, Preston wordlessly enfolded her in his arms.

Tucking her hands inside his ill-fitting coat and head under his chin, he pressed fervent kisses to her snow-slicked temple. He didn't need to say a word. She knew he was overcome with relief at having her safely delivered to their destination.

Clinging to him tightly, she wept grateful tears into his coat, relieved that she was safe and thankful to have met this man. He felt her sniffling and pulled back to gaze at her with concern.

"Is something distressing you?" He cradled her wind-chapped face between his icy hands. Elara turned her face into his palm, nuzzling and pressing her frozen lips to the centre.

"I am happy," she managed, her voice trembling.

Unexpectedly, his expression became frigid.

She frowned. "Is something the matter?"

Preston traced his thumb along her trembling lower lip. Fatigue seemed to overcome him suddenly.

"Let us get you warm and rested. We're not free from peril and should seek shelter away from prying eyes. I'll not relax until you're nestled once more amongst your family."

"Might they still be in pursuit? We have not seen a soul in the past two hours."

Solemnity clouded his countenance. "It does seem unusual that they have not come after us. We must assume, however, that they're searching for us. Go inside and wait atop the stairwell. Make no eye contact or sound. I will secure us a chamber and join you soon."

Eagerness lit her eyes, knowing they would not yet part ways. Perhaps she would have enough time to work up the courage to ask about their future. Did she dare to dream he may offer for her before she raised the question?

Elara entered the inn tremulously, afraid the fiends might be waiting for her. To her relief, the common room was quiet with not a soul. Mindful of each creaky floorboard, she stole up the wooden stairs with the utmost care. There she waited, listening intently for Preston. Some minutes later came the jangling of the entry bell, sounding repeatedly until shuffling steps approached.

"How may I be of service, sir?" a gravelly voice inquired.

Preston's voice spoke. "Another gentleman and I require a chamber for the day. Your finest, good man."

"One-night stay? Very good, sir."

"My companion... concealed. I... allege... at cards."

Was he asking the innkeeper to conceal them?

"Quite so, sir. Leave all to me."

"A sovereign... good fellow... no man... were present."

"Mum as a grave, sir! Much obliged to ye!"

"In ten minutes, bring us provisions and drinks for two. Also, pen and paper."

"Very well. It shall be done."

The enthusiasm of the man's response somewhat relieved her worries, for he might honour such a well-paid discretion. Soon, she heard bounding strides and Preston appeared. With his countenance still solemn, he guided her by the arm to their chamber. He swiftly shut the bolt and the latch once they were inside. He shook the door forcefully to ensure its sturdiness.

Elara placed a hand on her stomach, anxiety building as Preston's visage remained severe. He approached the window and peered through the glass panes covered in ice and snowflakes.

"No ingress or egress here," he muttered. Rattling the latches, he shook each window. Seemingly satisfied, he inspected every furnishing methodically, as well as the gaps in the walls and floors.

"Whatever are you searching for?" Her voice was cautious in response to the tension in the room.

"Clues for secret passages. Naught amiss there."

Elara observed his practiced and seamless manoeuvres as she pondered aloud, "Clearly you have acquaintance with these procedures."

"Alas, too often have I put them to use."

When no further enlightenment was given, she asked, "Whence came that sovereign? I thought those scoundrels had stripped us of all we possessed."

"Indeed, they had. But I habitually tuck one within my leathers lest I find myself in such a plight as this."

When a sudden rap at the door startled her, Preston swiftly drew a pistol in hand, signalling Elara to hide behind the bed. She complied, doubting such precautions necessary. It was likely the innkeeper who was delivering their repast.

"Who's at the door?"

"Begging yer pardon, sir. I'm the proprietor of this inn," a muted voice spoke beyond the door.

"Have you another companion, or do you come alone?"

"I am accompanied by my wife, sir. Between us, we carry victuals for ye."

Cracking the door, Preston confirmed the man's claim before concealing his firearm from view. Admitting the couple, he took possession of the trays. He declined their offer to start the hearth fire, taking the necessities from them to do it himself. His vigilant caution amazed Elara as she pondered the man whom she knew so little about except for his name... if it was indeed his name.

"Fetch warm water for bathing in half an hour. Here, send for two complete sets of day ensemble." Preston handed the innkeeper another shiny coin, which the other man received gratefully. "Should the blackguards come looking for me, do not engage. Deny seeing us, but do not provoke them."

At the gravity of his tone, the couple bowed nervously and took their leave.

After starting the fire with practiced hands, Preston held a chair and bade Elara to sit. Sitting across from her at the small table, their knees touched. Neither shied away from the contact, and she derived solace from this. Surely, this was proof their bond was no illusion.

They quietly consumed the stew and bread, which proved delectably tender. This was likely the proprietors' fare from supper the night prior. Ravenous from having starved for days from coiled nerves, Elara ate with abandon until naught remained in her bowl. Glancing up, she met Preston's amused smile. She delicately dabbed her lips with the serviette.

"Pray, do not stand on false airs now for my benefit."

She responded to his mocking by grabbing the remnants of his bread and making quick work of it.

"Fear not, for I have no pretensions to gentility." She chewed vigorously.

"Never have I met a more selfish woman." He leaned back and crossed his arms, his knees sandwiching hers under the table. Her stomach fluttered at the intrusion.

"Likely because you seldom enjoy feminine company," she retorted.

His smile was melancholic as he looked down at the candle.

"Quite so."

His low voice affected her in ways she did not understand. It made her skin tingle and even reached into her core and soothed it or made it weep. Elara observed his face and saw a frown. His mind was elsewhere.

Swallowing her unease, she asked, "What, no heated rejoinder? Where is your manly valour?"

Preston woke up from his reverie and held up his hands. "Only a fool argues with a lady. The quarrel is lost before it has begun." Offering her his remaining stew, he said, "Especially when I must sleep in the same room as the said lady warrior."

"You are wise indeed," she teased with feigned reverence. "Are you not famished?"

"I have little appetite presently."

The morsel vanished quickly before Preston's amused gaze. He laid the parchment on the table and began scribbling.

"What are you writing?" Elara took a sip of her ale.

"I'm writing to a friend, requesting his carriage and men for protection. They shall deliver us home."

"Where do you reside?" she asked cautiously, wondering if he would tell her.

"My office is in Slough, north of London. I live above my office. Look for my law firm if you need me."

"Only if I need you?" She tried to hide the stab in her heart. He was not going to offer for her. Was it possible only she felt this ordeal was a transcendent event to bond over? Could his tender words have meant nothing?

"Aye."

His simple reply clawed at her heart, rending a gaping wound. In her heart of hearts, she prayed fervently he might rescue her once more with his loving words, spare her the shattering grief. She knew not how she could find happiness without him.

## Chapter Eleven

# *Day: 3 March 1833 – five in the morning*

Elara stood and walked away from the table. She would preserve some dignity by hiding her tears.

"I thought our tender moments held greater meaning between us. Can feigned affection ring so true as yours did?" Anguish threaded her voice.

His tone was unfeeling and unyielding. "Our pretence was necessary."

Shock and ache bloomed fiercely in her breast. "You confessed ardent love when there was no compulsion to do so," she shot back.

"I wished you to feel loved during your first intimate encounter. I hoped only to gift you loving memories of our union."

She whirled around. "You uttered those words out of pity?"

"Not pity but concern and affection. I aimed only to gentle the wounds inflicted on your virtue." Calm pervaded his every word as if he spoke of another's plight entirely. He watched her steadily like a father anticipating a child's tantrum.

Elara gazed out the frosted window, eyes brimming with tears. A vice gripped her heart, slowly squeezing until every beat caused an ache so profound it stole her breath. She had envisioned lazy summer days picnicking in Kew Gardens, cosy nights nestled by the fireside in one another's arms. A future rich with joy, weaved with strands of their shared laughter and survival. Her foolish reveries drifted away with his words that pierced her soul.

He did not love her. He might feel affection in some small measure, but not the all-consuming longing that blazed within her for him. And he was not the honourable man she thought he was.

She wrapped her arms around herself tightly but could not stave off the chill creeping into her bones. She loved so deeply but must now shoulder this grief alone. The pain was almost too heavy to bear.

"Tell me the truth. Would any other maiden have received the same treatment in my stead?"

She knew the truth must wound but could not forestall the query. She wished he might yet surprise her.

"I confess, I would alter nothing were chance to repeat itself." No ambiguity clouded his decisive response. "I would've treated them with the same consideration, and I wouldn't have fallen in love with them either. How could I? I've known you for only three days."

"Sometimes it only takes one breath..."

The words wedged in her throat. Silent sobs trembled her body, but he shall not witness her vulnerability. She dried her tears on her sleeves and turned around.

"I care not a whit for your feelings on the matter! Although through no fault of your own, you have taken my innocence. I have no doubt search parties scour the land at my family's behest. None shall believe my virtue is intact. You alone can rescue my reputation by making me your wife!"

"Softly, my lady. You're supposed to be a lad."

The address cut through her like a blade. She was no longer his sweet tempting muse but "my lady," distant and polite.

"A life shared between us could never be. Were I of such inclination, obstacles would forestall any union, not to mention that I'm a poor solicitor. I cannot keep you in the comfort you're accustomed to," he said, his voice still even and reserved.

"I shall be comfortable as long as I have you at my side! Do not believe for a minute you know of my needs and wants, Nicholas. What conceivable barriers stand in our way other than your unwillingness?" she cried.

His icy blue gaze regarded her vacantly. "I am already married."

Colour drained from Elara's already pale cheeks. She swayed as if she had been dealt a physical blow. One hand flew to cover her mouth as she struggled to draw a breath.

"M-married?"

At last, the fractured words broke free, although her mind still recoiled from this newest cruelty. "You're married... You're bound to another..." Repeating it, she finally grasped the meaning. It felt impossible to will this anguished disbelief into acceptance.

"I am." His confirmation, devoid of feeling, tore through her chest.

"Why did you not apprise me sooner?" She forced her query through ragged breaths that seared her throat.

"Your trials were such already. Trapped as we were, I saw no recourse but to play my part. I wished only to spare you further distress where possible."

"You have a wife waiting for you at home... Have you any children?"

"Nay."

"Now, you shall return home and retire nightly to your wife's arms... to call her tender endearments..." Her own whispered words became the daggers that shredded her heart. Taking shelter behind her hands, her frame shook with sobs.

"Forgive me for hurting you," he uttered grimly.

"I resent that you have shown me something so wonderful only to take it away. Instead of remembering a kind man, I shall forever associate my first time with this betrayal and hurt." Elara wiped her cheeks with angry swipes. "What if I'm with your child? What then? Is my babe to be a by-blow?"

His eyes remained as inscrutable as marble. "I have a condition precluding fatherhood, so I was given to believe. Some slim chance remains you may carry life within you, but it is very unlikely. I have not impregnated my wife."

Elara's heart tore afresh at the mention of bedding his wife. She couldn't help but imagine him making love to her as tenderly as he had with her... night after night... speaking her name like a prayer.

"Do you love her?"

The words tumbled out despite how much she hated sounding so desperate. Was she not humiliated enough by his admission? Did she truly wish to increase her torment by listening to his confession of love for his wife? But she had to know. She needed the truth.

"Our marriage is complicated," he said after a long pause. "I need not ponder anything beyond that I made a vow to her."

Elara sank onto the bed, half resigned to their reality. Deep down, she knew he had done his best under the circumstances. Had he meant to mislead her for nefarious reasons, he would have taken advantage of her for another night before revealing his marital status. She supposed she ought to be thankful he had not charmed her into bed before his confession. She knew she would have fully given herself to him and another shard of her heart would have splintered.

"Should I indeed find myself blessed, would you wish to know of the babe?" She braced for the agony his words may cause.

His piercing gaze seized and held her fast. "Should you be carrying my child, I shall shake the pillars of heaven until the sky yields, and we are bound in matrimony."

## Chapter Twelve

# Day Three – 3 March 1833 – six in the morning

Preston remained stoic, hollowness veiling his eyes, whilst a woman who had imprinted his heart with a piece of herself now wept bitterly on his account. Any flicker of light within him was extinguished by despair, robbing him of joy. Was he foolish for believing she'd be better able to weather a heartache when the physical threat was eliminated? He had never meant to cause her pain. Yet, fate had shown neither mercy nor care for good intent.

As the sound of bathwater drifted through the door, Preston cradled his head in his hands. Six years have passed since his wife had quit their home. Such had been their agreement upon their nuptial. After one year of marriage, they were to go their separate ways should there be no child between them. Even after living as husband and wife for a year, he had harboured not an iota of affection or esteem for the woman. This had caused her much distress, believing her beauty was irresistible to all men.

In his years as a civilian, Preston had encountered no lady alluring enough to tempt him into intimacy more than once. Regular trysts risked personal entanglements, and he was determined to avoid this at any cost. His Slough office was his third attempt to conceal his whereabouts, and Preston was his second identity. Women, as far as he was concerned, were unnecessary risks for a man who had endangered his life to live freely, away from the constraints he was born into. Thus, since his wife's departure, he had remained without any lasting female companionship.

He had devoted his life to justice for the poor and was fearless in challenging any powerful men on behalf of his claimants. His first notion was that the kidnapping was a retaliation by a man who had lost to him in court. Was it possible Elara became the unfortunate victim because of him?

Elara... He found himself near crazed with longing, consumed by fears of life bereft of her quiet vitality. He yearned to know everything about her. What did she do when she awoke in the morning? What did she like to read? What did she think of Ceylon and Saint Helena being exempted from the Slavery Abolition Act?

And he wished to worship every inch of her until she cried out his name in rapture. He could not deny her impact on his carnal desires. Clearly, the dire circumstance had moved him to play the gallant rescuer, but nay, that could not wholly explain this phenomenon.

Could it be the surprising passion she possessed? He had not dreamed of encountering a zealous virgin. But surely no virgin had ever loved with such openness. Even some experienced women with vivacious personalities had lain with emptiness behind their eyes even while they found their peak. But Elara...

He closed his eyes, conjuring up her eager mouth and smouldering eyes, not to mention her sensual moans... His cock jerked at the thought.

A sudden chill cascaded through his thoughts. Dear God, what if she had conceived? Highly improbable, given his wife's barrenness throughout their year of conjugal relations. Yet if by some chance she was carrying his child... Preston scarcely dared to give rein to such thoughts. No child of his would enter this world an illegitimate, and he would not allow her to suffer alone.

A choking numbness descended upon Preston's chest. He was desperate to flee the ruin imprinted on an innocent heart, however, he could not abandon her. He needed to look upon her, breathe her in, and ensure her safety. At the same time, he needed to let her go and pursue her own bliss. Heavens strike him down if he stood between Elara and her happiness.

He moved to the door and listened intently for footfalls or sounds of stealth. Afterward, he scanned the frosted panes draped in snow crystals and discerned no shifting shadows outside. It was curious none had searched the inn for them. Nothing of these strange events formed a sense or pattern.

As this thought took grim root, Elara emerged from the bath in a borrowed nightshirt. Her face was ashen beneath the pale light. The sodden amber tresses hung limply, the shade still a stark contrast to the gloom within their chamber.

"I shall leave the door ajar while I bathe," Preston informed her as he walked past. He pulled his shirt overhead, noting her gaze trace the musculature of his torso before she glanced away. He moved toward the bath, unfastening his breeches.

He sank into the water, welcoming its warm embrace and gentle strokes. Despite his willed restraint, wayward thoughts winged back to tender caresses traded between them. What a rascal he was to grow a bulge after the ordeal she had been through and the heartache he had caused.

Under the soapy water, he gripped his rigid rod and stroked to the images of her erotic expression, his name on her lips, and the heavenly feel of breaching her maidenhead.

She belonged to him. She had enshrouded him and drawn him in. How delicious it had felt to thrust against her heat within the tight grasp of her chaste inner flesh. Unlike other women who usually recoiled in pain when they joined, she had welcomed him despite it with a passion equalling his fierce hunger. Granted, he had not fully buried himself inside her, but he knew she'd eagerly receive anything he had to give. Their mutual desire had pushed everything and everyone into oblivion, leaving them with only each other.

Rising out of the metal tub, he confirmed Elara was resting in bed before closing the door to the water closet. Taking care not to make a sound, he recalled his hand stimulating her sensitive bud while entering her from the side. A minute or two were all he needed for the release.

"Elara…" he whispered under his breath as he spent into the basin, easing the pressure but not the desperate longing that consumed him. "Damn," he muttered, noticing his cock was still tingling with arousal.

Donning the nightshirt borrowed from the innkeeper, Preston leaned upon the doorframe. Snow had not eased, and the air was as grey as a coal mine town. The sole lantern cast its pale glow over the wall, abandoning the bed itself to shadow. Though he discerned the shape of her form beneath the covers, he went to assure himself she lay safely. Standing over her, he seized her delicate features in his mind. He suspected that his mind's eye would behold her sleeping face for many days to come.

Preston situated a chair before the door and settled himself within, arms crossed, and head tilted back to rest against the door. Here he would rest and bar any sinister soul from gaining entry.

In a moment of weakness, his eyes strayed longingly to the bed which was wide enough to share. His feet would dangle off the edge, as was usually the case, but that lumpy straw mattress had sureties of comfort his rigid wooden seat could not provide. That and Elara lay in it, curled up like a scared animal. He quickly averted his gaze, quashing his impulse to hold her.

When he had braved the elements as a secret agent, taking the frigid night's blast fully as he propped himself up against an oak, he had only thought about his survival—food, warmth, and all the spirits he would drink. The past few days had confined him helplessly to an unknown fate, but he was only tormented by Elara's anguish and his want of her. Was this love, then? Love borne of shared struggles?

Mayhap it was no more than a fleeting fancy, shaped by dire circumstances and fanned briefly to brilliance between two souls. Within his depth, however, she was dazzling brighter with each passing moment. She was dawn's first radiance after an endless night. Losing her would fling him into the darkness again.

## Chapter Thirteen

# *Day Three – 3 March 1833 – half past seven in the morning*

Elara rose from the bed, shivering from the chill. Preston had stoked the fire in the hearth at dawn, but it was no contest against the icy air outside. He was sleeping in a chair, arms crossed, and head propped against the door. At the sight of him, a sharp ache pierced her chest and stopped her in her tracks.

She would never find peace, torn as she was between the heartbreak he unintentionally caused and the tenderness he showed her. Being near him elicited both joy and sorrow, peace and pain—emotions impossible to reconcile.

She walked towards the fireplace on the balls of her feet to add a log to it. She had taken only a few steps when Preston sprang up, pistol cocked and sweeping the room. Elara stifled a squeak behind her hands.

"It's all right, Nicholas. It's only me."

Relief flooded his countenance.

"Begging your pardon. I meant not to disturb you," she entreated, pressing a hand to her chest to still her pounding heart.

He lowered the weapon and leaned back against the oak door. "Think nothing of it. And be at ease. I'd never fire blindly."

"Of course. I was merely surprised, not frightened," Elara assured him. "It is not every day one spends the night with an armed man in their bedchamber."

"I am pleased to add excitement to your life, my lady," Preston said with a hint of a smile.

"Please, do not look so smug, sir. I had no complaints about my life before our... unfortunate encounter."

"Truly? I struggle to conceive of any hobbies that may provide such a thrill for a lady unwed."

Elara's lips thinned in resolution. "Perhaps not the import of your work. But I have my share of duties on Father's estate. And so many social invitations: balls, soirees, weeks-long gatherings. My dance card is always full."

Preston visibly tensed, though he kept his tone light. "I had the impression gentlemen kept their distance due to your reputation as the heartbroken woman."

She forced a cheerful countenance. "I may be too old for some gentlemen but remain pleasing to others."

He peered into her eyes ferociously, almost demanding her to deny the truth of her statement.

"I am delighted for you," Preston said after a long moment.

He didn't look pleased, Elara observed with perplexity. Rather, he looked greatly disquieted.

---

"Am I to expect you to be betrothed in the near future?" Preston asked casually, carefully masking the torrent of emotions.

Dropping her head, she sat on the bed and tucked her legs under her buttocks. Preston exhaled slowly, his eyes riveted on her bare legs.

They would likely burn the clothes they had been wearing for three days. Until the innkeeper brought them new clothes, he'd be plagued by the sight of her legs which led to... other parts.

Resigning to the torment, he leaned against the door and closed his eyes. He can't be tortured by what he cannot see. Except he was wrong. His mind's eye saw her round eyes as he entered her, her dewy lips whispering his name, and her bare legs...

The rap on the door had him bolt out of the chair. After interrogating the innkeeper at the door, Preston gratefully accepted the clothes and a message from his friend. He handed one outfit to Elara while perusing the missive.

"What is it?" she asked.

"My friend has advised me that a carriage is on its way. We shall stay here until their arrival. I believe they'd be here in three hours or so."

"I see." She sounded disappointed. Or was it his imagination? "Is it safe here, do you reckon?" she asked.

"Safer than traveling on horseback. Somerset shall send men trained in combat."

"Somerset? Do you mean the Duke of Somerset?"

"Aye. Are you acquainted?"

"Yes, a little. I like the duke and the duchess very much. However do you know them?"

"I represented the duchess in a trial recently."

"You are not the poor country solicitor you claim to be. You are well-connected."

Preston remained silent.

"Does that mean we may run into each other at gatherings?" she asked.

"No," he replied firmly as he hardened his resolve to avoid her at all costs. He could not fathom seeing her amongst the *ton*, as if she were a mere acquaintance. And to watch men fawn over her... He'd assault someone before the assembly was over.

Better to end it all here than face fresh agony with each stolen hour. To possess her again could never slake the thirst her taste ignited, condemning him to an eternal chase of her touch. In his heart, he knew he would forever yearn for just one more day in her arms.

He watched Elara, bathed in a faint light from the small fire in the hearth. How he would miss gazing upon her beloved face. He gave his head a mental shake. He must focus on more pressing matters.

"I shall follow behind you to ensure you reach home safely," he informed her.

Elara frowned without looking at him. "All the way to Stamford? Surely that is unnecessary with trained men guarding me."

"You may be right. Still, I would rest easier seeing you home safely to your father."

At the mention of her father, Elara sank. "What shall I tell him? The truth would devastate the poor man. His health had suffered much already."

Preston's heart constricted at her distress and his cursed marriage.

"I'm sorry I cannot do more for you," he murmured.

Elara shook her head, tendrils of red hair escaping her chignon. "You did all you could, given the circumstances." Taking a deep breath, she asked, "Had you not been wed, would you have offered for me?"

"Aye," he said without hesitation.

---

Preston's reply swept over her like a wave, briefly lifting the crushing weight from her heart and allowing her to breathe again. That he would have offered for her brought consolation, kindling bittersweet joy at what might have been.

His admission had soothed the raw ache of her longing. Though the flame guttered against the winds of circumstance, his words were a balm to her battered spirit. She would treasure this small gift of proof that what passed between them was not one-sided.

"I shall look into whoever orchestrated this vile crime. If you've cause to worry, I will send a word."

Elara nodded, swallowing the lump in her throat.

"You should refrain from attending the theatre or going anywhere unchaperoned henceforth."

"I don't believe I could ever enjoy such diversions again without remembering this nightmare," Elara whispered, twisting the hem of her nightshirt.

"I understand."

"Is this it, then? We never see each other again?" she asked, feeling panicked.

"Aye. I am a married man who has deceived you. Remember that, and it should not prove too difficult to forget."

Her eyes pooling with tears, Elara fled to the water closet, closing the door firmly behind her.

The luxurious carriages with a Somerset family crest displayed prominently arrived exactly three hours later. The eyes of the driver and footmen roamed the surroundings while Preston helped Elara board. Her swollen, red eyes did not meet his, and he could only see a handkerchief over her mouth. His heart shrivelled, grieving his loss and her pain. After a brisk bow, he spun on his heels and fled to his own transport before he could stop her.

## Chapter Fourteen

# *3 March 1833 – five in the evening*

Alone in the carriage, Elara permitted herself to feel the soul-crushing agony. Her heart paid no heed to what her mind told it and thrashed about wildly. What had she been thinking? It was her own fault for assuming a random gent trapped with her would be available and willing to wed her. It had not occurred to her that the honeyed words which melted her insides might have been feigned. She had believed he was in love with her. What a ninny she had been.

Deep in her heart, she knew he was right to withhold the information for their well-being. He was more concerned with survival than breaking a naive woman's heart. A lady of more experience may have suspected something or known what to ask.

Elara wanted to yell at her own naivety. But the love in her heart could not be unfelt, and the dreams undreamt.

She looked out the rear carriage window upon hearing gravel crunching under the wheels. She could see Preston's carriage following closely behind until they entered the circular driveway.

Disembarking from the carriage, Elara gazed back toward the shadows behind the gate, hoping to catch a glimpse of him. Despite feeling him in her very soul, his future would never converge with hers. The thought of him trotting toward his wife slashed her heart anew.

Elara entered the grand hall of the Stamford Manor and was greeted immediately by the butler's surprised visage. Mr Roberts' eyes quickly surveyed her breeches and coat but ignored them. Instead, he exclaimed, "Lady Elara! We did not expect you until the morrow, but we are grateful for your early return."

This threw Elara headlong into puzzlement.

"Had you not been searching for me?"

It was Mr Roberts' turn to be perplexed.

"No, my lady. The viscount did not wish for us to disturb you at such a prestigious festivity."

"I see..." But she didn't see. She gestured for the butler to follow. Setting a brisk pace toward her father's bedchamber, she asked, "So you believed me to be at the Acton Manor?"

"Aye, my lady. Were you not?"

"I-I was."

"It is just as the letter informed us then."

"A letter?"

"Yes, from the countess herself. Her ladyship informed us that you were departing the festivities tomorrow. Mrs Whytes and I were just discussing whether we ought to inform you about his lordship."

"Father? What has happened?"

"He has taken ill, my lady. Dr Hopps has been to see him."

"Is his condition dire?"

"The viscount spoke with the doctor. He is with the earl at present. Shelley returned only last night. She ought to be in your bedchamber."

It did not escape her notice that the butler had evaded her question.

Elara climbed the stairs, engrossed in thoughts about her father and how Lady Acton had known of her movements. A cold chill went down her spine. Perhaps there was no celebration at all. Her captors could have orchestrated it. But why would anyone go through this much trouble to capture her? To demand a babe from her? Or perhaps there was a celebration, and it was the kidnappers' design to seize her while her family expected her to be away. She shuddered at the notion of the beasts manipulating her life.

# ABDUCTED

She refocused her attention on her father and how to handle James. She had been wary of her cousin since the earl's health had begun to decline. He had been more insistent on marrying her and had refused to accept her rejection.

Her father had understood her objection, but he did not wish to lose his nephew's favour. James was an influential figure in the House of Lords, supremely popular and skilled at extracting secrets from the members. Unfortunately, Lord Stamford's strategy had been stringing James along, giving the impression he may consent. But with her father's illness and advanced years, she was certain James would not wait any longer.

She had loved him once, but now, the mere thought unsettled her stomach. More so since discovering how pleasurable the physical act could be. If only Preston was here...

Nearing her father's bedchamber, Elara suddenly felt a crippling fatigue, as though she had lived three lives in the last three days. The pain of losing Preston consumed her as she walked into the room where her father lay in bed with James sitting by his side. The viscount's dark eyes looked up and a smile spread across his face, a little too brightly given his uncle's sickbed.

"Ah, just the person I was hoping to see," James said, standing up.

"Hello, James. How's Father?" she whispered, approaching the bedside.

"Not well, I'm afraid." James came around to her side and kissed her cheek.

"What did Dr Hopps say?"

"Your father suffered an apoplexy. He may not regain the function of his right side."

The meaning of his words hit her unaware by the way he delivered them—with little emotion. Her hands flew to her mouth as comprehension dawned. She shook off James' attempt to comfort her and knelt by the old man. Gently, she stroked his creased cheek. The earl opened his left eye, his right side twisted and lacking life.

"Father," she said weakly and placed a gentle hand on his arm. He opened his mouth, and a raspy, incoherent sound came out.

"He cannot speak."

She turned her head to look at James, alarmed by his icy tone. The fear which had lurked in the background leaped forward when she saw his mocking smile. His smile said the very thing she had feared. That she would belong to him upon her father's death... or maybe before.

"But he can nod or shake his head," he supplied.

Elara looked down at her father who had closed his eyes. She opened her mouth to speak when James drowned out her voice.

"Uncle, it would be my greatest honour to take Elara as my wife as you have always intended. Will you give us your blessing?"

She stared at him, surprise turning into anger. Elara stood defiantly as she whispered, "James, this is not the proper time, and you ought to ask me first."

"We shall discuss it later, my dear," he replied smoothly.

"I am not your dear," she hissed.

James ignored her comment with a dismissive shrug and turned to his uncle. "Please, uncle. We would like your blessing."

Elara watched her father open his one eye and pierce James with a dagger. To her delight and relief, he shook his head almost imperceptibly, but they both saw it.

"Thank you, Father," she said as she exhaled. But the relief was short-lived.

"No matter. You shall be my wife, regardless." His voice sent a chill down her spine.

She stood facing him. "I. Will. Not."

He stepped closer until he cornered her against the wall. Stooping to her eye level, he gritted out, "You have no choice."

"I do have a choice. You are just ignorant of my choices." She stepped away from him, feeling threatened by his nearness.

"I am the most practical choice, and I shall marry you."

An urgent vocalisation from her father had them turn to him in unison. He was trying to shake his head, but his body was not cooperating. His left eye was fierce with anger as he glared at James.

"I am the rightful heir! What would a woman do with all that wealth? She will be deceived by all the vultures. You leave me no choice but to marry her and manage it before all is squandered!"

"What are you saying, James?" she asked, puzzled by his outburst.

"Your father left everything to you save for the cottage on the tiny parcel of land! When he dies, you'll be a very wealthy woman. But you are not capable of handling the assets. You will likely bankrupt the estate in short order!"

"I know the estate business. I shall manage it superbly as I've been doing!"

"Not alone, you won't. This estate has been in our family for generations. I will not watch you destroy the riches, or watch another man enjoy the harvest reaped by our ancestors! No, we are going to be married before the old man dies."

"How do you know what you believe is true?"

James smirked arrogantly. "That is what I do. I extract secrets from spineless men. Fortunately, everyone has something to lose. Your father's solicitor confessed with the smallest amount of pressure."

Elara's head tried to furiously make sense of what she heard. But it was all too much to bear. Her father planned to leave her everything? She almost wished he hadn't. How was she to escape James now that he was more resolute than ever?

"I cannot marry you. I have already accepted another man's proposal," she blurted. "He is wealthy and influential, so I urge you to think very carefully before you threaten me."

The earl slowly opened his left eye.

"You are lying!" James thundered.

"I am not! In fact, I have given him my virtue and may carry his child," she confessed with a wince. The wound gaped open as she said the words, but it was the only weapon she could think of against James. What man would want to question the legitimacy of his child?

She turned away from James' scowl and reached for the earl's hand.

"He is an honourable man, Father. You can be assured he will treat me kindly. He loves me and I..." she trailed off, overcome with the truth of her emotion. "I love him so much."

The old man's weak squeeze on her hand gave her hope in a heart mired in despair.

"Do not worry about me. I will be very happy with him."

"Who is he? What is his name?" James barked.

Without looking at him, she feigned all the confidence she could. "I cannot reveal his identity until I discuss it with him first."

"If you are telling the truth, why has he not called on the earl?"

"He planned to once I returned."

"I look forward to meeting him." James' eyes squinted with suspicion.

"I shall ask him to delay his visit until Father has improved."

"No. Summon him tomorrow," he said sternly.

"I will not. Not when Father needs his rest."

"Then I will assume you're lying."

"I just returned home to discover my father in his sickbed! Give me a moment to breathe!"

James yanked her upright, his eyes crazed and nostrils flaring. He opened his mouth then halted upon seeing the look in her eyes.

"What happened to you, James? We used to be friends," she said softly.

His jaw flexed, but he surprised her by releasing his grip.

"I grew up," he replied gruffly.

Turning away from her, he stood motionless with his hands on his hips. Elara waited wordlessly, holding her father's hand, and sensing a shift in James. Finally, he turned around.

"I am sorry. Please forgive me," he said with his head bowed. "I've lost my senses, myself. I've behaved most abominably." He raised his head and looked at her. "If I may be permitted to explain myself, I suppose I'm hurt by Uncle's low regard of me and the rest of the family. I never imagined he would leave me so little as if I didn't matter enough. I dare say the rest of the family would feel the same."

"Of course you must feel betrayed," she replied although she had her doubts where his sincerity was concerned. "If I may speak for Father, he holds you in high regard and believes you to be extremely capable. You already have a large fortune, and the rest of the family enjoys prosperity as well. Wielding influence as much as you do at your young age, he has spoken to me many times about how you shall eventually rule England."

James shifted his focus onto his uncle, surprise in his expression. Whether he believed everything she said, his self-serving arrogance couldn't help but believe her at least a little. It had always been his weakness.

"I appreciate the sentiment, but it isn't enough to placate the sense of abandonment," James said.

"Think about it, James. I have nothing. I am a woman. Would you not wish to protect your daughter if you were in Father's position?"

James nodded. "Why, of course. But I would protect you once we were married. I know I made a grave mistake in my youth, but I'm still a bachelor despite having many prospects. I've been distraught over our broken engagement. There is a part of me that will never recover unless you marry me, El."

Elara suppressed the laughter in her throat. "One day, you'll make a lady very happy, but it will not be me, James. At present, I need time to care for Father. Will you please give me the time and peace to do a daughter's duty?"

He nodded. "I will. Again, my deepest apologies for being brutish with you."

Elara smiled innocently. "I knew I could count on you, Cousin. Thank you."

James dipped a shallow bow and exited the room. It did not escape her notice that he had not offered an apology or deference to her father.

Elara bent down and whispered in her father's ear, "Do not worry, Father. I am not fooled by his act. I shall be well. Nicholas will protect me. You may have heard of him. Nicholas Preston, the solicitor and barrister."

## Chapter Fifteen

# *6 March 1833 – seven in the morning*

Elara gave up sleeping and rose from the bed. She donned her thick robe and sat at her escritoire in her bedchamber. She had slept fitfully from nightmares. When she awoke, her mind whirled with questions about how she would proceed with the lie she started.

She needed to find someone influential to be betrothed to if she were to have any hope of keeping James away from her. He had already moved into their home despite living in the next estate. He behaved like the master, ordering the servants about. Naturally, the staff deferred to him on decisions, assuming James would inherit the title and the current home they occupied.

Sighing deeply, Elara pondered the possible husbandry candidates she could tolerate. The Earl of Willoughby had sought her hand thrice in the past two years. His stomach would drape over her in bed, and she would need to manoeuvre the treacherous path of being a stepmother, but he was a kind man. She could learn to love a kind man. After all, she harboured no fanciful notions about marriage or spinsterhood. She desired a husband and a family of her own with shared respect. The earl was only forty years old. He would be agreeable to siring more children if she wished.

Then there was Viscount Hugh who had offered for her once before. He was much older, approaching sixty, but he has never been married. Her understanding was that he had thought of family as a distraction from politics. Thanks to his devotion, he wielded quite a bit of power in Parliament and the House of Lords. Father had approved of him, and she had heard of men as old as seventy siring children. The viscount still admired her from afar. He had accepted her refusal with grace and still sent her flowers on her birthday.

But Nicholas Preston, he was the one she wanted. He is not the powerful man she claimed her betrothed to be, but that did not matter. He would let his presence be known to James. Her fingers itched to pen a letter to him, but she knew she ought not to.

He had a wife. Even if he could pretend to be her fiancé, how long could he continue the sham? They'll be found out sooner or later. James was a patient man. He would use every ammunition in his power to discredit their nuptials before giving up on what he believed to be his. For now, he was cautious in case her fib about her fiancé was true. It shall not be long before he suspected her lie.

Elara's vision blurred at the thought of Preston. Not now. Not again. She irritably wiped the tears off her face.

The next question was how she would approach the gentlemen about offering for her again. It would be scandalous for her to call on them or make the suggestion directly. She would need a mediator. Her aunts had been her mentor regarding delicate matters, but they agreed with James that the earl's wealth ought to be kept within the family. It was a shame Elara didn't have a distant cousin who could make a woman feel protected and cherished during trials and tribulations. And one who could pleasure her...

She tapped her finger on the desk as she pondered asking her father's solicitor for help. He could make discreet inquiries. He would be reviewing her marriage contract, anyway. Or... Elara's pulse began to race, and she stood from excitement. She could use this as an excuse to contact Preston. She could see him once more.

She then wondered to herself, what was the purpose of seeing him again only to have her heart broken?

There was no purpose other than that she missed him. Buoyed by her soaring spirit at the prospect, it was easy to ignore the possibility that he may not welcome her in his sphere.

Preston watched the fresh snow on the ground turn to slush beneath the carriages passing by the inn's window. His every moment not occupied by work was consumed by thoughts of Elara. The images of her tear-soaked face and pink-tipped nose plagued him, and he felt himself drowning in her anguish as well as his own. He had, at one time, prided himself on maintaining a healthy detachment. Such stoicism was no longer within his power.

"Mr Jones has arrived, sir," a young lad said, standing formally at the threshold of the private dining room of the inn.

"Show him in," Preston replied.

An elderly gentleman, tall and lean with greying hair entered. He was garbed in a fine woollen greatcoat with a spine that looked to have been bolted upright with a broomstick. Irritation simmered off him as he took a seat.

The lad poured brandy from a crystal decanter and presented the glass to the visitor. Once the servant quit the room, Preston took a seat across from the gentleman and raised his own glass in greeting.

"To your health, Father."

"Four years of silence without any knowledge of whether you lived or perished, only to summon me a mere one day afore our appointment?" his father remarked irritably. "Du hast Nerven, Junge."

"Advance notice would only have provided an opportunity for your meddling," Preston returned coolly. "Besides, you likely knew I'd request an audience even before I did."

His father ignored the barb with a dismissive harrumph. "I had hoped you sought me out to declare you had wed and sired children."

"Not precisely."

"Then surely you have come to your senses and intend to assume your rightful place."

Preston scoffed. "Do not try your luck, old man."

His father's face hardened. "What is your purpose in summoning me?"

"Are you aware of Julia's whereabouts?"

"Your wife? Nay, why should I?"

"Very little slips your notice, as a rule."

His father bristled. "I make no habit of monitoring you."

Preston smiled sardonically. "One of your endearing qualities is denying the obvious. Your men have been trailing me for years. I do not mind. It keeps my mind sharp and my skills polished. You ought to train your lackeys better, however. They're too easy to elude," Preston needled.

"They are the finest in the nation!" the old man blustered.

"A sad commentary on the state of espionage."

His sire waved a hand. "What need have you of your wife, anyway? I thought you wished no connection."

Preston kept his expression neutral, although he felt anything but. "I'd like to seek an annulment."

Surprise flickered in the old man's eyes before delight overtook his features. "Have you a girl you wish to wed, then?" Hope tinged his tone.

"I have no lady."

The man scowled. "Do not say she is some penniless chambermaid or fallen woman."

"I shall say nothing whatsoever."

"Are you ashamed of your intended?"

Preston pierced the old man with an icy stare. "I have no wish to make any woman a widow."

His father gasped. "How dare you give voice to something so wicked! After what your mother and I have endured... to jest of such things... Why, you must have a heart of stone!"

"You'll have only yourselves to blame if I were driven to stab my own heart," Preston returned coldly. "Hear me, Father. Meddle in my affairs again, especially involving women, and I shall leave you devoid of another son."

His sire stiffened, face reddening. "I've a mind to summon my men to restrain you this instant!"

In response, Preston placed a heavy chunk of metal on the table.

"A bullet to my head would cause quite a bit of scandal," he said evenly.

His father's eyes studied the pistol. In the next moment, his expression transformed into a benevolent, grandfatherly smile.

"Really now, must you be so intense always? Let us put the past behind us. But you have not answered me. Why seek an annulment after so many years have gone by?"

"If any ill should befall Julia, I've no wish to be held responsible for her children."

"Ah, yes. Caring for another woman's offspring would make for an awkward marriage once you have your own heirs."

Preston's eyes flashed with frustration. "Your ambition far exceeds your grasp of reality, Father. The physicians have declared me incapable of begetting children. A fact you seem unable to accept."

His father drew himself up, visibly affronted. "Mind your vulgar tongue, boy! Those licenced men declared a possibility, however remote."

"A pronouncement made because you pressured them, and they feared your wrath, you temperamental arse!"

"My influence merely hastened their conclusions!"

"If I have not got a single woman with child since my military discharge, common sense says the fault lies with me. Especially considering Julia bore another man three children. Do you understand?"

"Are you saying you did not employ sheaths with any of those women?"

"I did except with Julia, but we know of their inadequacies." Leaning back in his chair, Preston spoke with gravity. "Let us discuss why I sought your audience. Will you aid me in locating Julia?"

"Not unless you accede to my terms."

"You have already muzzled me in politics. What more do you require?"

"Are you claiming your legal cases against the wealthy and powerful are apolitical in nature? You might achieve the same purpose if you were to hold up a sign indicating you are 'anti-monarch' or 'anti-aristocrat'."

The two men sat in tense silence until his father spoke. "Fulfil your duty into which you were born. Assume your rightful place as my heir and cease tormenting your mother so."

Preston shook his head. "After your fanatical interference, it is impossible to tolerate you and Mother in my life."

The old man waved a hand. "We apologised for that years past. At minimum, keep us apprised of your whereabouts if you plan to disappear again."

"Your apologies are meaningless when you knowingly repeat the offence."

His father looked away unrepentantly. "I was trying to right the wrong. And it was obvious you would not be siring any children with her."

Preston scoffed, no longer shocked by the man's twisted logic. "Precisely why I refused a divorce so not another woman would suffer your tyrannous ways. And of all the women, you had to choose her!"

"Let bygones be bygones, son. I shall aid you in this pursuit, but you must return home."

"I am surprised you have not broken down my office door."

"Yes, well, you have ogres guarding the place at all hours of the day and night."

"Are you developing some finesse to your approach, Father? Or becoming acquainted with common sense? I must admit, I am impressed! Well done, sir."

"Pfft. You know very well I cannot make a scene. Imagine if it was known that two of my sons were assassinated and I misplaced the last one. I would become a laughingstock."

"It is almost comforting to know that my wellbeing and privacy had not influenced your decision whatsoever." Preston stood abruptly. "If you wish to reconcile, you might start by giving me the information I have every right to instead of withholding it for bartering." His jaw was taut with tension. "It seems we have reached an impasse. Good day, Father."

Preston quit the dining room as his father shouted, "Best of luck with your Sorbonne trial tomorrow!"

---

Leaning back in the supple calfskin chair in his modest abode, Preston mused how mere weeks ago, none could have named him anything but a ruthless officer of the law. Indeed, his detached disposition had rendered him ideally suited to covert service and to defend the unfortunate in the courtroom. He had been perfectly content with his life, escaping his father's machinations and achieving the lifelong aspiration of meaningful work and autonomy. That was before he met the woman he could love. Now, he doubted he would feel joy ever again.

Since returning home, he had not known a moment's happiness. A restless disquiet permeated his body and mind which nothing alleviated. Not work, riding, drinking, nor scouring his skin until he resembled a pig. Most perplexing and vexing of all, he had not even contemplated dalliances with other ladies, though comely lasses abounded both in town and country. The sole woman occupying his thoughts was she whose passion burned as fiercely as her flaming locks.

Now his shell lay shattered, its jagged fragments piercing his core. No wall stood firm against the siege of softer sentiments once alien to his world-wearied heart. Long submerged beneath disillusionment, tender shoots now strained toward the sun that was her beloved countenance. There lay the axis upon which his world now spun, ceaseless, fixed, as inevitable as dawn's golden light. Strange, indeed, when once no living lady could compel him beyond a fleeting fascination. He shook his head disbelievingly. One woman's gentle smile alone could now beckon the complete surrender of his spirit.

A soft rap at the door seized his attention. Drawing his pistol, he moved cautiously to the entrance. The coded knock came again, identifying the caller as Smith, his protection officer. Preston replaced the firearm in the holster and opened the door.

"Good evening, Mr Preston," Smith greeted with a brusque nod as he followed Preston in.

"And to you, Smith. Will you take some refreshment?" Without waiting for a reply, Preston poured the man a drink. "Your duties are completed for the day, I presume?"

"Aye, sir. Davies is standing guard in my place."

"Then sit and be at ease. Have you any news of Julia?"

Smith sat on the settee, dwarfing the furniture. "We have confirmed that the lady and her children left England on a train three years ago. The ship captain remembered her because of her forceful character and her beauty."

"Aye. That sounds like her. Where was she headed?"

"France. We plan to track her from there."

"Spain."

"Sir?"

"She's likely in Spain."

"Aye, sir. We shall begin the search in Spain."

"Approach it with extreme discretion, Smith. We do not want to stir things up with Spain and God forbid, France."

"I understand."

"And now, tell me about Lady Elara."

Smith removed folded papers from his pocket and scanned them before answering, "We espied her only once."

Preston paused with his glass nearly at his lips, gazing sharply at the man. "Whyever?"

"The Earl of Stamford has taken ill."

Preston felt the tension ease from his shoulders. Unfortunate to be sure, but she was unharmed. "Is it serious?"

"Aye. He suffered an apoplexy. He is paralysed on one side. The servants don't expect him to survive much longer."

Preston nodded solemnly. He knew the man as being honourable and generous. He felt a rush of sympathy for Elara. How she must suffer, so shortly after her own ordeal. When she should be the one to be comforted, she was acting as a pillar for her father and the household.

"Is she receiving many visitors?"

"No. According to the servants and neighbours, it is unusual as the relatives are a self-interested breed, not the comforting sort. It seems that she has one regular visitor, her cousin. James Frances."

His jaw clenched. Possessiveness stirred in his chest for the woman whose innocence he owned.

"Does he stay the night?" The question scraped through his throat.

Smith searched the paper for notes. "He has for at least one night. Their properties border alongside each other. It is difficult to decipher at night."

Preston resisted the urge to break something.

"Give me the details of Lady Elara's movements," he said instead.

Flipping through the notes, he said, "She went out one afternoon to the local parish. Her ladyship was striking..."

Smith's complexion reddened. Preston speared the man with an icy glare.

Smith's normally unflappable composure faltered. "That is, viewed objectively, she might be deemed comely... no improper fancy factors into such assessment."

Grimness settling on his brow, Preston ignored the man's comment. "Pray keep vigilant watch over the lady, Smith. Apprise me directly if any ill winds dare disturb her peace."

"Aye, sir."

"And be extra cautious around my vicinity. I may have stirred up the muck."

"Certainly, sir."

"And if you find yourself drawn to Lady Elara, know that I do not blame you. However, I would expect you to dismiss yourself from the assignment immediately."

Smith flushed, then accepted his payment with effusive thanks before hastening towards the door.

Preston watched his old friend leave with unease in his gut when he heard him exclaim, "My lords! Your Grace!"

He drew his pistol. He did not like unexpected guests especially the kind that startled his protection officer. His gaze shot to the three large figures.

Lowering his weapon, Preston chided his friends who stood frozen with hands aloft. "What the devil are you about, arriving unannounced?"

"We've come to rescue you from misery and heartache," proclaimed the Earl of Carlisle who was a self-made man of prodigious wealth acquired through tireless industry and shrewd manoeuvring. Carlisle's physique and coffers were equally massive. Still a bachelor, his unwed state remained a mystery, for Carlisle had long sought a bride and was quite eligible. With his newly earned title a year ago, nothing ought to stand in his way.

"I'm quite content as I am," Preston said.

"What the devil are you doing brandishing a pistol? Is there an irate husband after you again?" Cameron Pembroke, the Duke of Somerset, asked.

"No. I haven't bedded a woman in two years."

"And you claim to be content?" Arthur Redesdale, the Marquess of Salisbury, shook his head.

"As content as dung beetles with their fare," Somerset commented wryly. Still resembling a living Greek statue, he was besotted with his exotic bride, Asilia.

# ABDUCTED

There was a time Preston could not have fathomed how any man could be so profoundly altered by a woman. Did not a grown man of worldly experience already possess all he needed to view the world clearly? A man may want a woman but never needed one. How ignorant he had been. His heart was now upended entirely in the past week as Somerset's had.

If he was a different man now, how much more would having Elara as his wife change him? The notion warmed his heart, quickly inflamed by impatient longing.

"I'm a man quite content with the law as my mistress," Preston said unconvincingly.

"Only because you have never known true happiness," Salisbury contended. "Your notions of contentment are basic. You cannot envision what joy might await in a wife's embrace after the day's toil, rather than doxies in some club."

Though still brooding and intimidating to outsiders, Preston knew how peaceful Salisbury had grown since marrying three years prior. He suspected that the security in Salisbury's home life lent him the strength to advance astronomically in politics. He was headed to become a prime minister not far into the future.

The friends sat knee to knee upon the settee in the cramped quarters.

"Good Lord, man. When shall you cease dwelling like a schoolboy and secure proper furniture and space?" Somerset grumbled.

"I confess, it is gratifying to see you discomforted. Feel free to take your leave if it irks you so," Preston said.

"At least he keeps quality brandy," Andrew Whittingham, the Earl of Carlisle said approvingly, settling himself upon the floor and stretching out his legs. He distributed the glasses and decanter.

"We called upon you because suspicious figures have been lurking around here," Salisbury said before raising his glass in salute.

Preston's brows arched. His father's men have been watching him for months. "Is that so? When did you first take note of them?"

"Perhaps three days past," Carlisle replied casually.

"You waited three days to inform me?"

Carlisle shrugged, unrepentant. "We had no need of you prior to now."

Preston shook his head incredulously at their self-interest and his father's incompetent spies.

"I've forgotten how selfish you devils are," he muttered, taking a liberal swallow of brandy.

"We didn't hurry because the men resembled your father's men from three years ago," Salisbury said.

"Oh, yes. That day when we came to your rescue. I can't recall why you were hiding from him," Somerset drawled.

"He is fanatical about controlling my every movement." The bitterness rose within Preston like bile. Were it not for that blasted union, he might be making love to Elara rather than quaffing drinks with these bastards.

"What is it that had you seek me out?" Preston asked Carlisle.

"I have need of your services on my sister's behalf." Carlisle sat cross-legged with shoulders spanning the width of two men.

"Regarding what matter?"

"That scoundrel, Byron, withdrew his betrothal, claiming Autumn's virtue was compromised. I aim to sue the scoundrel."

"Hmm..." Preston furrowed his brow in thought. "The difficulty in domestic affairs unrelated to crime is the lack of precedent to determine compensation."

Carlisle nodded. "My goal is to publicise her innocence. I care not if we win, so long as I can show the court, and thereby the *ton*, that Byron's claims were dubious enough to warrant a trial. I'll involve the gossip columns too, naturally."

"I understand. The reality is no barrister would accept a case he knows will lose. Even if the case doesn't reach the court, one still needs to demand compensation. Without precedent, evaluating damages is still troublesome. What sum remedies a ruined reputation?"

Carlisle's bluntness was unsurprising. "What of the cost for housing an aging spinster?"

"No judge would hold Byron accountable for your sister's spinsterhood when he meant to save her from it. One cannot fault a Good Samaritan for rescinding charity," Preston pointed out brutally.

Carlisle grunted unhappily at this analysis.

"Would it not prove more effectual to proclaim her innocence through society's gossipmongers?" Salisbury mused. "Byron has hardly proven an honourable fellow. I confess I am unsurprised."

Carlisle nodded reluctantly. "I misjudged the blackguard in my haste to secure a match for Autumn."

Somerset eyed Preston shrewdly, a knowing smile playing about his lips that reputedly could melt any young lady. "Speaking of which, have you happened upon a suitable lady, Preston?"

"Whatever makes you ask that?" Preston fully intended to deny all.

"It shows in your face and manner. A certain restless energy," Somerset pronounced. "You seem rather discontent, old boy."

"And unfocused. Your thoughts are constantly elsewhere," Salisbury added.

"Merely my advancing years, I expect. I do contemplate settling down these days."

"Capital news!" Somerset raised his glass.

"Don't be foolish, man!" Carlisle snapped.

Somerset waved a pound note eagerly. "Let us wager on who marries first! Carlisle or Preston. Come now, who wants the bet?"

Salisbury nodded. "Put me down for one hundred pounds on Preston."

"My money's on Carlisle. No one achieves his ends faster once resolved," Somerset said, flashing a wad of bills.

"Confound it. Have you both lost your senses? Wagering on a friend's matrimonial felicity?" Carlisle grumbled.

But Preston hardly heard, lost in a pleasing daydream about taking Elara as his bride.

## Chapter Sixteen

# *8 March 1833 – six in the morning*

Elara awoke to the bright sunlight streaming through the window. The house was even quieter than usual as if her father was gone from them already. She hastily rose from the bed and rang for her lady's maid. She needed to check on her father, then meet his solicitor about estate matters.

She chose a brown dress with a high neckline to preserve modesty in her father's honour. Shelley was quieter than usual.

"How is Father this morning?"

"I believe his condition has not changed overnight," her lady's maid replied grimly. Elara studied her face for a moment. "Is there something else that is troubling you?"

Shelley's brows furrowed, and she feigned intense concentration on the buttons of Elara's dress.

"Shelley, tell me. What is wrong? You know you can tell me anything."

Her lady's maid finished buttoning the back of the dress and came around to face her. Her fingers fidgeted. "I don't wish to speak ill of your relatives, my lady."

"I know that. You are a kind person who doesn't speak ill of anyone unless warranted."

"Thank you. I'm afraid I must say something about your cousin, the viscount."

Elara's shoulders tensed. "Go on. What has he done?"

Shelley lowered her voice. "He has instructed all the staff to prevent you from going out or receiving guests." She stepped closer and whispered, "He also told the footmen and Mr Roberts to watch the female servants who might disobey the orders. And he wants to see all your correspondence before they're sent or received."

Elara's chest filled with rage. "How dare he!"

"Please don't let it be known that I told you so," Shelley pleaded.

"I will ensure your protection, Shelley. Thank you for telling me."

She had no doubt James had threatened the staff with demotion or the loss of their job. As much as she felt compelled to confront James, that would not do her any good.

"We must go shopping today, Shelley. Ask for the carriage to be readied."

"But what of Lord Frances' orders?"

"I shall deal with my cousin. Do as I say."

"Yes, my lady."

While her lady's maid left to do her bidding, Elara gathered the essentials in her reticule and donned a bonnet. With her heels treading lightly, she made her way down the long hallway to her father's bedchamber. Since her mother's passing years ago, he found living in the marital suites unbearable. Thus, he had given over the rooms to Elara and relocated himself to the farthest end of the corridor.

His bedchamber was dark and smelled of illness. The air was stagnant, even though two nurses were moving about and tending to his needs. Elara waited for him while his valet shaved him.

"How is he?" she asked one of the nurses.

"There hasn't been much change, my lady. He's had a few spoonfuls of broth but not much else."

Elara sat at his bedside and held his hand while the nurses vacated the room. The earl opened his left eye slowly. She smiled, summoning all the warmth and light she could muster to her countenance, hoping to ease his mind.

"Are the nurses treating you well, Father?"

He closed his eye and nodded once.

"I'm glad to hear it. You must drink more broth if you want to recover. Could you try?"

He did not move. It likely required great exertion for him to reply.

"I plan to call on your solicitor today to get your affairs in order."

The old man opened his eye again and nodded once.

"I am grateful you have trusted me with the estate."

He pressed her hand weakly, but it was enough to express his love for his daughter. Elara dabbed at the welling tears with a kerchief.

"Ne…" The earl tried to speak. Surprised, she stood and bent over him, her ear at his mouth.

He sighed and tried again. "Ne…"

Elara stood back and studied his face. "No?" she guessed. He shook his head slightly.

"Newton?" She named his valet. The earl shook his head again.

With a pensive frown, she thought of the name that had been in the forefront of her mind ever since she returned home. "Nicholas?"

He nodded.

Elara was delighted her father had understood and remembered their previous conversation. Following closely was panic. With James, she could have chosen anyone to be her betrothed, but if her father believed she was engaged to Preston…

"You want to know more about him?" He shook his head, bewildering her.

She asked doubtfully, "Do you wish to meet him?"

He nodded, and her pulse beat wildly from panic and feverish anticipation. What if he refused or couldn't accompany her? What if he agreed to meet her father? She would be elated and crushed at the same time. At this moment, however, she did not care how or why. She only wanted to see him, touch him.

"I informed him you may need time to recover, but if it's your wish, I shall ask him to visit."

The earl nodded and squeezed her hand. Then he drifted off to sleep.

Elara descended the long sweeping staircase with her head full of when and how to approach Preston. Approaching the front door, she was distracted by Shelley exhibiting clear distress in conversation with the butler. Her maid appeared quite unnerved and indicated her dismay with urgent gestures.

"What is the meaning of this?" she asked the butler.

Shelley pointed accusingly at the man. "Mr Roberts tells me that Lord Frances has forbidden the use of the carriage in his absence."

"My apologies, my lady. I am following the viscount's orders." The butler sounded genuinely regretful.

# ABDUCTED

"But the carriage belongs to the earl not the viscount," Shelley whispered, looking around to ensure no one was eavesdropping.

"Shelley, might I have a word with Mr Roberts alone? Give us a moment, will you?"

Her faithful lady's maid stood to the side within an earshot. Elara drew Roberts aside discreetly and spoke in hushed tones.

"Shelley's right, Mr Roberts. This is my home, and all belongs to my father. The viscount has no authority here."

"I understand, my lady. I find myself... in an extraordinarily awkward predicament regarding the instructions issued in the earl's absence," he replied heavily. "As the viscount insists with such adamance that he is betrothed to you, and as the eldest male relative awaiting inheritance... he has made rather binding decrees concerning the household affairs." Roberts exhaled, his gaze averted as though the words themselves carried troubling weight. "I assure you, these orders forbidding use of the carriage distress me greatly, Lady Elara. However, to defy the master of the house in its present state of leadership poses grave concerns regarding my own position and welfare if... well, in event his lordship's claims prove legitimate."

The butler finally met her eyes, resignation and unspoken apology writ on his brow.

Elara's voice was stern from shoving down her indignation. "The earl still lives, Mr Roberts, and I am the only other relative who can call this home. Therefore, you shall listen to me, not the viscount. He has no legal rights here. Besides, I need to prepare for mourning should the Lord decide to summon Father. I am certain I can convince Lord Frances of the necessity of this shopping excursion."

A surprised smile touched Robert's eyes, although he did not relent. She was getting fed up. "Refuse me, and I shall have to dismiss you, Mr Roberts. What will it be?" The old servant acknowledged defeat with a bow. "Of course, my lady. I shall have the carriage come around."

When the carriage arrived, Elara glared at Mr Roberts' discomfited countenance, feeling betrayed by the man who had twirled her around the great hall as a child. He had caught her a few times too when she had decided to slide down the banister instead of climbing the steps. How had James so thoroughly coerced him? She would have to speak to him but not until she had a betrothed ready to rescue her.

Elara had no intention of shopping. Her wardrobe was full of black mourning clothes worn since her great-grandmother's passing and thereafter. Unbeknownst to Shelley, she was headed to see Mr Frankland, her father's eccentric solicitor.

"This is not the direction towards Mrs Barnell's shop," Shelley mumbled.

"We are not going shopping. I only said that to secure the carriage. We are going to see Mr Frankland."

"I see." Shelley's face fell.

"I am sorry you were looking forward to shopping. If we have time, we can stop by, but I would rather get home before Lord Frances does. I will need the carriage again this week, and I don't want to provoke him more than necessary."

"Where are you headed next then?"

Elara's face heated at the thought of Preston. She cleared her throat. "I plan to see a different solicitor."

"Doesn't Mr Frankland look after all matters for the earl?"

"Yes, he does. This is a personal matter. I would like a second opinion."

"Very well, my lady."

The carriage travelled for an hour, then twenty minutes on a narrow and muddy path to reach a small house in the middle of the woods. Elara disembarked while Shelley waited with the carriage. She rapped on the bright yellow door with colourful flowers painted on it.

"Lady Elara!" The solicitor's sister, who was also his secretary, greeted her warmly.

"Good day Miss Frankland." Elara stepped into the parlour and held the woman's hand. "Forgive me for calling on you without a warning."

"That's all right, my lady. Luckily, Mr Frankland is in the office today. You might have missed him if you had come any other day this week."

The kind woman tidied up the newspaper and quilts around the room. Upon her invitation, Elara sat on the settee, folding her hands primly on her lap. While Miss Frankland disappeared to fetch tea, Elara arranged her thoughts regarding the matters to be discussed with the solicitor.

"Is everything all right, Lady Elara? We have not had the honour of your company in a long time," Miss Frankland yelled from the next room.

"Unfortunately, everything is not well, Miss Frankland. Lord Stamford suffered an apoplexy three nights ago and is indisposed presently."

"Oh my heavens, I am so sorry. That is very distressing. How is he now?"

Miss Frankland appeared with a tea tray and sat beside her. She handed a teacup to Elara, impressively recalling how she liked her tea.

"He is paralysed on one side of his body and is unable to speak." Elara's words emerged unsteady as welling tears clouded the room.

"Poor dear, how frightened you must be," Miss Frankland enfolded her in an embrace and patted her back.

"Thank you," she said as she pulled away from the kind woman. "I came today to ensure all of Father's affairs are in order."

"That is very wise. How impressive that you would think of such a thing instead of letting despair rule."

"I need to keep my mind occupied, not to mention my relatives are waiting for the opportunity to pick the estate bare."

"Common story, that. It's most unfortunate." Miss Frankland clucked her tongue. "I shall tender your request for an audience to Mr. Frankland and inquire if he can receive you directly. I daresay he retains the same halting address as ever—full of fidgets and heel-turning when discomfited. And all females appear to render him most awkward."

Miss Frankland swiftly disappeared into another room whilst muttering something to herself.

Shortly after, Elara was escorted to the solicitor's office, where he sat at an enormous desk with enormous piles of parchment. He shot up from the chair upon Elara's entrance, his gaze darting fretfully.

"L-Lady E-Elara. How wonderful to see you. I'm sorry to hear about his lordship. I wish you, I mean him, a swift recovery."

His gaze floated around the room while his fingers drummed upon the desk.

"Thank you, Mr Frankland. I am sure he'll be grateful to hear your well wishes."

Elara did not wait for the man to invite her to sit. She chose a plush green chair and sank into it.

Sitting rim rod straight, she eyed the nervous man severely. "I felt the urgent need to make my position clear, Mr Frankland. I understand you've divulged some confidential information to Lord Frances, my cousin."

Frankland's visage turned ghostly while his ears turned crimson. His voice shook when he spoke. "Please forgive me, my lady. I feel most horrid and have had nightmares about the incident. I was weak and afraid, you understand. When Lord Frances confronted me, I couldn't help but become the helpless boy of nine... up to sixteen."

Elara sighed, no longer able to sustain her anger before the poor man who must have been scared out of his wits.

"Mr Frankland, is it true that the earl has left almost everything to me?"

"Aye, my lady. Nothing is entailed except for a small cabin on the estate border."

"Very well. In that case, you do understand that I, alone, shall be your client and you may not speak to any of my relatives about my affairs."

"Aye, my lady."

"If you fear Lord Frances' retribution, perhaps you'd consider hiring a protection officer."

Frankland brightened at the suggestion. "What a marvellous idea, my lady. I think I shall. Judging by his character, I'm certain he will return. However did he find me, I wonder?"

"My cousin is gifted in unearthing secrets. His brutish approach seems quite effective. Now, I'd like to ensure, in haste, that all of Lord Stamford's affairs are in order."

"Yes, of course. Very wise." Then, noticing he was still standing, he abruptly plopped into his chair.

"Let me see..." He sorted through the piles of parchment and pulled out sheets of paper without toppling the whole thing.

"The last service the earl asked me to provide was to register most of the holdings into a company bearing your name," Mr Frankland said pensively as if talking to himself.

"Would you kindly apprise me of why Father would create a company in my name?"

"Certainly. The company allows you to own properties, stocks, personal goods, and obtain credit completely independent from your husband should you wed. It secures your future regardless of your marital status."

Elara placed a hand on her heart, overcome with gratitude. She suddenly felt the burden of an uncertain future lift from her shoulders. Her father had planned to gift her financial freedom.

"However, this document is not binding until his lordship signs it. Will he be able to receive me tomorrow?"

"I'm not sure. Lord Frances has forbade me from receiving visitors or leaving the house. He may bar you from calling on Father."

The solicitor visibly paled. "Is he living with you now?"

She nodded. "As the head of the family, he has taken liberties at my home."

Frankland dropped his head and began to puff air.

"Are you unwell?" she asked the suffering man.

"Forgive me, my lady. Any thoughts of confrontation leave me feeling giddy and sick in the stomach."

"Oh, I am sorry. Do not worry, Mr Frankland. You need not suffer so. I shall ask another solicitor to help me on the matter."

His puffing slowed, and he raised his head. "You will? I must admit I am relieved."

Elara took the envelope containing the document and put it in her reticule. She thanked the Frankland siblings and hurried home before her outing was discovered by James.

## Chapter Seventeen

# *8 March 1833 – eleven in the evening*

Preston set his emptied glass upon a footman's salver and snatched up a fresh port. Just one hour more before departing, he bid himself, lest Somerset and Carlisle divest him entirely. Foolishness had led him to gamble against these card sharks when he could ill afford a housekeeper. Yet here, connections were forged, and fellowship nurtured. At least Lord Frances or Lord Whorepipe, Preston preferred to call him, kept him company.

Preston disliked the man even before meeting him, but more so now that they've been formally introduced. He had contending farmers and labourers filing grievances, claiming the viscount breached contracts. Clearly, there was no honour in this man, only greed.

Those murky, swamp-like eyes infuriated Preston, though they shared the verdant hue of Elara's. Albeit hers shone like emeralds, whilst the viscount's bespoke a blackened soul. That smirking mouth had kissed her sweet lips... and had access to her now.

Preston's grip bent the cards near to tearing.

"Tell us, Frances, when shall you wed?" Salisbury inquired.

Preston stiffened. Impossible. He refused to believe it.

"As soon as I obtain a special licence. I shall visit the archbishop in a few days." Whorepipe's tone was smug.

"What is the precipitous haste about?" Carlisle's brows knitted.

"My uncle, the bride's father, has taken ill. My bride wishes to rush the wedding to put her father's mind at ease lest he does not recover."

"I am grieved to hear that. He is a gentleman of fine character," Somerset remarked solemnly.

Preston felt his blood turn to ice within his veins, its sluggish flow toiling dread with each frigid pulse. Could the rascal be truly betrothed to Elara? Surely, she would not accept this scoundrel again. Or was she desperate with child and lacking options? He shot up from his chair, toppling it to clatter upon the marble floor.

"I say, whatever is the matter?" Somerset exclaimed.

"What ails you?" Salisbury grasped his shoulder with a steadying hand.

Preston scanned the wood-panelled room distractedly. "Apologies. An argument for a case struck me."

"You are a rare man who battles both tiers of the law," Whorepipe remarked. "What led you to practice both?"

*To imprison reptiles like you*, Preston thought bitterly. Aloud he replied, "I serve mainly labourers too destitute to engage both solicitor and barrister. So, I opted to become both."

"I've heard you've taken on some wealthy patrons," the rascal probed.

"Aye, I've bills to settle."

"And how did you become acquainted with these three influential gentlemen?" Whorepipe asked, looking around.

"We rescued him from a dire scrap," Somerset proclaimed.

"I was in no jeopardy," Preston retorted.

Salisbury scoffed. "Five ruffians pursued you. Surely you cannot believe you'd have escaped unmanned?"

"They were creditors come to collect," Preston said.

"Do not believe that for a moment," Carlisle blurted out. Somerset's boot collided with his shin under the mahogany table. Carlisle had plainly forgotten his oath never to breathe a word of Preston's flight from his family's estate.

"I do not," the serpent echoed suspiciously.

"Ruffians sent by creditors, then," Preston amended.

"The four of you took on five men?"

"That we did," Carlisle grumbled into his glass.

"I was running away from the fiends when their carriage passed me by. They opened the carriage door, and I leapt upon their moving vehicle."

Whorepipe surveyed the men. "Is that the sum of it?"

Four heads nodded equivocally as one. The scoundrel leered humourlessly.

"What has delayed your wedding to your cousin these five years past?" Carlisle interjected.

"Parliamentary duties, one thing after another. I admit Elara had been hesitant, but with her father ill, she has made her decision,"

Scowling, Preston rose and strode to the mahogany bar. He drained one crystal tumbler of scotch and promptly poured another.

"I could never wed a cousin. It would feel akin to marrying one's sister." Carlisle grimaced and warmed Preston's heart.

The rascal looked rather displeased but dared not retort. Carlisle did not notice or care, being thrice the man in bulk, wealth, and consequence.

"Each match is unique. None can predict what shall make it thrive," Somerset opined sagely, swirling his port. Preston swore he would murder the duke in the most painful way possible.

"And you, Preston? Why remain unattached still?" Whorepipe scrutinised him sharply.

"I suppose the right lady has eluded me thus far." Preston had no desire to answer any of the rascal's questions.

"You work overmuch and frequent not where eligible ladies gather. You'll find no wife in Newgate or Old Bailey prisons." Salisbury's tone took on his Speaker of the House persona as if Preston was a diaper-clad member he could rule over.

"On the contrary, there is a new comely barrister, Miss Morton. Either she seems more winsome for her keen intellect, or she is objectively a beauty. What say you, Carlisle?" Preston asked.

At the name, Carlisle's countenance visibly hardened. His eyes narrowed and jaw took on a granite-like rigidity.

"I may call on Miss Morton myself. We've much in common, and she could use an ally whilst you old cronies seek to destroy her career. I should like to offer my support." Preston took petty pleasure in the scarlet flush creeping up Carlisle's neck.

"Westminster exists to be her white knight. He must be fucking her to speak in her defence when no other would," Whorepipe sneered contemptuously.

Carlisle's fist slammed the mahogany table with a resounding thud. "Mind your vulgar tongue, and go to hell, Frances! You insult both a member of the Inner Temple and myself!"

"Oh, do unclench, Carlisle. We are among friends. This is how boys talk," the foolish snake derided scornfully.

"Then perhaps it is time you became a man, my lord, and not a boorish boy," Preston suggested mildly over his cut crystal glass.

"How dare you! You will mind that impertinent mouth when addressing your betters, you jumped-up charlatan!" Whorepipe's face mottled an angry scarlet.

Preston merely regarded him with an icy blue stare. "And you had best mind yours, Frances, if you wish to maintain your current extravagant lifestyle."

Preston noticed confusion creep into his haughty expression.

"I am intimately acquainted with thousands of honest, hardworking souls, including tenants of yours nursing ample grievances." Preston mindlessly swirled the amber liquid in his crystal glass. "After making your acquaintance this eve, I'm tempted to create difficulties for you."

The scoundrel's florid face turned positively purple, and he looked beseechingly to the others for support.

"Do you hear him uttering threats? This impertinent nobody dares threaten me!"

Carlisle frowned over his cigar. "I heard nothing untoward."

"Nor I," Somerset assured him.

"Nothing amiss reached my ears," Salisbury echoed.

Whorepipe quieted but continued glowering sullenly. Preston's fleeting sense of triumph evaporated like morning mist. Imagining this reprehensible lout joining with Elara filled him with impotent rage. Could she truly desire a life allied to this wastrel? He had already lost her to this scamp without ever having a chance to win her affections.

Once the other gentlemen had departed, the four bosom friends relaxed together before the crackling fire, reminiscing on their youthful exploits and folly. Yet, talk inevitably circled back to the apparent friction between Preston and Frances.

"I sense some animosity there, Preston." Salisbury observed his friend pensively through a wreath of fragrant cigar smoke. "Is there a matter we ought to know?"

"What else but a woman?" Somerset deduced knowingly. At Preston's cocked brow, he elaborated, "I noted your thunderous looks anytime Frances mentioned his supposed betrothed. I have never seen you reveal your hand so nakedly, Preston. She must be a singular lady indeed."

"Are they truly affianced?" Preston asked tightly, unable to mask the bitterness and panic in his tone.

"Rumours of an understanding have persisted these five years past, though her father never confirmed nor denied it publicly," Salisbury mused.

"Have you any intentions of offering for the lady yourself?" Carlisle's blunt query jarred Preston's insides. Only if he could.

Preston considered his friends and hesitated. Her name seemed too precious, their tale too profoundly intimate to be carelessly repeated. Yet, the joy and anguish of longing for her alone could be borne no more.

"I have compromised the lady in question," he confessed softly with no hint of remorse darkening his words.

The others traded astonished looks. "You scarcely leave your office twice a year! When did you encounter this lady?" Carlisle exclaimed while Salisbury whistled his surprise.

"A sennight ago, at the theatre."

"You compromised a lady after knowing her for merely a week? Good God, Preston. I misjudged you entirely!" Carlisle cried.

Fondness softened Preston's habitually stern features as he recalled their first fateful meeting when she had appeared to him a true vision. That profound moment was too sacred to share, even amongst friends.

"And you formed an attachment, clearly," Somerset said, reclining into the leather chesterfield.

"I did," Preston confirmed gruffly, taking a bracing gulp of port wine.

"Enough to offer for her?" Salisbury pressed, cigar smoke coiling above his head of tousled dark hair.

"Aye, I would make her my wife if I could."

"Well, why the devil aren't you betrothed? Did you misplace my invitation?" Carlisle demanded.

"I have not yet proposed."

"And whyever not? Does Frances stand in your way?" Salisbury showed his puzzlement. A rare occasion indeed.

Preston surveyed his friends with gravity.

"Because I am already wed."

"Blazes!" Somerset nearly upended his crystal glass.

"I am dumbfounded. Truly!" Carlisle's face crumpled in astonishment. "Did either of you know?"

Salisbury and Somerset both shook their heads, appearing equally perplexed.

Carlisle's brow furrowed severely. "I don't recall celebrating at your wedding breakfast, you duplicitous knave."

"There was no ceremony. It was a simple affair with my parents and witnesses. We've been estranged for six years. But now…" Preston paused, jaw taut, "I aim to locate the woman with all haste and petition for a divorce if not an annulment."

Somerset gave a low, ominous whistle, twirling his brandy slowly. "By the time you find the lady and manage to dissolve your matrimony, your intended may well belong to Frances."

Preston shook his head despairingly. "It is impossible she would accept that scoundrel's proposal."

Salisbury nodded thoughtfully, exhaling another wreath of cigar smoke. "I hear Frances has relocated himself to the lady's home, ostensibly to manage her ailing father's affairs."

"That explains his absence from Parliament of late. Too busy fattening his prize goose, no doubt," Carlisle pronounced.

The notion of the snake so near Elara, his gaze upon her unguarded form at dawn and dusk, scalded Preston painfully. Did she welcome the man's attention? *Bloody hell*, could they be intimate?

It was possible her heart still belonged to the knave. He was her first kiss, the first to awaken tender feelings in her heart. Though the cad had abandoned her, a lady's memory often lingered fondly on such first attachments. The idea twisted in Preston's chest like a dagger's blade.

"She could not desire a match with Frances if she lay with you mere days ago," Salisbury reasoned.

"Unless she desires a marriage of wealth and title and is merely indulging carnal pleasure with you," Carlisle pronounced bluntly.

Salisbury and Somerset traded uneasy looks at this indelicate speculation.

"Come now, I speak only the plain truth," Carlisle said, helping himself to brandy.

"How could she consider a life with such a bloody fool?" Preston raked a hand through his hair in torment. "I must take my leave," he announced abruptly, rising from his chair.

Smith had not been able to uncover much about her wellbeing in recent days. The servants became mute, fearing retribution, and Elara had left home only once since the last report. Being ignorant of her circumstances and heart was driving him to the brink of madness. He had to do something.

"Where are you off to at this hour?" Somerset inquired with brows furrowed.

"No destination in particular," Preston shrugged on his greatcoat. "Perhaps I'll clear some fences, join a hunt, or find a good tavern brawl."

Salisbury grinned roguishly. "In that case, I'm coming along!"

"The night is young, gentlemen!" Carlisle declared.

The four comrades proceeded shoulder to shoulder into the moonlit streets, their drunken voices ringing out tunelessly in the crisp night air.

*For the blare of his horn brought me from my bed;*
*And the cry of his hounds which he oft time led;*
*Old Peel's 'View, Halloo!' would awaken the dead;*
*Or the fox from his lair in the morning.*

## Chapter Eighteen

# 9 March 1833 – seven in the morning

Elara sat at her writing desk, head cradled hopelessly in her hands. She feared her spirit might flee her anguished body at any moment. Had she not already been weakened by the abduction, heartbreak, and her dear father's illness, she might rally more forceful resistance. She took small comfort in the company of her faithful lady's maid, but James' oppression created extreme tension and discontent in the household.

Not only that, when he was home, James insisted on passing every waking moment in her company. Though cordial outwardly, his restraint from pressing Elara for her betrothed's identity struck an uneasy chord. In due course, he would execute his plan, whatever it may be.

Shelley gleaned from the coachman that the viscount was planning to meet with the Archbishop of Canterbury, meaning it could be mere days until Elara is forced into a nuptial with James. She noted a distinct evolution in James' gaze as well. Those eyes once alight with lusty suggestions had sharpened to something harder, more expectant, like a diner with silverware in hand, waiting for the roast to be served.

Revulsion churned her empty stomach. She had no more tears to shed or strength to resist. But most of all, stark terror paralysed her mind.

She must swiftly settle on a more suitable union—with Lord Willoughby or Lord Hugh mayhap. Not only to escape a lifelong destiny with James, but securing a matrimony might allow her to gain reprieve from Preston's hold on her heart. Perhaps she would find refuge in an amicable attachment with her husband. An all-encompassing ardour such as that shared with Preston was too fraught with longing and misery.

Elara was suddenly startled by a loud thud emanating from the master's empty suites.

"Whatever could that be?" Elara exclaimed, pulse racing.

"Mayhap a rodent of unusual size, my lady?" Shelley said as she came out of the water closet, her eyes wide.

"It must be gargantuan to produce such a din."

With Shelley trailing apprehensively, Elara unbolted the door to a shared parlour and swept through the room into the imposing bedchamber. She almost wished it had been a rodent when she found James presiding over a man installing a new lock on the door. A footman and his valet were unpacking his trunks.

"James! What is the meaning of this?" Panic cracked her voice.

"I am relocating, clearly," he drawled.

"You cannot reside here. It is wholly improper!"

"And who shall stop me?" His eyes were shards of ice in pale green, and his smile resembled a serpent.

She was helpless, she realised despairingly. With no recourse against his superior strength, she whirled around wordlessly before she gave in to her urge to claw his smug face. Safely in her room, she turned the lock with trembling fingers while Shelley groaned woefully.

"What shall you do, my lady? His eyes were positively bestial," her lady's maid whispered fretfully.

"James is leaving this morning for London. I must quit this house and seek help."

---

Preston awoke with a pounding headache, having behaved as recklessly as a youth first away at school. Once out on the streets, the foursome had caroused and sang bawdy tavern songs, dared one another to clear fences, and ended in a tangled heap upon Mrs Baker's manicured lawn. He had slept fitfully, his dreams suffused with restless longing and stark fear, all centring on her face.

He had dreamt of Elara shivering in dread. An image seared into his mind since their shared ordeal. To think she was sequestered alone with that reptile in her home, with only her incapacitated father as protection, burned him with fury, jealousy, longing, panic...

He bet his firstborn that the snake had barred others from visiting the earl. He prayed she was not fooled by his whispers of love in her ear or worse, his vile caresses. Lord help him if the knave was forcing himself on her... A bleak voice in Preston's mind posed the most chilling query of all–was it too late?

Unable to contain his impotent rage, Preston screamed and punched the solid wooden door of his bedroom. He relished the relief he felt from the physical pain eclipsing the savage torment of his mind.

It was only when he heard someone kick the front door open that he halted his screams and backed away. Smith and three other guards burst through the bedroom door, wooden splinters flying from where they had kicked the latch free. After confirming their employer was in no danger, the men backed away carefully, eyeing each other in confusion.

Preston could not give a rat's arse about his men's quizzical glances. The thought of facing the endless hours ahead without confirming Elara's well-being was excruciating. His course was clear. He had to see her and ensure she remained unharmed.

Preston whirled around and stormed out of his bedchamber, shouting, "Smith!"

A *whoosh* of red appeared out of nowhere, colliding into him. Preston threw open his arms instinctively to capture the form. He pulled her fast against him, his back meeting the wall as she melted into his arms.

"Elara..." He whispered her name as a benediction and homecoming at once.

Laced through with the sweet essence of orange, her hair brushed his nose as their hammering hearts pressed chest to chest. Elara's delicate arms tightened around his waist with the same desperation churning inside Preston. At long last, she was here. Safely here. They drew together into stillness, all frenzy suspended, breaths syncing as one.

He peered at the woman he had dreamed of every waking moment since their release. Except he could not see her clearly amidst the squall of emotions brewing inside him–longing, regret and hope. He saw the dark circles under her eyes, her pale complexion, and the woman who would suffer more if he permitted himself to take what he wanted. He could not summon enough hope to make her a promise.

How naive was he to suppose that one more embrace could satiate him? Scrutinising Elara's countenance, Preston fathomed the true depths of yearning she awoke in him.

"Elara, you are here," he muttered huskily.

"Yes." Her voice was barely audible and her expression unreadable. Releasing her reluctantly, Preston gestured towards the settee. Her eyes roamed the room and fixed on the broken door.

"Have you forgotten how to pick locks?" she asked, returning her attention to him.

At this unexpected jest contrasting starkly with his inner tension, Preston burst out laughing, throwing his head back and walking away from her for more air. Pressing a palm to his forehead, he turned back to her quizzical face.

"It appears so," he replied with the rest of the laughter lodged in his throat. His mood quickly became solemn when Elara didn't crack a smile as if it would shatter her completely.

Heavens help him. He hoped she didn't come to announce her engagement or to hire his service to scrutinise her marriage contract.

She gingerly took a seat on the settee. Her eyes reflected frustration, anger, hurt... He schooled his features to reflect how he ought to present himself. Unbothered, charming, married.

"This is a most unexpected pleasure," he said. She lowered her eyes and stared at her hands. His eyes roved over her form, appreciating her delicate curves, remembering how she had felt. She was clad in a modest brown wool dress, doing nothing to dampen her vibrant hue. The earl had not passed away, then. "I'm sorry about your father's illness. How is he?"

Surprise registered in her eyes before she smiled faintly. "He's not well, but he still fights. News travelled even to your ears."

Preston nodded. "I had the pleasure of Viscount Frances' company last evening at the gentleman's club. He mentioned the earl's illness."

Elara stared down at her hands again, the delicate fingers fidgeting. "I see."

When she did not speak, he prompted gently, "What has brought you here?"

He kept his voice neutral. Now that her safety was confirmed and the immediate shock of her presence had passed, his sense of duty returned–the duty to protect her heart.

"I am sorry to call on you unannounced. It hadn't occurred to me that your office might be closed. I would have waited, but the guards insisted."

"Did you travel alone from Stamford?"

"No, my lady's maid accompanied me. Your guards wouldn't permit her in your private quarters."

"Did you travel in your family carriage?"

"Yes."

"Good... My apologies if the guards' presence startled you."

"Not at all. Your caution is understandable after what we've endured. Have you any news of the captors?"

"Not yet, but I have investigators on it."

Elara obviously had spent hours in the carriage to see him, but she was rendered mute and as nervous as a country mouse.

"Shall I congratulate you on your betrothal to Lord Frances?" His voice was calm, and he hoped his smile betrayed the tumult in his heart.

She looked at him wide-eyed. "Did James tell you we were engaged?"

"Aye. He said you would be tying the knot with a special licence."

Preston studied her face which seemed to be on the verge of bursting into tears. When she spoke, her voice trembled. "I refuse to marry him. But I need your help to keep him away."

Awash with relief, he stood and walked to the window. Confirming his guards were keeping watch of her carriage, he returned and leaned against the wall across from Elara. She raised her eyes and became riveted on his linen trousers.

*Damn*, he was aroused. Her eyes blatantly surveyed the muscles on his thighs, then his bulge. Her lips parted.

*Damn it all!* His cock was flattered by her stare, apparently. He had to distract her from his groin before he embarrassed himself. He cleared his throat, and her eyes flew up to meet his.

"What is it?" he asked.

"Nothing. I was, um, just admiring how soft your trousers looked," she said hastily, her face colouring.

He furrowed his brows as if he was confused. "Thank you, my lady. I was referring to the help you were seeking."

"Oh! That. Yes, of course." She flustered and flailed like a scarecrow in the wind.

He was a scoundrel, but it was effective and enjoyable.

"I saw Mr Frankland, my father's solicitor," Elara said hastily, "and he informed me that I need my father to sign a document to make this official." She withdrew the parchment from her reticule and extended it to him. He studied the document and smiled.

"Not many fathers would do this for their daughter," he said, handing the paper back to her. "What is it you'd like me to do?"

"I'm afraid James would interfere if he found out what Father has planned. He would easily overpower me. Can you help?"

"Is your father lucid?"

"Yes."

"Good. I shall accompany you to have the document signed and witnessed."

Elara took a deep breath, presumably with relief, but it was short-lived. Her gaze faltered as she said, "There is something else. I, um, I would like you to initiate a proposal on my behalf."

Preston stared.

"As soon as possible," she added.

He walked away, unwilling to let her see the emotions on his face. He dug his nails into the cuts he sustained earlier. "What... kind of proposal?"

"A marriage proposal," she said softly, her hands crumpling the skirt.

Preston felt a strong compulsion to put her on a ship and take her across the ocean where no one knew them. They could live as husband and wife.

"I assume you mean to employ my service as a solicitor. Could you explain?"

"There are two gentlemen whose offers I had declined in the past. I believe their interest in me still holds true. Considering the recent events, I've decided either of those gentlemen would be preferable to marrying my cousin."

"Who are these esteemed gentlemen worthy of such high regard?"

"Lords Willoughby and Hugh."

The air seemed to thicken as Preston sat, leaning forward with his elbows on his lap, recalling everything he knew about the men. Images of Elara panting beneath their weight flashed past, and he thought this was how he was going to lose his mind. He focused on steadying his breaths.

"I am sorry, but I can't help you," he said briskly.

"You can't or you won't?"

"Given our history, I cannot remain impartial."

"You said what we shared was all pretence. Everything that happened was under duress and... you are committed to your wife. I hardly think negotiating a marriage contract would require that much impartiality."

"I am sorry, but I must decline. I am certain there are unofficial and easier channels for you to go through rather than hiring a solicitor."

"Do you think involving a solicitor is not ideal?"

"No. There are two reasons for it. First, the moment they receive the solicitor's letter, it becomes official. Once the offer is made, rescinding it would be in poor taste. You would need to come to an agreement no matter the terms. Second, solicitor fees can be costly. That is all I will say on the matter."

"Please. I have no relations or friends who can help. And it is humiliating to approach a random solicitor. I'm afraid I will wake up wed to James one day. I..."

Preston was torn between helping the woman he cared for and keeping a path clear that, someday, may return her to him. The prospect of securing Elara as his own tempted him acutely. The longing gave rise to a war within himself–honour that bade him to act selflessly for her welfare versus a traitorous spark of hope that she might be reclaimed. The path ahead stood plain, however, no matter how agonising it may be.

"Do you fear for your safety, my lady?"

She flinched at the use of her title but did not comment. "Yes. A little."

Preston would have preferred to howl and break something, but she needed him. This was not the time to lose his temper.

"Which gentleman is your first choice?" he asked.

She dropped her head. "Lord Hugh, I think."

He rocked in his seat, trying to subdue the agitation cracking his control. "Do you know of a gathering where you can reacquaint yourself with Lord Hugh?"

"I do. Still, I cannot approach his lordship and request that he offer for me."

"Which event will you attend?"

"The Lullingstone Castle spring festival. I was planning to decline the invitation given Father's condition, but he insists that I represent him."

"Is your father's condition stable?"

"Yes."

"I believe it is a week-long gathering. You should be able to solidify an agreement by the end of it."

She bit her lip and concern shadowed her face. "Would you make the introduction? If not as my solicitor, then perhaps as a friend? An acquaintance?"

Rage descended like a crimson mist. He pushed it down deep until he could unleash it somewhere else. "My invitation must have got lost. There must be a gossipmonger you can influence to start a rumour."

"I'm afraid not. This celebration is exclusive to the most influential men and their wives. I'm uncertain how I would broach the subject."

"I can speak to Lord Salisbury. Lady Salisbury would not hesitate to assist you. She may even negotiate on your behalf."

"That would be wonderful if you could arrange it." Her voice laced with hope clawed at his chest.

"Well, that is settled. I shall make myself presentable so we may depart for Stamford straight away."

Without waiting for her response, Preston turned on his heels and disappeared into his bedchamber.

---

With hands clenched at her hips, Elara paced the confines of the parlour, her clipped steps belying the tempest whirling within. What foolish fancy to have raced here with naive hopes, only to gaze at the indifference in his eyes. She felt herself plunge straightaway into some dark abyss at his detachment. Small wonder he could readily agree to accompany her to Stamford without a flicker of former longing. He clearly regarded her as merely another transaction to mediate.

"Let us be off."

Preston appeared, dressed for travel, accompanied by trunks. After the guards carried them out, Preston asked, "Is something amiss?"

She shook her head and cleared her throat.

"No. I was only curious about your wife."

His face hardened as if she offended him somehow. She looked closer at the mayhem. Perhaps she ought to be more cautious. How well did she know the man after all?

"Were you violent with your wife? Is that why she's not here?"

Preston stared at her incredulously. "Of course not. Why would I break a perfectly innocent door if I wished to harm her?"

She eyed him curiously. "Did your wife do this, then?" She gestured towards the broken door.

He smiled reluctantly. "No. I stubbed my toe, screamed, and the guards broke the door down. Shall we?" He picked up his hat and overcoat.

---

Elara settled in the carriage dreading the awkward silence ahead. She would rather have joined Shelley and Mr Smith, but Preston wanted to ride with her alone. How silly of her, she thought. She had raced to him with her heart pounding, but now, she wanted nothing more than to avoid him. A part of her did not wish to be reminded of the man she had lost. She wrapped her arms around herself, feeling profound loneliness.

"What is tormenting you so?" His voice washed over her, gentle and caring like when they had first met.

"Naught is bothering me." She shook her head without looking at him. "I am happy to have your assistance."

"It's my pleasure," he said while he shuffled through the papers on his lap.

"Doesn't your wife mind that you travel for days with an unwed woman?" she asked.

Preston stilled briefly before answering, "I work with many women, married and unmarried. She has come to expect it."

"Have you travelled far to meet with them? Alone?"

He paused before replying, "No." He looked up and met her eyes. "Are you concerned for my marriage, my lady?"

"Not exactly. I only feel remorseful for taking you away. If I were her, I would not be happy at all especially when…"

"When?"

She turned towards the window. "When we shared intimacy."

"You do not need to worry. This is my work. She understands that."

"What is she like?"

She was aware it was foolish of her to want to know more, but she could not help herself. The idea of another woman plagued her day and night. Mayhap if she could picture her, turn her into a real person instead of a mirage, she would accept his situation and stop dwelling on him.

Preston sighed and pinched the bridge of his nose. "I think I should keep my private life to myself. It is not helpful for either of us to discuss my marriage."

"You know all about my affairs."

"Yes, out of necessity."

"I told Father we were betrothed," she blurted. When no response came, she glanced at him, fearing he may be cross.

He was watching her in stunned silence. "Why?"

"James was... threatening me, telling me he would take me by force... in front of Father."

She covered her face in her kerchief and stifled her sob. Her resolve to stay strong crumbled in front of a man who had been her protector. She wanted the same protection from him against James, against heartbreak.

She didn't see him approach, but his strong arms circled her and pulled her to his chest. He was on his knees on the floor and kept her secure in his arms through the bumps and sways until she could speak again.

"I told him I was betrothed to a powerful man and I've given him my virtue. I thought it might give him pause before he carried out his threats. It seems to have worked, but he will see through me if I wait too long. I wanted to give Father more reassurance. I thought a name might make it seem more real so... I gave him your name. I am sorry."

"Has he touched you?" His voice hissed so softly Elara wondered how she had heard him.

"No." Emerging from behind the kerchief, she glanced up at him and was startled to see his seething countenance.

"That was clever. I'm glad you thought to deceive him. Do you wish me to pretend to be your fiancée?"

Surprised and relieved by his ready offer, Elara nodded eagerly.

He resumed his seat. "Very well. How will you explain your betrothal to Lord Hugh?"

"I have not thought that far yet."

"I suppose you could always break off our engagement for a better match," he murmured.

## Chapter Nineteen

# *9 March 1833 – quarter of one in the afternoon*

The carriage rocked gently as they neared Stamford Manor. After four hours of fuming silently with rage, Preston was glad to see the manor in view. He prayed that the knave was in residence so he may murder him. Brutally. The thought of the snake putting his hands on her and threatening her with... His fury once again threatened to ignite the hellfire.

The carriage stopped, and a footman held open the door. He swiftly gathered his things and exited first so he could help Elara alight. He reluctantly released her gloved hand and did not offer his arm as she ascended the front steps ahead of him.

The Stamford Manor was as grand as any palace by Preston's measure. The edifice displayed hundreds of windows across the frontage, with a towering portal serving as an entranceway. Years of habit prompted him to swiftly assess his surroundings. How might he quit this place in haste should it prove necessary? Craggy stones and jagged surfaces on the exterior wall made it easy to slip out from any window.

Having completed his observations and found multiple routes of escape, Preston followed Asilia to the grand doorway. His guards promptly stationed themselves at the door and the side of the building.

The door swung open, and the butler exclaimed, "Mr Preston!"

Preston winced. He will need to explain himself sooner than he thought.

"Mr Roberts," Preston acknowledged with a nod.

Elara eyed them suspiciously. "How do you know each other?"

The old man shrunk visibly, only just having realised what he had revealed. Preston stared at the man to see what he would come up with.

"I am certain Mr Preston would provide a thorough account of our acquaintance."

Preston narrowed his eyes and mouthed the word, "Coward," as he followed Elara up the stairs.

"Please explain," she said.

"I came down to speak with your butler after Smith, my protection officer, told me your cousin had moved himself in."

Elara's sprightly pace came to a sudden halt. Preston stared back at her puzzled expression.

"You came to Stamford? Why would you wish to meet with our butler?"

"I wished to put certain security measures in place for your safety."

Her eyes became hard-edged stones. "Meaning?"

"I, um, planted protection officers among your staff to safeguard you," he replied hesitantly.

Her eyes flashed furiously. "You spied on me without my approval?"

"Not spying... Monitoring," he said weakly.

"Which is spying."

"Well, spying implies some nefarious purpose... My intentions were good. Every single one of them," he said, his sheepish speech suggesting backpedalling.

She crossed her arms. "Tell me the truth. How many and where?"

"One in the kitchen, one chambermaid, four footmen–"

"You have women spying on me in my bedchamber? Why would you discuss my security with my staff instead of me?"

He rubbed his chin, pondering the most placating reply but not finding any. In the end, he decided on the truth.

"I was afraid of misleading you. I hoped you would not misunderstand my wish to protect as something more than plutonic."

"Plutonic..." She mauled over the word. "You wanted to protect me from falling in love with you. I am so grateful you stopped me before it was too late," she said and resumed her brisk walk.

Preston thought it wise to keep his mouth shut.

"Where are the footmen stationed?" she asked.

"Outside," he said.

"Where outside?" She stopped in front of her father's bedchamber and waited for Preston's reply.

"Sides and back of the house when not in motion. On the carriage with you on outings."

Her mouth and eyes gaped open with realisation. "You! You are the one who's been restricting my use of the carriage, not James!"

"Remember. My intentions were good," he said with a boyish smile.

"Thank you, Mr Preston. Rest assured that I will not fall in love with you," she said firmly before pushing open the carved door.

The earl's chamber was empty except for the frail man disappearing into the mattress. Elara went to her father's side and clasped his hand.

"Father, can you hear me?"

The earl's good eye fluttered open and joy gradually lit his features.

"I am sorry I've been away. I brought Mr Preston to meet with you. Father, allow me to introduce my intended who is also a solicitor in Slough."

Elara reached for Preston's hand. The old man's wan features brightened at once upon beholding her betrothed. Preston grinned as if greeting an old compatriot and shook the earl's good hand.

"What great fortune to see you again, my lord."

The earl's head twitched, one corner of his cracked lips curving into the ghost of a smile. Elara stared between the two men, astonishment writ on her face.

"You are acquainted?"

"Indeed. Though in truth, our last meeting was over a decade ago when I was still a youth."

"You never spoke of it."

"I knew him by a different name back then. I thought there was something familiar about your eyes, Elara. I had not made the connection until now." Turning back to the earl, he said, "What fortune to be betrothed to the daughter of a man I had admired all those years ago."

The earl was still smiling, his eye bright and alert.

"You are proving to be a devilish tough one to finish off. Powers above and below have tried," Preston jested.

The earl made a guttural noise which Preston recognised as laughter. Elara stared at her father incredulously.

"I shall keep his lordship company whilst you fetch what is needed for his comfort," he offered. Then, turning to the reclining man, he said, "We have some catching up to do, old man. One thing is certain. I know I can beat you now."

Elara stared at her father's laughing face once more before quitting the room in bewilderment.

Preston took a chair by the bedside, still clasping the earl's hand. He had known him as Lord Balestra at the fencing club. The earl was nicknamed as such for his lunging attacks. The earl pierced him now with a lucid glance. Neither of them could believe the coincidence.

"What are the chances, Lord Balestra? It seems that we cannot be rid of each other." Preston took out a kerchief from his pocket and dabbed the saliva from the old man's mouth. Stamford's fingers pressed his feebly in reply.

"It has been a long time since we last met. I confess feeling astonished you knew me straightaway. I assume you recognised my name as that of our mutual friend."

The earl allowed his eye to drift shut as though traversing the faded pathways of memory.

"Never shall I forget the counsel you imparted onto me that day. 'No man who forsakes his principles truly lives. He merely exists.' Those words shaped the course of my life entirely."

The earl released a heavy sigh.

"I see the thought plain upon your face. You fear your words drove me to ruin. Banish such misplaced guilt. My fate was sealed with or without your advice, wise though it was. Though conventional happiness eluded me, I still found satisfaction in pursuing life's purpose. My work endowed me with meaning beyond mere decoration or symbol. And now, by the grace of your magnificent daughter, I have found love as well. What more could any man desire?"

A wistful smile crossed the old man's countenance. Preston studied his features and gave a solemn nod, divining the unspoken request in Lord Stamford's eye.

"I love your daughter beyond words, my lord. I vow to do all in my power to ensure her happiness. And if it should come to that, I shall."

---

Preston wasted no time in discussing with the earl the document he needed to sign. He made several copies and had them witnessed by Smith and Davies. Elara was elated that her father stayed alert as long as he did. Preston summoned one of his men to deliver a few of the copies to his secretary in Slough.

After Elara ensured the earl's comfort and left the nurses in charge, Preston exchanged words with an extremely burly and intense man named Davies whose gaze did not stop roaming the environment. They then headed downstairs to introduce him to the staff. There, he won the hearts of all men and women with his humour and charm. They took a liking to him instantly, and Preston did not shy away from reminding them that legally, Elara was in charge of the estate.

Merely by being present, Preston reduced the tension in the household and some lightness returned to the servants' footsteps. This gave Elara the chance to write to several physicians, requesting consultations for further medical opinion.

Learning that Preston was taking his supper in the library, his temporary office, Elara asked her meal to be brought there as well. She wished to discuss any outstanding issues from the day. She had hardly seen him since they had arrived in the afternoon and noticed how her breathing was becoming shallow. She paused in front of the door and placed a hand on her stomach. Drawing another breath, she entered the room, awash in orange glow, and gaped. Preston was sprawled across the chaise in his stockinged feet, his boots gathered neatly to the side.

Staring at her gaping mouth, he said, "Sit down, sweetheart. I shall never become a proper gentleman if you stand there with an open invitation."

A *whoosh* of inhale accompanied her gasp while Preston laughed.

"Your audacity is out of this world!" she exclaimed.

"I am behaving as your betrothed now that I've vowed to your father to keep you happy. Do you not want me to be convincing?"

"You do not need to be a rake to be convincing."

"I may be a rake, my lady, but even more shocking is your knowledge of such an obscene subject matter."

"E-everything I know is theoretical. You know full well you took my virginity," she said, placing her cool palms against her heated cheeks.

"Yes..." he said as his gaze darkened, and a bulge appeared out of nowhere under his breeches. The ghastly man did not even try to hide his arousal.

Sucking in a sharp breath yet again, she turned away–mortified, excited, and surprised all at once. It was thrilling to know she still had that effect on him... endlessly thrilling. Elara took refuge in the nearest chair, fearing that her trembling limbs might betray her nervous excitement.

*He's married. He's married. He's married.* She dared to look up and saw his lingering smile, looking pleased with himself.

He sat up and adjusted his breeches before reaching for the glass of wine. "Do not concern yourself with my anatomy, my lady. It happens when I'm in the company of women."

Not knowing what to say or where to look, Elara reached for her glass and took a slow sip. "Any woman?" she asked.

"Unfortunately."

Swallowing her disappointment, she redirected the conversation. "Could you tell me how you know my father?"

Preston sliced a piece of the roast and put it in his mouth. He washed it down with wine before speaking in his rich baritone, instantly transporting her back to their past tender moments. Her heart ached to have those moments back.

"I first met your father when I was fifteen at an underground fencing club. They were extremely secretive and discerning about their members. I had the fortune of being invited by my cousin who was a member at the time."

"Why were they so secretive?"

"Because there were no rules."

"No rules involving sharp objects? That sounds dangerous."

"Aye, hence the secrecy. It was a freeform sword play with no protection whatsoever. If someone was injured at the club, no one spoke of it outside the club."

"I cannot believe my father was part of this club. He never mentioned it. In fact, he hardly discusses his days as a young man."

"He was one of the founding members and instructed young men. He started it to prepare men for battle with Napoleon, but the allure of danger spread to one member at a time. Eventually, it became a brotherhood. When I shared my desire to enlist in the army, Balestra, your father's alias, told me to meet him for private instruction. We met every day for a month, during which he became my mentor, teacher, and a father-like figure."

A wistful smile appeared on his face while Elara listened. "He encouraged me to pursue other forms of training if I wished to survive the battle. So, I learned every style of fighting I could."

"When did your acquaintance end?"

"After a month, my family travelled to another country, but we returned for two more summers. I trained with your father as much as I could during those times. His advice saved me more than once on the battlefield. My father, on the other hand, was occupied with choking out any happiness my brothers and I may have enjoyed."

"I am sorry. May I ask what he has done to make you so miserable?"

"Nay, it is not important." Preston brought the wine glass to his lips once more before saying, "But I will tell you that he was ambitious, detached, ruthless, and manipulative. Not an ounce of softness in him. And he married a woman just like him."

"I am sorry," she said again.

"I'm fine. I am no longer a lad in need of nurturing," he said with a smile.

After supper, Elara went to her private library to look after the household affairs, estate matters, and confirm her attendance for the Lullingstone gathering. When slumber threatened to overtake her, she returned to Preston's "office." Through the jarred door, she spied Preston pacing barefoot.

He had his shirtsleeves rolled up, dispensed with stockings, and was muttering an argument aloud. She watched with amusement as he paused occasionally to close his eyes and tap his forehead with his fingers as if to dislodge the information. Upon her belated knock, his handsome face turned to her. His silky hair glowed in the amber light.

"I'm sorry to interrupt," she said from the doorway, "but I'm retiring to bed. Shall I show you to your bedchamber?"

"That would be helpful. Give me a moment to gather my things." Preston stuck his barefeet into his boots, placed some piles of papers in the trunk, and gathered other piles in his arm. Finally, he collected his discarded clothing. Elara picked up the lantern and led the way.

"Do you still plan to work in your bedchamber?" she asked, eyeing the papers.

"Aye."

"Please allow me to assist if you need help."

"Why, thank you. It seems you have a fair bit of responsibilities yourself."

"Yes, estate and household matters. It is getting easier now that I've had some practice."

A brief pause followed before he queried, "What made you settle on Lord Hugh as your husband?" His voice was even and pleasant, causing her throat to constrict. If she had held any hopes about his romantic feelings towards her, she did not now. Not after he spoke so casually of her marriage plan.

"He is older but in good health, distinguished, and interesting."

"Interesting? That is a high praise indeed."

"We have not spoken in quite a while, but our last conversation included the Reform Act, farming, tenant issues, and magic shows. And he is young enough to father children if willing."

Preston was quiet, but Elara did not dare look up, for her eyes threatened to tear.

At the top of the stairs, they turned right in the direction of the earl's chamber. She stopped two doors down, in front of Preston's guest bedchamber.

"Here we are. If you need anything, don't hesitate to ring the bell."

"Where is your chamber?" he asked.

"I am in the opposite wing," she said, pointing.

"Why am I not staying near you? We are betrothed, and it is you I came to protect."

"Yes, well, I am in the mistress suite since Father vacated the master suite. James now occupies his rooms."

Preston's eyes filled with such violent rage so unexpectedly that she became afraid. He paused to massage his temple, then schooled his features to something more benign.

"Has the snake injured you in any way?"

"No, only threats..." Elara watched Preston wage an internal battle, sinews standing taut in his neck.

"Would you disclose it to me if he had?"

"Yes."

"Are you sure?"

"You have my word." Her earnest avowal seemed to placate him. His rigid jaw relaxed a fraction.

"Very well. Wait here," he said and walked into his room. Within seconds, he exited holding his trunks. "I'm taking the master suite. Lead the way."

"But James has already claimed it."

Preston began striding towards her chamber. "Good. No doubt his clothes and shaving tools are of better quality than mine."

"He will be angry," she said nervously, trying to keep up with his pace.

"Even better. I'd like nothing more than to pummel him."

"You are staying only the night. It hardly seems worth the trouble."

He swung abruptly to face her, causing her to step back. His expression was hot with fury. "Do you want that scoundrel to see your body clad in a thin layer of fabric? Do you want him sleeping next to your room?" he barked.

"Of course not! Nevertheless, I'll be alone with him after you are gone! Angering him will not help me at all."

Noticing her voice shake, Preston reached her with one long stride and enveloped her in a tight hug. He whispered, "I will get him out of this house, and my guards will ensure he never returns. You'll be safe."

Before Elara had time to relax into his arms, he released her and resumed striking his heels on the marble floor. Elara stood watching his back profile. Her spirit had buoyed momentarily with the promise of his protection, but his impersonal exit left her plunging back into the cold shadow.

## Chapter Twenty

# 9 March 1833 – ten in the evening

Holding her had been a mistake. It underscored what he stood to lose should he fail to secure an annulment from Julia. Preston's heart ached at the anticipated grief he would cause them both.

In tense silence, they proceeded down the corridor with Elara eventually overtaking him and leading the way. The entire wing consisted of only four large doors. She opened one door revealing an enormous bedroom with fire blazing in the hearth large enough to roast an entire pig. Around it were two green chairs and a chaise on top of a luxurious rug of deep burgundy.

Preston studied the canopied bed shrouded in the sheer pink fabric. The virgin white of the luxurious silk counterpane on the bed shimmered, and Preston imagined Elara's naked form writhing on top of the quilt, shrouded in the sheer fabric. He could envision her breasts and pink nipples teasing him through the fabric. The fabric would glisten with moisture from her sex as she opened her legs apart for him. What he wouldn't give to pound into her until her breasts heaved and legs trembled. He would bind her to the bed and suck her, lick her, and eat her until she begged him to stop because the pleasure was too much. She would feel marked by his desire and scorched by his possessiveness. He would ensure she knew in her core to whom she belonged.

"Is something amiss?" Elara's hesitant voice asked.

Hell. He was too aroused to turn around. Instead, he clicked his tongue. "This will not do at all," he muttered.

"Whatever do you mean?"

"There appears to be nowhere to restrain you properly."

Elara gasped, bright colour suffusing her cheeks. "Nicholas!"

Preston flashed her a grin, unabashed as his mind recalled the soft flesh of her cunny that had sucked in his cock and pulsed around it. *Heavens, she was lovely.*

"I suppose my crude jape was ill-timed. Perhaps you'll find it humorous another time," he said smoothly.

"I would like to pretend you did not say that," she murmured, cheeks scarlet as she led the way to another door.

Preston was relieved to follow behind her with his raging erection. She opened the door to a cosy private parlour with another enormous fireplace and a sitting area around it.

"Capital, we even have a private withdrawing room! It is grander than my entire lodging," Preston enthused. Looking around the room, he pointed at a door on the opposite side of Elara's chamber.

"Is that the master suite?"

"Yes."

Preston strode to it and turned the door handle. Finding it locked, he asked, "Do you have the key?"

"No. James has it with him."

Feeling another surge of anger, he was tempted to break down the door. But he'd fall flat on his arse. Preston felt around his collar. Finding nothing, he extended his palm to Elara. She grasped his intent and handed him a hairpin from her chignon. He swiftly picked the lock, the mechanism clicking open.

Striding inside as though he belonged there, Preston set about tossing James' belongings into the hallway with relish. He began by flinging out undergarments and clothes. A great mound amassed in the corridor while the stupefied servants and James' valet gathered to watch. Cravats, pocket watches and cigars were left untouched, but pipes went sailing through the air to land who knew where. Having emptied the bedchamber sufficiently, he ordered the footmen to toss them at the front door. Preston ordered the dumbfounded valet to unpack his meagre belongings and sat by the fireplace.

Elara hovered uncertainly by his side. Without a word, he gripped her small hand and guided her onto a chair beside him. He revelled in the feel of her small hand, skin to skin. Before they had a chance to enjoy the quiet, however, Whorepipe's indignant howl rang in the hallway.

"What the devil is the meaning of this?"

James arrived with two of Preston's guards trailing him, puffing with fury. "Who dares to handle my possessions thus?" he barked as he advanced towards Preston.

"Excellent timing, my lord!" Preston replied amiably, standing up and smiling. "You made the error of occupying my bedchamber. An innocent misunderstanding, I'm sure. Do take a moment to pack properly."

"Preston?" James shouted aghast. "You? You are the wealthy and powerful fiancé Elara spoke of?"

"Yes, I am," he said, pulling her against him tightly. His body sang at the contact.

James suddenly chuckled, shaking his head. "When I heard you were fetching your powerful fiancée, I feared you might be telling the truth. You had me fooled, El. That was clever. But he really is no one without his law licence. I could have him disbarred with one letter. And to think I was on my best behaviour for this country mouse while I could've taken you again and again."

Scarcely had the words left James' lips than Preston acted, years of hardened experience lending him startling speed. In an instant, he had seized the slighter man by the cravat and slammed him to the wall, before flinging his wheezing form to the floor. Though they matched in height, the viscount's more gangly frame was no match for the fury of Preston's onslaught. Keeping the cur from cracking his skull on marble, Preston nevertheless bloodied his jaw with efficient blows. A red haze gripped his mind, demanding more violence, each blow proving less satisfactory than the last. He was stopped only by Davies and Smith pulling him away. He would have lunged for the knave again if not for the light pressure of Elara's hand upon his back. At her soothing caress, clarity pierced his muddled senses.

Leaning near the cowering man, Preston ground out through gritted teeth, "Quit this house lest I truss and roll you outside, you damned blackguard. She is under my protection now. Never again will you threaten or even look upon her, or you shall taste my fists once more."

Rising, Preston pulled Elara close with one arm while James clambered slowly upright, dabbing at the blood trickling down his chin.

"You will pay for this," James gritted out. "I will ensure you are shackled like an animal and dragged to the dungeon if it is the last thing I do!"

"Are you threatening me, Lord Frances? A peer was intimidating and coercing an officer of the law through rank and influence. That is why I defended my honour. Why, some might construe it as placing yourself above the law, even beyond His Majesty the King! I doubt the lords would look kindly on such a man."

"What boll..." James trailed off at the sight of Davies and Smith closing in on him.

"The keys," Preston bit out. "All of them. Now."

After a fraught pause, James silently obeyed. At Preston's subtle signal, the guards escorted the viscount from the premises.

Preston released his arm around Elara with an immense effort. She stepped in front of him, appearing for a moment as though she might bestow a kiss. But propriety reasserted itself, and she drew back with a demure whisper instead. "I thank you. Now I must see to Father. The commotion might have startled him."

Craving her nearness, Preston followed her wordlessly like a pup. Observing Elara tend to her slumbering father, he wished he could bundle his reckless passions and sink them to the ocean depths. Listening to her gentle voice whilst soothing her father aroused an ache. How easy it'd be to go to her, enfold her in his arms and slake this pounding thirst upon her willing lips. But no.

This urge shall pass. He would leave once the Stamford estate was registered under Elara's business and there was no incentive for James to wed her. It remained to be seen if he would pursue her for any other reasons. He would leave his small army behind for her protection.

In the interim, perhaps the monastery beckoned. Or else redouble the efforts to locate his errant wife. Briefly, the urge gripped him to extract her whereabouts from his father by any means necessary. He even contemplated conceding to the old man's demands in exchange, though it would mean surrendering his autonomy and life's work... relinquishing all he had sacrificed and achieved. Alas, he could not betray himself or those relying upon him after striving so tirelessly to reach this point.

Preston escorted Elara to her room with a silent prayer for strength. Even as he willed the desire to ebb, it lingered on, a bittersweet longing for a woman logic could not erase.

## Chapter Twenty-One

# *10 March 1833 – two in the morning*

Tossing and turning in the space between reality and dream, Elara was awakened by the call of her name. The voice was deep, soft, but urgent. She quickly sat up, her nerves tingling with alarm. Was it her father calling for help? But impossible. He was too far away unless he had crawled down the corridor somehow. She listened and heard it again.

Quietly, she followed the voice to the adjoining parlour. She opened the door and found the room unlit and cold. The faint light from her bedchamber overflowed into the withdrawing room, faintly illuminating the figure on the divan. She covered her mouth to stifle her gasp.

Lying on the divan was Preston, completely nude. His eyes were closed, and his lips were muttering her name. One hand extended towards the floor, holding a drink. His other hand was wrapped around his stiff member–large and intimidating–stroking it slowly.

Elara watched, unable to look away, both fascinated and mortified. She understood now why it had hurt to be breached by him and why it had felt like he was piercing her centre.

Suddenly, Preston's eyes flipped open, and she jumped. His half-hooded eyes twinkled, and heat flushed over her as they held each other's gaze. His strokes slowed but did not cease. She told herself she ought to leave, but her feet stayed glued to the rug.

With a pained look, he slurred, "Hell. I'm seeing visions of you now." His lids fluttered closed again.

Elara felt a primal awakening thunder through every fibre as she floated closer, moth to a flame. Preston's eyes opened slowly, the barest embers enkindled and searching hers through the dusky darkness. No word was uttered, no motion made save the steady cadence of anticipating breaths.

His gaze lingered over gossamer cotton barely shielding her. He scorched her silhouette beneath and ignited smouldering trails down her spine. Elara tremored under his sensual assault, her nerves plucked exquisitely taut.

His eyes sharpened on her breasts, and his hand moved a little faster. His superb muscles rippled impressively as the orange glow glided over the bulge. Elara braved another step forward and stopped just beyond his reach. Preston stopped breathing and stroking. His eyes opened wide as she slipped one loose sleeve over her shoulder and revealed her breast. His breathing was laboured now, and his eyes drifted down between her thighs.

"Sit," he rasped.

She obeyed.

"Bring your legs up on the divan. Face me."

When she did as told, he exhaled a deep breath and resumed stroking. "Show me the other breast, love," he said softly.

Elara tugged on the other sleeve of her night rail and pushed it down to her waist. He let out a soft moan as her creamy flesh and coral-tipped nipples glowed in the faint light.

"I wish I could hold your tits, take them in my mouth and suck..." His grip on his cock tightened. "Fondle your breasts, Elara," came his low command.

Elara stared at him, her eyes as big as the full moon.

"Now," he said sternly.

Slowly, she raised her hand and touched her nipple with a finger. She then circled the peak slowly, broadening the caress to the areola.

"Yes, just a light touch. Yes..." His eyes were rivetted on her finger, and she sensed his appetite growing.

"Lift your night rail," he ordered.

"I can't." She shook her head, embarrassment flushing her skin and his demands heating her from the inside.

"You can and you will. I need to see your pussy before I go mad."

Hesitantly, she lifted the soft fabric to her hips.

"Higher, love. To your stomach so I may feast on your cunny."

Turning her head to avoid his eyes, she obeyed.

"Mm... spread your legs all the way... more... more. That's it. My sweet darling, you are exquisite." His lips parted, and his eyes fixated on her most secret place as his hand moved the length of his cock rhythmically. Becoming audacious with arousal, Elara moved her hand to her clitoris and began to stroke.

"Fucking hell... What you do to me, Blossom," he said with ragged breath.

"Do you think about me often?" she asked as her dainty fingers moved over her folds and clitoris.

"Every damn night, love. I dream about drinking you in, burying myself deep inside you, filling you with my seed... your pussy drenched for me, your come dripping from need of me."

"I need you, Nicholas. I want you inside me."

"God... what I wouldn't give to be inside you, Elara... take you hard from behind..." His hand pumped his cock at a surprising speed, his abdomen contracting admirably from the effort.

Elara chased her own pleasure, and her body swelled from the vision of him wanting her. He had been detached during the day, but at night, he craved her. She would need to be content with that.

"Nicholas," she whispered, powerful sensation surging in her body. "Nicholas!" she cried out as her body climbed the peak and became weightless. Then the tension burst hot and silken. It flowed inside her as her inner muscles squeezed every ounce of delight from her body.

Preston got on his knees, his eyes glued to her euphoric face. "You are so beautiful," he said before an absolute stillness overtook him. His entire body stiffened, jerked as he spewed grunts and sharp exhales in quick succession. He ejaculated hot, white fluid over her breasts and pussy.

Still quaking from pleasure's dying echoes, Elara darted away to her room with little modesty intact.

## Chapter Twenty-Two

# *10 March 1833 – seven in the morning*

Elara stole occasional glances at Preston's strong profile adjacent to her at the breakfast table. Her body was heated from suppressed mortification of the night while longing welled powerfully within her breast. Lingering beneath mere lust, however, lurked the tendrils of a deeper attachment, one she feared voicing even to herself. Last night, it had required all her self-restraint not to return to him and nestle into his embrace.

Preston's eyes were glued to the morning papers, and Elara kept her eyes on the plate. He had barely glanced in her direction at the table. It now seemed like a fantasy he would desire her every night. She was beginning to suspect he said that to coax her cooperation.

This morning, she had dressed to impress. As shy as she was about the events of last night, her spirit had leapt for joy because he still wanted her. With Shelley's stammering approval, she had donned her lavender gown with low decolletage and the stiffest corset. Now, she was desperate to stir longing in his heart or lower. She leaned forward with her hands folded neatly on the dining table, pushing her breasts up farther.

While he ignored her, she surveyed him shamelessly. His coat was a perfect shade of blue for his chestnut hair and fit his body like a second skin. She leaned back in her chair to get a better view of his lower half and internally groaned at the sight of his cream-coloured breeches moulding snuggly to his long, muscular legs.

Elara wondered if he was harbouring an erection under the table at this very moment, but she couldn't see it. Having given up on breakfast several minutes ago but unable to abandon his company, Elara dropped her fork on the floor. She ducked down when a footman swiftly came to her aid and picked up the utensil. She sat up awkwardly with a mix of embarrassment and disappointment.

"What are you scheming?" came his deep voice.

"Scheming?" Her startled voice croaked. "I am not scheming."

"Then why did you pretend to drop the fork?" he asked, meeting her eyes for the first time.

"I... I don't know what you mean."

He leaned back in his chair and smirked. "You've been studying me," he said with amusement. "Correction, you've been admiring me."

"Don't be ridiculous!" she shot back. "How would you know? You've been ignoring me all morning."

"I have not."

"You have."

"How would I know you've been watching me if I hadn't been watching you?" he asked, his gaze returning to the papers.

"Yes, but... You haven't said a word or even looked at me."

He was silent. She felt pathetic to have him so near only to be unnoticed. Just when she thought he had no intention of continuing the conversation, he said, "It is called self-preservation, Elara."

She stared at him, and his gaze flew to her face then to her mouth, darkening instantly. Blushing, she looked away and stuffed her mouth with bread as she seemed to do with some regularity in his company.

She swallowed the mouthful of bread and sipped the cold tea. Glancing at him cautiously, she noticed his expression was no longer indifferent. Her fingers itched to smooth away the burden carved in his brow, but she knotted them tightly in her skirts instead.

"About last night..." he began, and her pulse skipped a beat with panic. She hated the thought of him apologising. "You fled afterwards. I wanted to ask if you are all right with what happened."

"Um…" Thoughts fought to emerge in her head but became scrambled. Instead, she placed her hands on her cheeks.

"Did I shock you? Repulse you? Or were you insulted in any way?"

"I was surprised and embarrassed but not offended."

"Good. I am relieved."

Squirming in an uncomfortable silence, Elara was about to excuse herself when he spoke.

"You are tempting no matter what you wear but today…" He glanced up and let his eyes fall to her cleavage. He shook his head slowly. "You shall ruin me, Elara."

She studied his powerful hands holding the papers. Those long fingers had been inside her once… had stroked her… She wanted them again. "Were you deep in the cups last night when I saw you?"

He grimaced as he replied, "I was properly foxed. A mistake."

"Last night wouldn't have happened if you were sober, then?"

"Most likely not."

"I see," she said, deflating. "Did you mean what you said? That you think about me every night?" She forced herself to lift her head, fear and longing gripping her.

Instead of responding, Preston folded the newspaper and asked in a low rumble, "Do you think about me when you pleasure yourself?"

Her eyes darting to everywhere except his face, she replied, "No."

"No?" Surprise was obvious in his tone. "Who then?"

"A man I had known for a long time."

"Don't tell me it's James," he gritted out.

"No, of course not! His name is Captain Wentworth, Frederick Wentworth."

"When and how did you meet?"

"When I was about twenty-three. We met through his mother."

"What happened?"

"I fell in love with him right away. He was kind, tall, handsome, wealthy, and so charismatic."

Preston narrowed his eyes, displeasure obvious in his countenance.

She did her best to refrain from smiling, thrilled to witness his jealousy. "But he was in love with someone else. A woman named Anne. I couldn't compete."

"Is he married to this Anne, then?"

"Yes. I see him sometimes, but he does not know I exist."

"You sound as though you pine for him," he said coolly.

"I do."

Stiffening, he said firmly, "You may end our involvement once the business registration is processed at the courthouse. We shall need to be honest with Lord Hugh about our sham betrothal."

Her chest squeezed tightly, and the earlier thrill evaporated instantly. "How long will the registration take?"

"Likely a week or so."

"Is that when you will leave me for good?"

"Likely sooner. Mayhap in a day or two."

"Why so soon?"

Preston's eyes pierced hers with stoic hardness. Embarrassed by her pleading tone, she quickly added, "I understand. Your clients and... wife..."

"Today, we will go to the local rector, so you have refuge if required. It may also help to cultivate the tenants' goodwill. Let us then head to the bank in London and establish your status as the heiress."

"London?"

"Aye. I do not trust the local bankers to keep your information confidential. I don't know your cousin well, but I'd rather not take any chances. I have a banker I trust. We shall go to see him."

"I see. How long will I be away? I don't wish to leave Father for too long."

"Two nights. Is that acceptable?"

Elara nodded in agreement. Just then, Mr Roberts appeared and whispered in Preston's ear. Preston promptly excused himself, leaving her alone to ponder the intricacies of her heart.

---

Preston found Smith just outside the dining room with news from London. He lowered his head and asked in a hushed tone, "What is it?"

"Your campaign was effective, sir. Thorn spotted a Mrs Julia Martin on a Spanish ship, arriving in Plymouth with three children yesterday evening. The children are a girl of six years, boy of ten, and a boy of thirteen."

"Those are the right ages. Who is on her trail now?"

"Thorn and Dupont, sir."

"I assume she's headed to Lullingstone?"

"Yes, sir."

"Very well. I shall leave for the office today. Go lend a hand to Thorn and Dupont. Be diligent about Jones' men."

"Yes, sir." Smith took a few steps then turned around. "Another matter, Mr Preston. It seems that Lord Frances is having our men followed."

Preston groaned. "That is shite on my shoe I could do without."

"How shall I handle it, sir?"

"Let them follow and mislead them when necessary. What else is Frances scheming?"

"He is meeting with the Master Bencher and an Archbishop this week."

"That whorepipe!" Preston spat under his breath. The snake was going to be a rock in his kidney. He meant to have him disbarred if he had to speculate. The Master Bencher being a man whose morals were as crooked as his teeth, Preston needed to prepare for the worst.

The bencher could falsify his record and accuse him of something truly appalling such as bigamy which could destroy his career and Elara's reputation. If this were the case, he and Elara must abandon this sham as soon as possible.

Failing that, he may need to use his ancestral influence to evade this trap.

This was for the best, he told himself. It wouldn't do anyone any good to prolong this agony considering the slim chance of an annulment. Julia would not grant his wish easily. Nay, she would require something unobtainable by money.

Picking up his leaden feet, Preston returned to the dining room and was surprised to find Elara still at the table.

"I am sorry to have left you alone. Smith brought me some news that requires my return to the office."

"Nothing terrible, I hope?"

"No."

"Good," she said, standing.

"We leave within the hour."

"I will be ready. Shall I bring my maid with me?"

Preston rubbed his chin, vaguely discomfited. "I fear there is scarcely any room to accommodate your lady's maid in my humble abode."

"Oh," she averted her gaze. "Shelley may remain here to attend to my father," she said.

"Very well. Let us be off to the rector and speak to some of the tenants if you wish. We have much to accomplish today."

He was about to offer his arm to her but hesitated. Elara's nearness quickened his blood as if no dam existed. Desperate to anchor his wavering reason, Preston clasped his hands rigidly behind his back as yearnings clung as close as his own shadow. His sense of duty to protect her must dominate his lustful weakness or she would suffer for his deficiencies. With his heart clenched against traitorous impulse, he strode with stalwart step to ready their departure.

---

As Preston gazed pensively at the passing scenery, Elara willed his glance to meet her own. When at last his eyes turned her way, she swiftly passed a hand through the strands of curls she left down. She had been told by a man or two that they liked her hair like this. Her effort may be futile, but she did it anyways. To lessen the heartache, she chanted silently, he had thought of her last night, not his wife. He had wanted her, not his wife.

She knew her heart would be irreparably shattered when this charade of intimacy between them ended, but for now, her heart strained at its tethers to answer his slightest call.

Their first visit was to the chapel on the estate grounds. Elara presented Preston to the new rector as her solicitor and Preston praised her as a woman of compassion and generosity. "My dear lady wishes to ensure this parish lacks for naught," he proclaimed.

Elara then offered the astonished clergyman a large sum. After profuse thanks, the rector praised her Christian charity before God, vowing the church doors would stand open night and day should she require refuge.

They then spoke to a few tenants who had not cooperated with Elara since her father's illness. She had discussed with the earl the need for a steward, but he had not heeded her warning. The earl distrusted anyone to care for his tenants as well as he cared for them. Besides, he enjoyed the work, he had said.

With good-natured cheer and subtle threats, Preston obtained cooperation from the tenants who had not respected her authority before. With their promise to hold her in high esteem, they embarked the carriage and settled in for the long journey.

Elara removed her shoes and sat with her feet on the seat. She arranged the cushions around her and placed several blankets over her lap. She ignored Preston who was observing her with amusement.

"Are you afraid you may be dislodged and thrown from the carriage?" he asked.

"Not at all. I am already weighed down by my troubles."

"What trouble is in the forefront of your mind, my lady?"

*Fondle your breasts, Elara. Spread your legs all the way. I need to feast on your pussy...* He had said those things only last night. And now, it was *my lady*.

"I wish I was marrying for love," she said honestly.

"Tell me, when you allowed girlish imaginings about marriage, what manner of gentleman did you envision?" Preston asked cheerfully, interrupting her whirling thoughts and emotions.

Elara lowered her hands, revealing her heightened colour. "I had thought a well-educated man possessed of wit and devotion would bring me felicity."

"Sounds like me..." he murmured under his breath.

"And preferably unmarried," Elara appended delicately.

Realising she had heard him, Preston tried to make a light of it, waving a hand as if swatting a gnat. "A trifling detail."

Elara smiled melancholically. "I suppose Lord Hugh meets the requirement."

"My secretary, Mr Campbell, shall guide you in your duties should you wish to be involved while you wait for my business to conclude," Preston said abruptly.

"However do you sustain a practice without wealthy patrons?" Elara probed delicately.

Grasping her intent, Preston replied frankly, "I take on affluent clients upon occasion when in need of funds."

"Enough to sustain an army of protection officers and investigators?"

"Oh, the opium dens and brothels pay for that," he said with a shrug.

Laughing, she asked, "The wealthy patrons do not object that you often advocate against landowners?"

"Complaints abound, but none refutes my results. And a privileged circle employs my services with some regularity." He slanted an oblique look her way. "You may also, someday."

Flustered by his intimation, Elara demurred, "Gladly, if ever it were my choice."

"Best to find a progressive sort of husband, then."

"If such a paragon exists."

"Would you still seek marriage, knowing you must relinquish autonomy?"

"Indeed. Freedom holds a small joy when devoid of beloved family. My dear mother perished in my birthing, and thus I have no siblings for companionship. James and my other kins had long provided friendship. Alas, no more, as you have witnessed. Soon, I shall stand bereft even of Father's presence. Therefore, I find myself dreaming of a family of my own."

---

Anguish squeezed Preston's chest as twin visions unfurled—him in a loveless marriage whilst she found love and family in another man's arms.

When they arrived at the London Bank, Preston hastened from the carriage, welcoming the distraction from his desolate thoughts. He offered her his arm and resolutely ignored his riotous pulse at the contact. There were more pressing matters at hand.

Schooling his features into a smile, Preston entered the bank and introduced himself as Lady Elara's solicitor. He then asked the clerk if they could meet with Lord Carlisle, the owner.

The clerk laughed lightly at the request. "You must have an appointment with his lordship, Mr Preston. He does not meet with just anyone. He is an important man. All your requests can be met by myself or the manager if you'll tell us what you need."

"Let his lordship know that Mr Preston and Lady Elara seek his audience, and he will make time. Do not tell me his lordship is not in because the man does nothing except work and separate me from my money at the gentleman's club."

At Preston's insistence, the clerk disappeared with a disapproving huff. Shortly after, a sharply turned-out man who Preston supposed was the manager came hurrying.

"Mr Preston, my apologies for keeping you waiting. Lord Carlisle is anxious to see you, sir. My lady, this way, if you please."

As they neared Carlisle's office, the roar of an angry beast echoed in the corridor.

"I was untitled and worked on the docks until a year ago, you toad! Am I not good enough for you either? Does my past shame you, Toad?"

The group found the pathetic figure disappearing into himself while Carlisle towered over him, his spittle flying in all directions as he shouted.

"That will do, Carlisle. The man holds you in high regard, though I have no idea why," Preston said smoothly.

Straightening out, Carlisle dismissed Mr Todd and approached with a good-natured smile. He was only a few inches taller than Preston but seemed to tower over him, nonetheless. He shook Preston's hand and kissed Elara's, grinning and winking at her conspiratorially. Preston narrowed his eyes at his friend, wondering how much of his flirtation was sincere.

Preston placed a possessive hand on Elara's back and tensed when she chuckled shyly at Carlisle. The banker was as large as a house and as solid as a ship. His hands were larger and thicker than Preston's. Standing in the centre of his empire, if there was any time for Preston to feel emasculated, this was it.

Carlisle jovially invited them to sit and barked at Toad to bring tea for the guests while he poured brandy in his glass. "This is an unexpected pleasure. I've heard so much about you from Preston, Lady Elara."

"You have?"

"Yes. He–"

"We are here on business, Carlisle," Preston said sternly.

"Life is short, Preston. What is the point of work if we cannot extract pleasure from it occasionally? Do you not agree, Lady Elara? You ought to get out some time, Preston. You look to be growing algae."

Elara laughed again, ignoring Preston's menacing eye.

"About the business–"

"Lady Elara, for how long are you in London?" Carlisle asked.

"That depends on Mr Preston's schedule," she replied.

"We are heading up to Slough immediately after this appointment," Preston said curtly.

"That is criminal! You cannot bring a lady down to London and not take her to the opera, the vaudeville, ballet. I'd be happy to escort you, my lady, should Mr Preston be too occupied with his business."

"Why, I, I don't know." She looked at Preston carefully as if the wrong answer may set her aflame.

"That is enough, Carlisle. I know what you're trying to do but you are only embarrassing yourself."

"You may think you know, but I am a very eligible bachelor in need of a wife, Preston." Carlisle grinned at Elara who dropped her gaze after his forthright comment.

Preston wanted to lunge at his friend and demand satisfaction for flirting with her, coveting her, for making her laugh. "I am here as Lady Elara's solicitor to ensure smooth transfer of her assets," he pressed in a low rumble.

He murdered Carlisle in a dozen ways while explaining the situation with the Earl of Stamford. Carlisle smiled back steadily, wholeheartedly enjoying Preston's jealousy.

As it turned out, Frances had already paid Carlisle a visit, appointing himself as the man to contact. Regarding Frances as a bothersome gnat, Carlisle needed no convincing to appoint Elara as the sole steward of her father's accounts.

"I very much look forward to getting to know you better, Lady Elara. If there is anything I can do to assist you, you only need to say it. Nothing is too big or too small," Carlisle said sincerely as he bent over Elara's hand once more.

"Watch it, Carlisle," Preston threatened in a hushed tone.

"How is your lovely wife?" Carlisle asked just as quietly, chuckling at his own retort.

As they quit the bank, Preston felt some satisfaction at having restored control and security to the woman he cherished. Though still wary, she walked a trace taller, visibly bolstered by having her independence restored. The first steps had been taken, but securing her future would require continued vigilance. For now, Preston permitted himself a small measure of contentment in seeing her burdens lightened.

"What happened in there?" Elara asked after she settled in the carriage with cushions and blankets.

"What are you referring to?"

"I am referring to your mood shifting between ice and barely contained blaze."

Preston's lips pressed thinly. He did not deny it. The thunderous realisation that Carlisle would make an ideal husband for her had chilled his blood. His friend was an honourable man, and he had no right to stop a good match for her. But it will nearly kill him to witness her future unfold in the arms of his friend, cradling their babe together while he tried to contain the ever-expanding abyss in his soul.

"You didn't seem to mind Carlisle's flirtations," he observed, trying to sound as casual as possible.

"I suppose not. He is not the typical banker one would expect."

"He is not just a banker. He has a shipping company as well. He opened the bank because he was surrounded by money. He has earned his peerage by thinking five steps ahead of his competition and putting himself in a position of power."

"That is most impressive. How did you become acquainted?"

"I met him through mutual friends." Preston let the next words tumble out because her happiness was more important than his selfish desires. "He is an extremely eligible bachelor. He is a decent fellow even though he seems the rough sort. He would make a good husband."

Elara's eyes widened then her face fell before turning away from him. "Perhaps."

## Chapter Twenty-Three

# *10 March 1833 – four in the afternoon*

Upon arriving at the office, Preston handed Elara down from the carriage. They passed the lengthy queue of common folk waiting to seek Mr Preston's counsel pro bono. Some had journeyed from distant villages just for a chance to petition the renowned barrister. Elara observed the hopeful, nigh worshipful looks these people bestowed upon Preston as he greeted them genially as old friends. Never had she felt such pride in another person. As her heart swelled with admiration, an ache bloomed alongside—he would encourage her to wed his friend, to lie with him and make a life without him. Swallowing the bitter draught of truth, Elara fixed her thoughts upon the task at hand.

Grievances deemed simple were attended by Mr Campbell and pupils studying law. Elara gladly assisted the former in recording clients' troubles, organizing them by urgency and type. For the first time, she experienced the profound satisfaction of living amidst humanity and exercising her intellect fully. This felt wholly unlike distributing alms from afar. She had never felt so engaged.

After a gruelling seven hours, the queue finally dispersed. Elara was tidying up the desks and filing papers when Smith entered the office.

"Mr Smith, is Mr Preston expecting you?" inquired Mr Campbell.

"Aye," Smith rumbled.

"Please follow me. I shall alert him to your arrival." The secretary ushered the man into the inner office and withdrew. Smith acknowledged her with a shallow bow as he passed her.

Elara watched Smith's broad back disappear into the doorway, almost filling the entire span. What was he doing here? He had not journeyed with them.

Elara stacked the remainder of the documents and hoped desperately to see Preston, who had scarcely glanced her way since their arrival. Such detached treatment was only to be expected given their awkward start to the day and how consumed he had been with work, yet she felt a maudlin melancholy creeping upon her.

---

Preston gave his final orders to Campbell and turned to face Smith.

"Mrs Julia Martin has agreed to meet with you tomorrow morning," Smith said.

"Good. How miserable were the Salisburys?"

"Sufficient degree, sir. I've never heard a woman shout like her."

"Yes. That is her talent. Did she have men with her?"

"No. I believe she was trying to be inconspicuous."

Preston scoffed. "As if that's possible. How many are guarding her?"

"Four. I can be there if you require."

"No. I assume Jones' men are lurking around."

"Aye."

"Be on guard, Smith."

"Why would her brother want her back?"

"Because she is the only effective diplomat to France."

"I see."

"And for leverage against me. He doesn't wish to lose his bargaining chip."

After Smith confirmed he would be accompanying Preston to meet his wife, he turned to leave.

"Wait," Preston said. "I have a man I need you to find. I want to know everything about him. What he likes, dislikes, how he proposed to his wife, if he's a good dancer, everything."

Smith's brows furrowed, creating deep creases on his forehead.

"Do not look at me like that. I am not going mad. You didn't look at me like that when I declared war against my parents."

Smith said nothing.

"His name is Captain Frederick Wentworth, a military officer. Apparently tall, handsome, and wealthy. He is married to a woman named–"

"Anne," Smith interrupted.

"How did you know? Do you know the man?"

"Aye," Smith stared at Preston with a… Was that a smile on his lips? He'd never seen Smith smile except when he won a prize fight.

"Well? Tell me what you know," Preston said impatiently.

"I believe he was born around 1817…"

"Impossible! That would make him only sixteen!"

"His mother's name is… Jane… Austen."

"What?" Preston paused then slapped his forehead and hissed, "That minx!" He walked around his office a few times before asking, "How do you know about the novel?"

Smith shrugged. "It's the best way to start a conversation with a woman. You ought to as well if you fancy a lass."

"I did. Of course I've read her books. Pride and Prejudice, Sense and Sensibility, but who reads an obscure novel like…"

"Persuasion."

"Persuasion? Even the title is unremarkable."

"Miss Austen didn't think so. Neither did my lady at the time."

"Are you telling me you've read all her books?"

"Aye. I had to. I was told we were to take turns reciting the lines from her books or I wouldn't get to kiss her for a month."

"A month!"

"Aye. She was tough, that one. But I studied hard. Made patrolling more enjoyable."

"You were memorising romance novels while patrolling for me?"

"Aye. Kept my mind sharp. You want your guards to pay attention and not fall asleep? Have them memorise Miss Austen's work. They're quite entertaining."

"All right, Smith. I think I've heard enough. Let us forget this conversation ever happened. But feel free to share your knowledge with the rest of your men and demand whatever you see fit."

"Aye, sir."

"Ask Lady Elara to come to my office, will you?" Preston tidied the documents murmuring, "Minx, how dare she."

"Is everything all right?" Elara's voice came from the door. Preston looked up and tried to stop his heart from melting when his eyes took in her lovely face. It was hopeless.

"Yes. Why?"

"Mr Smith just smiled at me."

"Oh, that. He's very proud of himself for being well read." Preston breathed and let the impulse to hold her pass. "My affairs here are settled for the evening. I shall dispatch someone if you require anything."

"You are most considerate, but I brought all necessities with me."

"Does chicken soup suit you for your repast? My skills in the kitchen are limited. And it grows late to attempt anything more elaborate."

Elara raised her brows, looking pleased. "You prepare your own meals?"

He gave a shrug. "My modest means make it difficult to perform unpaid work whilst paying a cook regularly. She attends one day a week, for more complex affairs and heavier cleaning."

She grinned and said enthusiastically, "Then I confess I am eager to sample your efforts."

He waved this aside with a smile. "Hush, let us not heighten expectations overmuch. And you shall assist, not simply await being served. This is my domain, my lady."

"Anything you ask, I shall most gladly oblige," she said, looking delighted.

## Chapter Twenty-Four

## *11 March 1833 – past midnight*

After issuing instructions for provisions to a local lad, Preston led Elara upstairs to his private rooms. He ignited the oil lamps, and she walked about scrutinising every little thing as he gave a brief tour of the cosy lodgings. Elara could not quite smother a small gasp of pleasure at everything she saw no matter how trivial. She even delighted at seeing his washbasin and shaving tools.

"I promise you shan't get lost in so modest a space," he remarked. "Pray wash up if you'd like whilst I commence preparations. Your assistance shall not be required just yet. Soap cake is already present beside the basin."

Doffing his coat and waistcoat, Preston set to work briskly on the simple knot of his cravat. As he rolled back his shirtsleeves, Elara stopped and watched him from behind the wall. When he looked up, she graced him with a shy parting smile before disappearing into the water closet.

The instant Elara quit the room, Preston leaned heavily upon the counter, burying his head in his hands with a muffled groan. Here, amidst cramped quarters, sans servants, naught but divine intervention could preserve him from taking her in his arms.

It was true he had claimed her maidenhead whilst imprisoned, but such duress granted him no enduring rights. Now free of confinement, he must consider the consequence of his actions, as though they were but newly acquainted. She was an innocent, himself a married man—that solitary fact must suffice.

Ironically, until Elara entered his sphere, Preston had lived much as a bachelor. His technical domestic status had not impacted his life. Yet now, this exquisite woman threatened his hard-won discipline most profoundly. Even clad in subdued grey or beige gowns deliberately plain, her vibrant palette of scarlet and emerald peeked through to rouse his senses. Tonight, she looked extraordinary in lavender with her hair loose from her chignon as if she had been thoroughly debauched. Her gentle grace and ready compassion lit such an ache inside as he had never known. He found himself bereft of defences before such enchanting temptation.

Work had always proved distraction enough. He would have to toil at his desk until he collapsed from exhaustion. Failing that, he must simply seal her from his thoughts, permit not even the most innocent fancy.

Thankfully, the lad soon returned with his purchases. Preston busied himself preparing the simple fare, fixating his thoughts upon the domestic tasks at hand. He tuned out his mind further by half consciously humming snippets of nameless melodies.

"What may I do to be of service?"

Elara breezed into the kitchen, a wafting trail of soap and her citrus scent slicing through the pungent spice of the soup. That delicate fragrance struck the very depths of Preston's being, for it conjured his most searingly intimate remembrances of her graceful neck, her enticing décolletage... Those recollections could warm him from within on brighter days or haunt his darker nights like the most savage of spectres.

"Have you..."

Preston's voice faltered as his gaze lit upon her, clad now in a gossamer night rail and a silk wrapper. He had no doubt the diaphanous fabrics cloaked her form whilst subtly displaying every alluring curve and dip. Her loose wrapper gaped open above her waist, unveiling the glimmering alabaster flesh of her bosom, its delicate lace trimmings summoning him to caress.

His eyes trickled over her with the languid heat of warm honey. He watched her throat convulse as she swallowed under his brazen appraisal, his gaze clinging to the responsive peaks of her breasts.

"I say, whatever became of your gown?" he managed weakly.

"I did not wish to risk soiling it. Do forgive me if my dress disturbs you."

"Nay, you are... quite all right," he assured her, rather than demand she change lest he drape her across the table like a plucked fowl.

Attempting to distract himself, he returned to vigorously chopping chicken limbs with the dangerous blade. Alas, even that conjured wholly inappropriate visions, his blood surging traitorously. Good Lord, was he so far gone as to lust after poultry now? The woman had unmanned him entirely.

"I pray you, slice these vegetables," he stammered. "I'm preparing a simple chicken broth."

"That sounds most delightful."

Taking up a stem of purple broccoli in one dainty hand whilst wielding the knife awkwardly in the other, Elara hesitated, peering uncertainly up at him.

"Er, what specific size and shape ought I cut them?"

Despite inward warnings, Preston moved behind her, gently covering her delicate hands with his own. Heaven help him, he had not the strength of will to resist. Her hands were so smooth...

Nay, not as soft as the silk of her unbound hair when he had knotted his fists within. Nor so fine as her neck onto which he had seared fervent kisses. Not so sleek as her womanly flesh whose hidden swells and valleys his fingers had learnt by heart...

Preston stared fixedly at the stout vegetable she clasped, imagining his rigid shaft equally blossoming, equally firm in her grasp. Hell, his cock was angrily pushing against his skin-tight buckskin which he had hoped would bind the useless appendage. A confounded nuisance it was, refusing to be mastered. Likely, his angry flesh matched the same purple shade of the broccoli, bruised from straining. But no garment could tame what her touch alone might pacify.

As she swayed, her shapely arse grazed his engorged anatomy.

*Blast it all!* The thin buckskin was no match for his mutinous cock. There remained but one recourse. He angled his hips backward, resisting the urge to rut against her softness like a cake of lye soap upon a washboard.

Turning the blade right-side up, he covered her fingers in his much larger grip and demonstrated the proper slicing technique, voice gone hoarse.

"Rock it so, with care... control comes through practice..."

"I see," she said rather breathlessly.

"And keep your fingers so... lest you lose a tip," he rasped near her ear, feeling her slight tremor.

"Very wise," she whispered.

"I have my moments."

"This is such fun," she murmured, leaning into him.

"Indeed," Preston agreed, his rough palms caressing the tender skin of her hands.

*Delicious torment, that's what this was.* He grunted silently. How his flesh remembered and thrilled at her softness.

Elara arched farther back with a quivering sigh, every luscious curve melting to him. The excruciation of holding her thus roused all his self-castigation. What madness had possessed him, to take such liberties when he had vowed not to reopen barely healed wounds?

He could withstand the constant hollow ache of longing which he knew well. But to hold her so intimately once more, only to lose her, would pose the cruellest torment. He would risk her heart again when he had naught of value to offer, no certain future. With a heroic effort, Preston withdrew, silently berating his unruly passions.

Elara resumed her ruthless assault on the hapless produce as Preston surveyed her efforts, quelling a wholly inappropriate envy of the innocent vegetable. He found crying over onions most satisfying, but what demon had possessed him to grant her a parsnip to grasp when her delicate fingers curled so suggestively around their rigid lengths?

Eventually, with the simple ingredients left to blend, they retired to the parlour with glasses of wine. Preston took the armchair whilst Elara reclined upon the settee, every alluring contour of her silhouette visible beneath the shimmering fabric. His gaze lingered at the juncture of her graceful thighs, where he had... No. He must not reminisce. Clearing his throat gruffly, Preston crossed his legs to conceal his body's indecent state.

"You would make for an excellent secretary, should you wish to continue," Preston ventured brightly over the aching hush, summoning her from reveries.

"You think so?" He saw that she was attempting levity despite her forlorn expression.

"Without a doubt. I've faith you shall triumph at anything your heart aspires to, Blossom." Preston flinched inward, the tender endearment having slipped out most unintentionally.

She heard it but did not comment. Instead, she said, "You have been my surest comfort in this trial." She nibbled her lip, and Preston barely quashed the urge to gently take that sweet flesh between his own teeth. "Without your stalwart presence these days... had I only James and sorrow for company, I do believe I would have perished."

"It brings me great pleasure to provide what meagre solace I can."

Recognising the inadequacy of his words, he halted his emotions from spiralling by returning to the kitchen and setting their simple supper.

After serving the soup with fresh, crusty bread, he took her hand as if she were arrayed for any ballroom and led her solicitously to the table. He disappeared to fetch the blanket and draped it over her slim shoulders. Preston brushed aside Elara's praise as she savoured the meal, finding deeper fulfilment by simply sharing this world with his Blossom.

As Elara ate, Preston's heart swelled painfully with overflowing devotion, then squeezed sharply with sudden dread.

They ate in pensive silence awhile, each absorbed in their pain, turning over quiet questions and unvoiced conundrums.

"Nicholas," she broke the silence. He looked up at her countenance layered with emotions. "Why is there no sign of a woman in your home? Do you have another home you share with your wife?"

"No... I only have this one," he said in a steely tone.

She did not query anymore on the subject.

They fell silent again before she spoke once more. "And please forgive me for being boorish, but how does a solicitor who cannot afford a daily housekeeper pay for all his protection officers? What are you not telling me?"

Raking his fingers through his hair, Preston looked into her large eyes, vulnerable and pleading. Peering into them, he waded into his past and let her in. "I left my family over a decade ago because I could no longer tolerate their obsessive control over me and my brothers. My brothers, being the heirs, lived like trapped animals with absolutely no choices over anything. I was lucky to be the youngest and dispensable. After completing my studies, I enlisted in the military, but even there, my parents tried to exercise their influence. So, I became a spy to elude them from locating me."

He stood and walked to the window, blankly observing the scenery outside. Talking came easier when piercing into the darkness. In the reflection, Elara nodded in comprehension.

"Have you been estranged from your family ever since?"

"Aye. I did not want any of the things I was born into. Not if it meant I could not live my life as I wished. My parents disowned me and cut off my funds. We had no contact for six years until I was sent home due to my injuries. By then, my brothers had been killed, and my parents grew desperate for grandchildren to carry forth the lineage. Whilst I lay senseless from laudanum, they had me wed to a stranger."

Elara's hand flew to her mouth.

"Once some semblance of sense returned, Father and I reached an agreement. I would try to beget an heir for one year's span. Thereafter, I could resume my former life entirely, autonomy restored. I was told the woman was a widow. Yet within weeks, I discovered the two children accompanying her were, in truth, fathered by a lover she continued taking to her bed even after our nuptial. Once appraised of the sordid affair, my parents intervened and compelled us to maintain the marital bed for the remainder of our agreed upon term."

"Oh, my. How perfectly dreadful," Elara murmured.

"In return, I would get my freedom at the end of the year. I didn't fully trust them, so when I was released from my obligation, I changed my name and began anew. Alone. Over time, I grew rather outspoken against tyranny and inequality amongst the societal ranks. My parents found me due to the publicity I garnered and forbade me from political activities."

"What would they have done if you had not obeyed?"

"Most likely force my hand into another marriage, lock me up in a tower, throw me in the dungeon. They wanted me to annul my marriage, but I refused. I wished to spare another woman from being forced into my world. To escape their grasp, I changed my identity yet again and studied law. They located me years later and their men now lurk around my office, but they cannot afford to cause a scandal."

"Are your guards for protection against your parents then?"

"It had been the main purpose in the past. Gradually, I used them to protect witnesses, protect me from disgruntled clients, etcetera."

Elara put her wine glass down and took a calming breath. "Have you been in contact with your wife?"

"She has come to see me twice in the early days. I have not seen her for several years, but I asked her to meet me tomorrow," he said.

Elara stilled, and he sensed her spiralling thoughts and emotions.

"May I inquire as to why?" she asked in a barely audible voice.

"I mean to ask her for an annulment. I'd like to marry you if you will have me."

Before he finished speaking, Elara shielded her face with her hands and began to sob. He went to her and knelt between her legs. Wrapping his arms around her, he pulled her down onto his lap and held her.

## Chapter Twenty-Five

# *11 March 1833 – two in the morning*

Preston pressed her body against his in a firm embrace. One arm wrapped tightly around her torso while the other stroked the bare skin on her neck. Her body tingled and shuddered at the contact. He was warm, firm, and unspeakably tender.

How she had craved this. Her body recognised him and sighed blissfully at his familiarity. As his lips claimed hers, Elara felt herself dissolve, no other world existing beyond his embrace. His mouth moved over hers with famished urgency, unspoken longing fuelling the fire between them. She opened for him like a flower to sunlight, a soft moan escaping as his tongue claimed hers in searing possession. He drank from her, as though she were a rich wine and he a wanderer long bereft in the desert. His large hands slid down to grasp her waist, firm yet reverent, pressing the soft cradle of her body closer until no breath of air came between them.

With tentative touches, Elara slid her fingers upwards to delve into the thick silk of his hair, thrilling at the groan it tore from his throat. Each probing caress revealed some new, exquisite sensation, threatening to overwhelm every scrap of her composure. The vanilla-tinged spice of his skin, the day's roughened abrasion of his jaw where it chafed her own. Each one illuminated her senses until she burned everywhere at once.

The kiss awakened a glorious, terrifying need within her very soul, melding her to him past all divisions. For these scintillating moments at least, Elara knew the utter joy of belonging in the circle of Preston's' sheltering embrace.

As their lips at last drifted apart, neither could find words to illuminate the sanctity of what had just transpired between them. Tongues and minds alike were mute from an excess. Even language itself proved too crude a vessel to contain.

Instead, hands spoke for them, attending to each other in unspoken rite. Elara undressed him with unhurried reverence, exposing the mighty expanse of his chest, firm with muscular slopes and hollows. Her eyes and mouth gaped at masculine terrain that seemed carved of living granite, smooth beneath her timid palms. She traced in quiet wonder the rugged curvature and dips bestowed by valorous combat, down to where his abdomen formed a lean, rippling plain.

There she continued her shy exploration, fingertips gliding with feather-light awe, secretly delighting when each brush and tickle tensed his iron muscles most deliciously. Curious as any coquettish debutante, she teased and tested until familiarity overcame hesitance. As her caresses grew bolder in claiming intimacy that was rightfully hers, Preston shuddered, enraptured by her provocative play.

Her delicate fingers drifted to the fastenings of his breeches, alighting upon the first pewter button. Green eyes lifted uncertainly to meet his simmering blue gaze. Her fingers moved deftly... and the next button slipped free.

---

When at last her hesitant caresses glided across the burning width of his chest, Preston shuddered, laid bare beyond flesh to the very bone. Even the lightest tickle of her tentative touch against his sensitised skin resonated through him like thunder. The sweet torture of her fumbling exploration racked him with pleasure beyond bearing, muscle and sinew clenching beneath her shy investigation.

As Elara's fingers worked free the buttons of his straining breeches, Preston could scarcely draw a breath, stunned by her boldness yet terrified to startle her into reticence. As she gradually moved lower to unveil new private sites, Preston lost all guise of saintly restraint.

The feather-light brush of her knuckles against his abdomen felt scorching as any brand. He quelled the urge to trap her hand and bring it to where he ached, as he would have done with casual encounters. Instead, he allowed her exploration to proceed at her own maddening pace. When at last the fabric parted, those slender digits slid tentatively, barely skimming along his throbbing length. She then held her breath as she ran a gentle palm along his erection from the root to the head.

"Sweet Lucifer..." he breathed.

With round eyes, alive with intrigue, she touched him in various ways and watched his reaction. How often, in lonely nights, had he conjured her precious face, imagining the exquisite torture of her touch? Little did he know, fevered fantasy paled before reality's fragrant fire. Each caress, however naively bestowed, lit his every nerve ending until sheer will alone leashed his desire to erupt then and there.

"This is why it hurt to have you inside me last time," Elara said conversationally as her hand continued its curious examination.

"I am sorry. I'm afraid it shall be painful for some time. It takes a little longer for women to become accustomed to me."

Elara wrapped her delicate fingers around his thick girth and began to stroke the tip of his cock. Preston sucked in a hiss, his eyes clamped shut against the blinding rush of sensation.

Placing his palms on both of her cheeks, he tangled his fingers within her locks and pulled her close for a deep kiss. The pliant softness of her yielding to him, the clean citrus scent of her unbound hair twined around his questing fingers.

"Grip it firmer, my sweet," he whispered, guiding her hand with his to slide along the full length of his pulsing cock. "That's it... Perfect... You're perfect..."

He took her mouth in his once more and sucked her in. He drank thirstily from her nectar-sweet mouth, affirming again and again she was no mirage but heavenly reality. Then, at the verge of exploding, as tempting as it was, he stayed her hand.

"Did I do something wrong?" she asked timidly.

"Sweetheart, you did too well. I don't want to come yet, although I could climax a few times tonight without any effort. You are glorious."

Reaching with reverent hands, he slowly peeled the gossamer silk robe from her porcelain shoulders. The sheer fabric sighed, a reluctant whisper as it slithered to the floor.

Beneath, her delicate night rail clung and draped in equal parts modesty and invitation over feminine curves.

As his fevered gaze drank in her beauty, Preston's breath caught, all eloquence fleeing before such flawless symmetry. No dream or desperate fantasy had done justice to her subtle perfection.

"You're striking," he whispered, meeting her eyes. "Do you know how ravishing you are?" he rasped, his breath shallow from arousal. Elara slowly shook her head. "Everything about you is... decadent."

Unable to resist temptation any longer, his trembling fingers followed where hungry eyes led. He swept aside the last veil of Chantilly lace to bare her fully, unveiling at last her bare form to his worshipping gaze. Her skin, akin to living satin that glowed pale as the moon, welcomed his adoring touch. Though she was slim and fragile as a fawn, her generous swells and dipping hollows evoked pure delight.

As she shivered beneath his reverent hands, Preston soothed her trembling form. His fingers drew delicate circles around her breasts, then around her nipples as a breath hitched in her throat. He ran his fingers over the pink buds as he worshipped her breasts with his mouth.

Rising with Elara's legs wrapped around his waist, Preston leaned his back against a wall. As she stood, he opened his legs wider and fit her between them. He firmly gripped her behind, kneading and fondling her delicious flesh. His mouth traversed to her delectable mounds once more, evoking the round breasts to flush pink and her nipples cherry red. He licked and sucked her peaks while groans escaped his throat from the lushness of her body. Shallow breaths and shy whimpers escaped her lips as he drew feather-light circles with a finger from her neck down to the back of her knees.

Elara shivered and opened her eyes, their verdant depths naked and pleading. Preston's heart constricted at seeing her lovely face so trusting as she awaited his lead. He gently cradled her cheek, his roughened thumb tracing lightly over the downy curve of her jaw. "Tell me, Blossom, what would bring you pleasure?" he whispered. "Where might I touch you?"

Elara's petal lips parted, but no sound emerged, a lovely blush blooming upon her cheeks at his frank query. Preston watched in fascination as her gaze darted away, eyelashes sweeping down demurely even as she leaned into his caress. When words failed, he saw her feminine yearnings betrayed by her graceful thighs subtly rubbing together.

Preston removed his breeches and stockings. Elara's eyes widened at his form, his thighs rippling with muscles and his large erection jutting up from light brown curls. He moved slowly, as if approaching a scared animal. He turned her and pressed her back against the wall. He loomed over her, confident and imposing, but his touch was gentle. He knelt before her and ordered, "Spread your legs, sweetheart."

She did as told, but he wasn't satisfied.

"More," he said and caressed her heat with a thumb. She flinched at the strangeness of the contact. Moisture pooled and dripped from her cunny as arousal gathered in her core.

"So wet..." he rasped, his breathing ragged.

Elara watched as he dropped to his knees with his hands on her hips. He then took her aching heat in his mouth. She gasped and tried to close her legs, but he held them firmly open. Soon, her eyes fluttered closed as a concentrated sensation poured from her centre to her toes. Preston gripped her arse and drank the moisture at her entrance. His tongue delighted her senses, making her desperate for more caresses, more licks, more and more.

"Nicholas..." She tried to rub her thighs together, squeezing out more sensation as his tongue stroked her clitoris in a steady rhythm.

"Patience," he chided.

His finger slipped inside her, then two, stroking her inner flesh without breaking the rhythm of his tongue. Elara writhed against the escalating pleasure while her hands pushed against the wall. Just when she thought she would shatter from euphoria, he added another finger, flinging her over the threshold.

"Nicholas!" she screamed as delicious sensation overwhelmed her completely. Her hands gripped his thick shoulders, the muscles flexing and straining beneath her touch. Just as she arched and stiffened, Preston went rigid with his mouth still cupping her pussy. Ecstasy flooded her, and her inner muscles pulsed furiously around his fingers. At the same time, Preston let out muted grunts, his chest heaving. Elara leaned against the wall, limp and sated. While her fingers absently stroked Preston's hair, she realised his body was shaking.

"Are you all right?" she asked with alarm. "Are you... crying?"

To her relief, Preston rose to his feet without a trace of tears. He scooped her up in his arms as she yelped and carried her to the bedchamber.

"I did not expect this royal treatment, but I am pleased," she said.

"I must be a saint, wasting my effort on a mere earl's daughter," he grumbled.

"A very reluctant saint," she observed.

With an expression of self-recrimination, he placed her down gingerly on the bed and lit the lantern. She feasted on his impossibly masculine form as the light danced over and around him.

"I shan't be making that saintly mistake again," he said.

"Not even for a reward?" she asked seductively.

Preston's eyes flashed. "You have a terrible habit of driving me mad. You ought to work on that before I return."

"Where are you going?"

"Stay in the room. I must attend to a matter of utmost urgency," he said and closed the door behind him.

"What is it you do not wish me to see?"

"Only the remnants of my desire for you, Blossom! Naught interesting!" he yelled from the parlour.

She frowned, searching her brain for bits of indecent information stashed away. She finally admitted defeat. "I don't understand!"

"I'm referring to what happens when a man reaches climax!"

"Oh... Why does that concern you?"

"It is perfectly normal for a healthy male... between the ages of fourteen and eighteen!"

Elara tilted her head in confusion. "I don't understand!"

Preston did not respond, but she heard the trickling of water. Shortly after, he entered with a wet cloth, his cheeks colouring slightly.

"You are blushing!" she made sure to point out.

"I do not blush," he said grumpily as he wiped her thighs.

"You are blushing now. I must know. What is so embarrassing about what happened?"

"Audacious wench," he said without malice. "I wasn't... you were not touching me. I haven't come without contact since I was a lad. At my age, I ought to have more control, lasting at least an hour inside you. I ought to be showing off my manly mettle, not coming prematurely like a schoolboy touching a woman for the first time. There. Are you happy?"

She nodded, stifling a laugh.

"You do know what my schoolboy prowess means, do you not?"

"Not exactly."

He crouched by the bed and pierced her eyes with affection. In a low, rumbling voice, he proclaimed, "The desire you stir within me has eclipsed all else I ever held dear... even my life's devotion to the law that once consumed me."

With that, Preston left to further rid of the shameful evidence.

---

When he returned with Elara's night rail, she was on top of the counterpane, displaying her deliciously bare backside to him. His cock reacted instantly, urging him to penetrate the depth of her, claim her.

"Lying on a bed with you brings back surprisingly fond memories of our capture," she said sleepily. "Am I sleeping in your bed tonight?"

"If you wish," he said, his breath catching as his pulse raced.

"I do wish," she said, stifling a yawn.

"You do realise I'm going to be in it, don't you? Me and the bed come as a package. No bed, no me," he said as he bent over her.

Turning to face him, her eyes widened at seeing his erection. He climbed onto the bed and hovered over her. Dotting kisses on her face and neck, he whispered, "I have handcuffs to keep you in my bed all night, all week, for a lifetime."

"Why do you have handcuffs?"

"To keep women from escaping my bed, obviously."

She forced him to look her in the eye. "Truly? You use them for bed sport?"

"No..." he said uncertainly.

With his cock throbbing, Preston rolled over her and settled his hips between her thighs.

"If the lady or I wished to use it in bed, we would discuss matters of that sort beforehand." He nudged his cockhead against her opening. "Enough talk. I need you now, Elara."

He raised her arms above her head and secured them in his grip. Taking care not to hurt her wrists, he kissed her deeply.

"I need you to know..." he rasped over her mouth, "the way I made love to you the first time is not my usual style. I've always taken women roughly, fucking rather than making love... You are the only one I've made love to, wanted to protect."

Seeing apprehension on her face, he said, "Say the word and I will stop. Until you do, I will screw you hard, imprint myself into you. Do you understand?"

She nodded.

As the pulsing in his cock became more desperate, Preston rolled her onto her side and bent her knees to her chest just as he had done the first time. This time, he could see her pussy clearly, her centre dark pink surrounded by lighter petals rippling around her entrance. When her opening glistened with her nectar, he grunted before thrusting inside her. Elara gasped and gripped his hand holding down her hip. He held his breath as he entered her deeper and deeper, savouring the vision of her centre parting for him, relishing every miniscule contact his cock made with her swollen inner flesh.

Surprising himself, he held still despite the urge to plunge deeper. "Breathe, darling. It'll get better."

When her breathing slowed and body relaxed, Preston moved inside her gingerly. As her inner flesh engulfed most of him, the sensation that shot through him was more potent than anything he had experienced. He was utterly overcome by the passion Elara stoked in him, rendering him speechless. He drove into her with urgency, pleasure surging as he watched her panting mouth, round breasts, and his cock breaching her pussy, again and again.

"Bloody hell, Elara... Fuck..."

The pleasure that overpowered his body wrenched his spirit away, flinging it into a realm unknown until it floated back in its place. When he became whole again, he gasped and puffed like a man taking his first breath after near drowning. More expletives were spat out in his gruff voice before his breathing returned to normal, and his vision cleared.

He rested his forehead against hers for a moment of tenderness when she whispered, "What sort of matters?"

"What?" Jarred out of his state, he lifted his head and looked at her.

"What sort of matters do you discuss before using shackles for bed sport?"

He stared at her in a daze. When he finally recalled their previous conversation, he erupted in laughter.

"What did I say that warrants this reaction?" she asked, looking puzzled.

"Cherry Blossom," he said.

"Yes?"

"Nothing mortifies a man more than impotence, premature ejaculation, and a woman who's lost in a conversation while he's making passionate love to her."

"Oh, is that what you were doing?"

He shook his head with mirth still on his lips. "You are more devious than you'd have me believe. You have utterly ruined me in one night."

---

By the time Elara finished her nightly ritual, Preston was sound asleep under the covers. He was on his side, one arm under his head, and the other extended into the empty space, as if he had reached for her. She was disappointed he wouldn't be holding her but remedied the situation by nuzzling her backside against him. His arm came around her chest and pulled her snuggly to him.

With all that had been revealed about his life and marriage, Elara's thoughts spun, and heart murmured with possibilities. She drifted off to sleep, wondering if she could be any happier.

Sometime in the dead of the night, Elara awoke in the dark at the feel of Preston's sturdy erection digging into her bottom. Seemingly in his sleep, he was grinding against her with a low moan. She pressed against him, thrilled to share more intimacy with him.

"Elara," he rasped, his voice husky and full of sleep. His arm tightened around her waist. "I need you again, my sweet. I need to fuck you."

She felt heat and delicious pulsing in her core from his words alone. His hand moved up, roughly fondled her breast and squeezed her nipple. The pressure sent shivers down her spine. His movements were needy and selfish as his hand roamed around her body and groped his favourite places–thighs, arse, and breasts.

In a blink, Preston was on top of her, grinding his hard shaft against her heat. He slid his hand between her thighs and ran a finger along her folds. A guttural moan escaped his throat. Sliding his finger deeper between the folds, he stopped at her entrance. "I'm going to take you hard," he rasped.

Elara opened her eyes and saw his dreamy expression, dazed and impatient to take his pleasure.

"Yes," she whispered. She wanted him to be a part of her, she wanted to feel him inside her for days, so she would not forget how they completed each other, in body and spirit.

Preston positioned his cock at her entrance. "Everyday, my body ached for you," he said before he plunged into her, making her gasp. He was stretching her to the limit, and the fullness of it stole her breath.

She realised then that he had not taken full possession of her before. He had been sparing her further discomfort. At this instant, however, he was taking all of her, fully, again and again. Preston thrust inside her, unapologetically lost in his pleasure. The deep plunges inside her core eased the ache.

Fondling her bottom with one hand, he bent over her and whispered, "Are you all right, Blossom?"

"Yes."

"Shall I stop?"

"No, but kiss me."

He devoured her mouth as he drove his cock into her. He pressed his mouth hard against hers, sucking, licking, and gasping for breath. As he wrapped his arm tightly around her hips and deepened the penetration, he let out a growl, violently jerking and heaving. The convulsion of his body continued, with climax rolling again and again.

His body limp, Preston released a muffled groan, burying his face in her hair. He lay on his side and pulled her securely against him. As she drifted off to peaceful slumber, she thought she heard him whisper, "I need you... forever..."

## Chapter Twenty-Six

# *11 March 1833 – nine in the morning*

Elara opened her eyes and watched a well-groomed man don a perfectly tailored coat in the most beautiful shade of green she'd ever seen. The cuffs were embroidered with gold stitches and the matching breeches accentuated his tall and lean form. She had not seen him dress formally before, not to mention having a tailor. She sat up in bed, pulling the sheets to her chest.

Preston turned and smiled warmly. "Good morning," he said as he approached the bed.

"Good morning. You look very handsome."

"Stop flirting with me, my lady, or I'll get nothing done today," he said, kissing her gently on the cheek.

"Where are you going looking so official?"

He sat on the bed and linked his fingers through hers. "I'm meeting Julia, my wife."

"Oh…" Ugly jealousy twisted and turned in her gut. "Are you still intending to ask for an annulment?"

"Aye."

His firm response somewhat soothed her insecurities.

"Elara, if we married, how would you like to see your life unfold?"

Her spirit hummed at the suggestion. "I don't know what you mean."

"Would you want to live in Stamford with all your servants? Or would you be content living here with me?"

She smiled brightly, her mind already planning their life together in a cosy one-bedroom dwelling. "I'd love to live here with you, just the two of us. Maybe a cook until I learn how. I want to help you at the office and meet your clients. It would be a wonderful life."

"And children? Don't you want them?"

She shook her head. "I want them only with you. Even if we can't have any, I wouldn't have any regrets."

Preston nodded but did not appear reassured. "I am not too optimistic if you understand my meaning," he said.

"Are you trying to protect my feelings again because you don't want me to raise my hopes?"

"Aye." He smiled sheepishly. He slid his fingers lightly between hers, in and out. "It seems that I cannot stop trying to protect your heart. If it's any consolation, I try just as hard to protect my heart. I am weak, Elara, when it comes to love."

"What does it mean to be weak in matters of the heart? Do you fall in love hopelessly or do you resist it wholeheartedly?"

Brows furrowed on his handsome face, signifying the question held gravitas for him.

"Both, if that's possible," he said. "I must go now. I shall see you this afternoon."

"Why do I feel like you won't come back?"

With a look of concern, Preston placed a hand on her cheek. "I will always come back for you. Always," he said. He raised her hand to his lips, kissed it, and quit the room.

---

Preston stopped to chat with Smith in his office on his way to the carriage.

"The trail has gone cold, sir," Smith said, snapping Preston's attention back to him.

"Already?"

"Aye. We confirmed with a few Scuttlers up north that they were indeed hired by the Muns to carry out a kidnapping. Our contact within the Muns confirmed they had recently orchestrated an abduction, but the request had been anonymous. Rare bottles of spirits were sent to them with written instructions. No signature, coat of arms, or seal upon it for identification."

"Did they keep the letter?"

"They claim they had not. I wrote down the names and years of the spirits, sir."

Preston studied the list, but none of them were helpful. They were not from the collection of any particular person, organisation, nor were they from any one region. He doubted there were any hidden codes to decode.

"Hell, they could still be out there somewhere, targeting innocent people," he said bitterly. "Did your contact have more information about the Muns' future activities?"

"He claimed he was warned of activities only on the day of."

"Filthy bastards. What I wouldn't give to bash their heads in. What of Lord Frances?"

"His men were seen at the foreign office and the home office. They asked about your past."

"He is sniffing in the right places," Preston said. "Devil take him! Guard the lady closely in my absence. Do not let her out of your sight, in or out of the manor."

"Aye, sir."

As the carriage bounced along the muddy road, Preston repeatedly rubbed his face with his hands, as if that would harden his heart to Elara or wipe his past clean. His mind splashed frantically through the murky waters of passion, fear, and tenderness. The height of happiness he experienced with Elara was terrifying.

With his head full of worry and heart full of turmoil, Preston disembarked the carriage and studied Lullingstone's entry, exit, servant's door—the front door thudded open.

"Welcome, Mr Preston. His lordship is waiting for you."

"Has he been watching me from the window?"

"Aye, sir. His lordship informed me that if I do not open the door right away, you would find all the ways to breach our security and rob him blind."

"I would if there was anything of value," Preston said.

"That is comforting to know," Salisbury drawled from one of the five hallways.

"For me as well. I can free my mind from scheming," Preston said.

"Touché, my friend."

"Where is she?" Preston asked gruffly.

"Are you sufficiently calm?"

"Why wouldn't I be? My life is in her hands."

"Calm yourself before you walk in there and throttle the woman."

"This ought to be the merest trifle to accomplish for a former spy," Preston said with confidence.

Salisbury gave him a doubtful look before he pushed open the double door and announced with a flourish, "Prince Maximilian, Your Royal Highness."

Preston flinched at the introduction.

Preston saw his wife in red sitting by the window. She was splendid, of course. Her long brown locks cascading in beautiful waves down her back contrasted dramatically against her blood red gown. Her big brown eyes, high cheekbones, and dark lashes all did their part to highlight her lush mouth and exotic beauty. Whereas Elara was delicate and bright, everything about Julia was big, loud, and dark.

She was tall, reaching Preston's nose, and perfectly proportional if proportional meant extraordinarily abundant breasts and very generous hips. Her mounds had overflowed in his large hands, and she was the only woman he'd bedded who could sheath his cock completely. It had not been difficult to tup her until she opened her mouth.

Julia approached him with poise and the usual sway of her hips, smiling seductively with an outstretched hand. He bowed over it only to drop it like a lump of hot coal.

She pouted. "I nearly perished with excitement at the prospect of seeing you, at last. I've been waiting all day. I even purchased a new frock for you. Do you like it?" She twirled and smiled radiantly.

"No. Let us talk. I don't have much time," he said coolly.

Giving him a wounded look, Julia stood with one hip cocked dramatically. "You are still as grumpy as ever," she said, her enthusiasm abating.

"I am. Only with you, however," he replied as he poured himself a drink... then two.

"Oh, Max. Don't be like that. It has been a long time. Five or six years. Can we not start over?"

Preston looked around the room for a chair that would put him as far away from the woman as possible. "You know how I feel about you," he said, sinking into a brown wingback chair.

Julia took the chaise across from him, lying on her stomach and bending her knees. The dip of her neckline was fully displayed and the roundness of her abundant derriere led his eyes straight to her stockinged legs with her feet in the air. His eyes took her in, but his cock didn't give a damn. It did stir and twitch at the thought of him taking Elara from behind while she was sprawled on his settee in the same position. This woman was between him and getting back to Elara and making love to her as soon as possible.

"You look handsome as usual, Max."

"You look well," he said.

"I am not well. I came only because you promised to legitimise me as your wife in front of the *ton*. The children were vehemently opposed to travelling, you know. They want a home. So, we're going to stay here for a while."

Preston lowered the glass from his lips. "I shall do as I promised. If you stay here, however, your beau will be heartbroken."

"He does not have a heart. You, on the other hand, have a big heart."

"Not for everyone. Why is it that you didn't marry him instead of making your children illegitimate?"

"Jacque did not wish to marry me. He said I am too unstable, maddening."

"I can relate," he said into his glass. "But he is still a scoundrel for evading his fatherly responsibilities. I am at a loss as to why you would return to him time and time again."

"I was mad to give you up, but I still want you, love you."

He studied her sorrowful face. "You have an unusual way of displaying your affection. Even if you had not betrayed me, you were never the woman for me." He gentled his tone. "A beauty like you ought to have suitors and admirers coming from all directions. Do you not wish to marry someone who can love you the way you want him to?"

She lifted her head, her eyes glistening with moisture. "I am already married. I am your wife."

"You have not been my wife for many years, Julia. What we have is not a marriage."

She rose from the chaise and approached him. She sat on the floor at his feet and rested her chin on his knees. Gazing up, she pleaded, "You do not have any children. Why can you not be the father for mine?"

Preston shook his head. She had not changed a bit. "Because you had an affair with their father while married to me. Because we do not love each other. And because I would like to have our marriage annulled."

Her eyes snapped up, alert and readying for an attack. "You have a woman?"

"I have a lady I wish to marry."

"Who?"

"You do not need to know who."

"Well, the more important question is, does she know you are married?"

"Shall we discuss the merit of our marriage? We have been estranged for six years. I believe you have a six-year-old daughter who looks exactly like Louis Thiers."

She waved a dismissive hand. "It wasn't my fault. You know Emiliano made me coax information out of Louis."

He frowned in distaste. "It does not change the fact that you hid it from me. You should have come to me when your brother gave you the order. I could have done something."

"You couldn't. He is too cunning. No one can outsmart him."

Preston sighed. "There lies our problem, Julia. Your unwavering loyalty and unreasonable worshipping of your brother despite resenting him."

"I do not worship him. You've always been jealous of him, that's all."

Preston scoffed. "I do not wish to discuss the issues of the past. You proved with whom your loyalty lay."

"I chose Spain over my personal happiness!" she exclaimed indignantly.

"You chose your brother over me. You chose Spain over Bavaria to whom you vowed loyalty."

"I am sorry. I couldn't disobey Emiliano. It still doesn't change the fact that I am your wife, and I wish to make our marriage work."

"It is too late for us," he said, trying to stay calm.

"This woman you wish to wed, she will be angry that you lied to her. She will believe you did not trust her enough to tell her. She'll think–"

"You don't know her at all. And I am not interested in your opinion."

He stood, forcing her back. He walked to the large windows and stared at the newly sprouting leaves.

"I have been good to you over the years. Despite your betrayal, I quashed the scandal that could have ensued to protect your innocent children. You had all the freedom you wanted and enjoyed all the privilege as my wife. Now, I'm asking you to give me a chance at happiness. Give me my freedom, Julia."

"What has you so enthralled about her?"

Refusing to disrespect Elara by discussing her with this disgraceful woman, he asked, "What was it about Thiers that had you smitten?"

She smiled fondly. "His power, charisma."

"He certainly has an abundance of power," Preston said.

"Is she beautiful?"

He remained silent.

"Who does she think you are?"

"Julia, I'm willing to forgive you for all your transgressions if you're willing to do this for me."

"No," she said firmly, getting up and wrapping her arms around his waist. He pried her arms open and walked away.

"Your reason?" he asked.

"You are mine, and I do not like to lose."

"Any logical reasons? One a mature adult might have?"

"No need to be sarcastic. I want you. I always have."

"How flattering," he said sarcastically.

"I have no intention of ever releasing you, Maximilian. *Du bist mein. Verstehst du mich?*"

"*Ich werde niemals dein sein*! I do not need your permission to annul our marriage. You know that, do you not? I only asked out of courtesy."

"Officially, yes. Unofficially, you know I can cause ample trouble seeing that the French foreign minister is my lover, and the King of Spain is my brother. What do you think will happen if you discard me?"

"Releasing you with riches to enjoy for the rest of your life is not discarding you. It's a gift."

"Well, I like being the Princess of Bavaria. I love being the wife of Prince Maximilian. Nothing makes me happier than to be envied by other women when I'm on your arm."

"I will not step into that role again. You will not be a queen. Your children will not have a father!"

"And whose fault is that? You could be their father, but you won't!"

"They are not mine! My father will not allow it! Thiers won't allow it!"

"You will never have your own! This way, at least your monarch will be secure!"

"It will be the opposite! The people and the council will not accept your son as their prince. The throne will be at risk. Your son's life will be in danger!"

"I will never agree to the annulment. Press the issue and I will convince Louis and my brother of your impending assault on their nations."

Preston's eyes turned clear blue of ice and fire. "You overestimate your influence over them."

"It is you who underestimate me," she snapped. "If you have nothing else to say, I believe we are done talking." Julia spun on her heels and quit the room, taking Preston's happiness with her.

"Blasted woman!" he spat under his breath. Engulfed in fury, Preston headed towards an uncertain future.

## Chapter Twenty-Seven

# *11 March 1833 – ten in the evening*

Preston removed his coats and cravat as he stood by the doorway to the water closet. Rolling up his shirtsleeves, he gazed at the woman he loves through the haze of steam. The lantern glow glistened on her skin like the first break of dawn. Elara sunk under water, holding her breath for so long Preston wondered if he ought to pull her back up. Once she re-emerged, she took a gasping breath then noticed him admiring her.

"Nicholas! When did you arrive?"

"Not long ago." He knelt on the tile before her and poured water over her hair. While lathering her hair with soap, he regarded her wordlessly as his hands massaged her scalp and his fingers ran through the silken strands.

"How did you fare today?" she asked hesitantly.

He rubbed his soapy palms over her neck, shoulders, and chest. She was fresh and vibrant, like a spring bud in the snow. "I missed you terribly," he said softly. "All day long."

Her eyes widened, and then a radiant smile brightened her visage. He scooped water in his hands and watched the liquid cascade down her hair, her face, neck, and to the swells of her breasts.

Offering a hand, he pulled her up to stand. With a hand at her nape, he took her mouth in his. With an aching tenderness, he brushed his lips against hers, his tongue against hers. He kissed her like a breeze. He kissed her with all the stormy passion. He kissed her like it was their last.

He shed himself of clothes with his mouth never leaving hers. Elara's eager fingers assisted with his buttons and soon, he was pressing her wet body against his bare skin. While they kissed, he covered her body with soap, his hands roving smoothly over her breasts, back, rear, and between her thighs. She moaned when his fingers found her clitoris.

With the grunt of a man taking his long-held breath, he stroked until her folds swelled and bud hardened. As she became firm and sleek, he increased his speed, stroking her with even pressure.

"Nicholas," she gasped breathlessly, pressure building within.

"Come for me, my love. I need to be inside you."

"Nicholas, I shall explode."

"Let it be, sweetheart. Take me in your pussy..."

She frantically clung to his neck and rubbed her heat against his hand.

A scream tore through her throat as ecstasy struck and flooded her body. Just as she began to descend from her peak, he inserted two fingers inside her hot flesh, then three. He stroked the spot in her quim that brought her flutters of pleasure. He groaned as her pussy squeezed his fingers again and again.

Preston guided her out of the tub and turned her toward the looking glass by the basin. Elara averted her gaze upon seeing her nude form. Standing behind her, he bent her over with a firm hand spread across her back. With his erection pressing against her rear, he stooped over her and brushed her silky hair to one side. Burying his face in her nape, he breathed her in.

"What you do to me..." he whispered. "You invade my thoughts incessantly, enough to drive me mad." He positioned his cockhead at her entrance and groaned. "I've been fantasising about your pussy all day." He entered her slowly, waiting patiently until her muscles relaxed around him. He inched forward until she sheathed him as much as she could. Grunting at the delectable sensation, he began to move inside her.

Elara looked over her shoulder to meet his eyes, and the arousal surged through him.

"Can you take more of me?" he asked hoarsely.

"Yes."

He hiked up her hips and thrust forward another inch and grunted, his eyes glazing over from the heightened sensation.

"Hell... Your pussy is dancing around my cock..."

With his eyes feasting on her perfectly peach-shaped arse, he kneaded her flesh greedily with his hands. The more he claimed her, the more he craved her essence, again and again. "I need to get you out of my head, fuck you until this obsession stops tormenting me."

His voice came out as a roar scraping out from the back of his throat. It was angry, desperate, and full of pain. "Watch us, Elara. This is me claiming you as mine. I own your pleasure."

She raised her head shyly and her eyes perused his rough hands on her milky skin, fondling her flesh and his thighs smacking against her rear.

Her pussy sucked him in, refused to let him go, and clung to him as he pulled away. He didn't know where he ended and she began.

Even then, it was not enough. It was not enough merely possessing her sweet flesh. He must own the very depths of her—mind and heart, soul and spirit alike. He coveted each breath drawn, tear fallen, peal of laughter given. All must be his alone to treasure and protect. In this rapturous joining of their bodies, he strove to leave no doubt. She belonged to him as utterly as he belonged to her. His engorged flesh buried deep in her yielding softness, their twin bloods molten as one, even his ragged breaths soon knowing no name but hers to cry aloud.

In her embrace, he discovered his life's only true purpose and meaning. All petty wants and childish hurts faded to insignificance beside this revelation. As blessed release broke upon him, brilliant and blinding as a thousand rising suns, Preston knew with bone-deep certainty—never again would they walk as solitary beings. All that he was, and might ever become, now stood wholly dedicated to this beloved woman who completed his soul.

Bundling her in a soft towel and warm coverlet, Preston arranged Elara snugly upon his lap, her head nestled cosily against his shoulder. He stroked her sunset-flame tresses, marvelling anew if ever before his rough hands had cradled such precious beauty.

After a while, they rested contentedly in silence before drifting off to sleep, their souls open and vulnerable.

## Chapter Twenty-Eight

# *12 March 1833 – ten in the morning*

Elara awoke wanting to chirp and sing like a bird. She was completely, unequivocally, head over hills, in love. She felt like she had a sack over her head except this sack was made of silk and smelled wonderfully of the lush green forest. She was surrounded by its tender touch, hypnotised by its alluring scent, and could not see beyond her love for him.

She reached for Preston beside her in bed but found it empty. Opening her eyes, she saw him in a full travel attire and boots as shiny as the looking glass.

"Nicholas?"

Preston turned amidst adjusting his cufflink. He had dark circles under his eyes as if he had not slept. Tension simmered beneath his skin, and Elara's stomach fell into the pit.

"What is the matter?" she asked.

He came to her side and knelt before her. His hand rested lightly on her bare shoulder.

"I'm afraid I must leave."

"Where are you going?"

"To meet with my parents."

"Where are they?"

"Oxford."

"Why do you look troubled?"

"Julia has refused to annul our nuptial. I must see my father and convince him to aid me in this endeavour."

She studied his expression that spoke of something deeply distressing.

"Nicholas, how did it feel to see her again?"

His eyes softened, and his thumb stroked her cheek.

"I felt only irritation towards her for keeping us from our future together."

Relieved, she placed her hand over his.

"What is the worst that can happen now?"

"I am uncertain. One does not enter Father's lair without giving up something precious."

Preston placed a kiss on her cheek and stood. Elara followed, encircling her arms around his neck. His arms tightened around her waist and pressed her against him.

"Is it possible you may not return?"

"Of course, I will return."

"Mayhap you do not need to go. We don't need to be wed. We could be lovers."

"Darling, patience. I'd prefer to make you my wife."

He placed his forehead against hers and whispered, "I must go now. I am leaving Smith and a few others behind to look after you."

He kissed her lightly on the lips and walked out of the room.

Elara stared at the doorway for an unknown period of time, sensing he may be lost to her forever.

## Chapter Twenty-Nine

# *17 March 1833 – six in the evening*

Preston disembarked the hack and approached Howick Hall with a sigh. The bliss he experienced with Elara had been eye-opening and terrifying. He now knew the height of happiness that could be reached, and he was paralysed with fear of losing it. He was afraid he would bring only tears to her eyes, that he would forever chase the fantasy of being with her.

He rapped on the door and was greeted by a butler.

"May I help you, sir?"

"Maximilian here to see King Ludwig."

The butler eyed him sceptically. "Wait here a moment, please."

Preston stopped the door from closing. "I'll wait inside if you don't mind."

Skimming his poor-quality coat, the man grimaced before walking away with an efficient gait.

Seconds later, footsteps hurried towards him and one of his father's long-time ministers appeared.

"Your Royal Highness," he bowed. "What an unexpected delight. His Majesty will be pleased to see you."

"Is he capable of being pleased, Count Montgelas?"

"True, Your Royal Highness."

"Why is he still here? Does he not have enough duties at home?"

The old man chuckled, his spine bent and barely reaching Preston's chest. "I'm afraid the unrest in France is keeping His Majesty here for the time being."

"I wondered when I might have the opportunity to thank Thiers for bedding my wife. Now, I may express my gratitude in person."

"These are delicate times, Your Royal Highness," the old man said with warning in his gentle voice.

"Yes, yes. I understand."

The double doors swung open, and he found his father sitting by the fireplace, cigar in hand.

"Son, this is a surprise."

"For me as well, Father." Preston sat beside his sire and accepted a teacup from a footman.

"How fares the Prime Minister?"

"Very well. A clever man. Louis Philippe, not so much. For a Citizen King of France, he is too ambitious. He should be careful, or he shall have another revolution in his hand." The old man finally turned to regard his son. "I'm sure you didn't come here to ask after those men. How fared the meeting with Julia?"

"She has refused."

King Ludwig nodded wordlessly, puffing cigar smoke in languid succession. "She is enjoying the comforts of her position away from the insane demands of her brother. And believe it or not, she is fond of you."

"Do you think Ferdinand will declare war if I force the issue?"

"Knowing her talent for manipulation, I would think so."

"Can you help?"

His sire eyed him pointedly. "My word! I never dreamed I'd hear those words come from you."

"Well?"

King Ludwig chuckled. "I knew she was a beauty, but I didn't think she would hook you so assuredly. I suppose you are helpless against a damsel in distress."

Preston felt like the ground dropped out from under him as the truth dawned on him. His stomach churned with a sickening blend of horror and outrage. Preston's mind raced as he tried to piece together the truth and resist it simultaneously.

"I do not believe... you are referring to Julia..." he growled darkly.

His sire cleared his throat, understanding his error. Preston rose to his feet as thunderclouds gathered in his eyes.

The door opened in that moment, and his mother sauntered in.

"Ah, my darling. At last, I can lay my eyes upon you."

Quivering with rage, Preston glared venomously between his parents and the solemn minister hovering alertly nearby. His voice shook low with wrath.

"I swear by all that's holy, if you two orchestrated the abduction, I shall have you committed."

The two Majesties exchanged uneasy glances.

"Do not be so dramatic," his mother scolded unabashedly. "We merely thought to hasten fate's hand a little. Desperate times called for bold action, what with the succession uncertain and the popularity of the monarch so precarious."

"Clearly you gave not one moment's thought to the innocent lady's future happiness amidst your reckless intrigues!" Preston roared. His jaw muscle ticked dangerously. "Abducting a gently bred woman remains reprehensible on its own. But then to force intimacies with a stranger through coercion and terror? You truly are mad!"

The monarch drew himself up, summoning the last dregs of regal dignity. "Whilst I shall concede to engineering this scheme, you wrongly accuse a pursuit of true harm toward either party. I merely sought to gently... expedite the natural course of affection. Any gross mistreatment enacted vastly exceeded the bounds of my directives."

"You entrusted leadership to those dissolute aristocrats! The vile Munroe brothers and their ilk! And to employ the Scuttle boys to conduct their vicious trade at the Muns' behest! Just how far will this depraved family go to secure the damned succession?"

The King erupted. "I've not clawed my way to the apex of power by being ruled by sentiments and delicate feelings! You ought to know how unstable a country can be in the aftermath of two assassinations and one son who refuses to return home! The nation desperately needs the joy of weddings, babes, and heirs! You ought to thank me for creating such a cosy cottage getaway when I could have thrown you both into a tower to do the deed!"

"Did it occur to you that you might lose me forever?"

"How dare you threaten me so after the loss we suffered?" his mother raged.

"Frederick and Louis were dead long before the assassins killed them! They ceased to live in your grasp, their mind and body imprisoned by you!"

"How dare you!" the Majesties thundered.

"How. Dare. You! Shame on you both! To abduct an innocent lady and your son! To force intimate relations! I never wanted the throne, but I feel compelled to now, so the country isn't ruined by a pair of lunatics!"

The parents and son stared at each other, breathing fire, until their ragged breaths began to subside. Then the Majesties looked at each other, disbelief and smile gradually replacing anger.

"Did you just say you would return and take the throne?" his father asked delicately.

Elara... his princess. The position of an heir apparent did not seem so suffocating with her as his wife. "When it is necessary to do so. How will you convince King Ferdinand to keep the peace?"

"With Germany and France as our allies, they would not dare attack," his sire said eagerly.

"It does not mean they wouldn't create trouble for the nation," Preston said.

"Son, you are thinking like a king already! You are correct, of course, but I shall make him an offer he cannot refuse."

"Which is?"

"A seat at the table with the four most powerful European nations. It will legitimise his status as the ruler instead of being a laughingstock."

His parents' eyes were fixed on Preston, studying every flicker of light in his eyes and every line of his visage.

"And if I said I'd be willing to ponder the idea if I were free to marry Lady Elara?"

"You shall be free to marry the lady after you sign an agreement."

"What are the terms?" he probed suspiciously.

His father gestured for him to sit. Preston sat down slowly, feeling tense and alert at the imminent danger.

"Return with your wife to show unity, my son. The people need reassuring symbols right now–the handsome prodigal prince restored, his reconciliation with Princess Julia shall be a hopeful beacon in trying times."

Preston dissented firmly. "Out of question. I shall have Elara stand radiant beside me instead–the Citizen's Princess comes to shift old orders into new. People shall rally to a fresh vision, to lift the fog obscuring their future."

"Our goal is to warn the people of overturning old vessels for new ideas that may conceal risk. You and Julia must symbolise the strength of the old union."

"Elara's love drew this stubborn prodigal son home. Might not my people welcome such unexpected affection into their lives as well? For I still believe my happiness aligns with those I would see thrive–my family, my nation."

The King stroked his beard, contemplating deeply.

Preston continued his outright refusal. "I'd rather live out my days with Elara in the colonies than deceive the hopeful public. Even if I agreed to act the happy husband to Julia, then what? Confess our fraud after breaking hearts twice over? Surely, Father, your savvy mind can propose fewer outrageous schemes than that ludicrous plan?"

His father winced. "Very well then. A compromise. Simply keep up appearances temporarily whilst I privately negotiate terminating your marital contract without embarrassing King Ferdinand."

Preston bristled with doubt. "And why should I trust you'll keep such convenient promises?"

The elder statesman sighed. "Neither of us can be certain, but we must rely on each other all the same or all is lost." Gaze firming, his sire declared, "From now on, flawless public conduct is essential. We cannot risk humiliation sabotaging this delicate work. Your duty begins now. I need your accompaniment for all the meetings and social assemblies until our business here is concluded."

"I need to speak to Elara before I commit."

"Impossible."

"I must!"

"There is a conference with the world leaders daily until a resolution is reached. Would you risk your matrimony with the lady just for an opportunity to confirm what your heart already knows to be true?"

Shutting his eyes and looking up at the ceiling, Preston acceded. "Maximum a fortnight. I need the annulment signed before I take my place as the Prince."

"Be seen with Julia, attend assemblies. Speak highly of her brother and foster good will towards the King of Spain."

"I need our agreement signed and witnessed before I perform my puppet duties for you."

"Of course. Now, off you go to a tailor. You look hideous."

## Chapter Thirty

# 20 March 1833 – three in the afternoon

Taking a deep breath, Preston entered Salisbury's private library. After a bow to his father and King Ferdinand of Spain, he seated himself beside his sire.

"What is delaying Julia?" King Ferdinand barked.

"She is likely bent over a chamber pot wondering how her flesh and blood could have used her like a common trollop," Preston intoned smoothly.

King Ferdinand bristled. "It was a matter of national security with a man she had children with."

"You encouraged the Princess of Bavaria to have an affair in the name of national security? Was she the only one who could seduce the man? You risked her marriage, her life, and orphaning her children!"

"Good afternoon, gentlemen," Julia strode in just as her brother shot up from his chair. Sensing the tension in the room, Julia spun and twirled the skirt of her bright yellow dress like butterfly wings. She smiled brightly at her brother.

Preston tried not to look annoyed when she walked over and kissed him on the lips.

King Ludwig cleared his throat disapprovingly.

"Oh, Papa. Relax. We are not spring ducklings."

*Papa?* Preston restrained himself from rolling his eyes.

"So, I understand you have a demand," the ever so humourless Ferdinand intoned after his sister took a seat next to him.

"Not a demand but a mere request," his father said amiably.

"You wish to annul the joining of our two families. That is no mere request, Your Majesty." Temper already infused Ferdinand's every syllable.

"We may find a mutually beneficial solution," Ludwig replied.

"How do you suppose? What good could come out of leaving my sister in ruins, neglected by her husband who had vowed to protect and honour her?"

Preston breathed deeply and slowly, counting to ten, then fifty.

"I've already done my part by inviting you," his father said sternly. "As a young king, you have a lot more to lose should I rescind your invitation to the table of distinguished rulers. Imagine the humiliation and effect on your reputation upon your return to the kingdom."

Ferdinand glared at the old king, his jaw clenched. "Do you expect me to throw my flesh and blood overboard for my reputation?"

"Not your reputation but your nation's peace, for your dynasty. You know very well what could happen if you show any weakness. Your relations are rather bloodthirsty."

Ferdinand grinned. "You forget that I, too, am bloodthirsty. War is what I depend on to show my strength as a ruler to my people. It is what would differentiate me from my father who was a coward."

"What your people remember will be their empty stomachs and the cries of their children during your rule if you waste any more resources on battles. How much longer could you last without the help of your allies? Do you believe Portugal will surrender willingly?"

Ferdinand leaned forward, one elbow on his lap, looking pensive.

"I do not agree to the annulment, Ferdi!" Julia exclaimed.

"Be quiet! This is not your decision!" Ferdinand barked.

"This opportunity shall solidity your reputation as an influential ruler, one who cannot be ignored, one who confers with the most powerful," His Majesty said. "The people will praise you for your foresight, for accomplishing something your father never could."

The young king's eyes sharpened into awareness.

"Your father strove to get France on his side but with Napoleon still strong, he could not achieve it. But you shall."

Ferdinand looked at his sister who shook her head. "No, I love him," she said.

"Like you love that ugly old man, Thiers?" her brother shot back.

"It served you well, Brother."

"You will agree to this annulment!" her brother said forcefully.

"No! If you make me, I shall tell the world, everyone, that all of you decided to punish Thier's children because of your hatred for France! I will not release you, Maximilian. Never!"

"It is settled then," Ludwig said brightly, ignoring Julia. "Now, off to the negotiation of lesser import. European peace treaty."

## Chapter Thirty-One

# *29 March 1833 – nine in the evening*

"He is not coming back. He has abandoned you, you understand," James said. "You'd be better off with me, in my household. I shall give you the freedom and independence you need."

"I am not interested," Smith said.

"Come, now. It cannot be that stimulating guarding a woman, following her around like a pup."

Smith looked at James evenly, standing by the door in Lord Stamford's chamber while Elara fed her father.

"Let him be, James. Let him do his duty."

Smith looked to be running thin on patience today. She feared for James' safety.

"I am giving him a better opportunity, El. He cannot be making more than forty pounds a year. I shall double it."

"I am not interested, my lord," Smith said curtly.

James walked over to the bed where his uncle was sitting up. "I am thrilled you are feeling much better, Uncle. But your illness made me realise how unprotected Elara is. Should you fall ill again, Heaven forbid, she needs a husband. It appears that Preston has disappeared into the thin air. I cannot find the man anywhere. He has abandoned his office, his clients, all his duties at the Inner Temple."

James leaned forward and met the earl's eyes.

"Don't you think it would be wiser for Elara to wed before another tragedy occurs? Would you not like to see her settled with a husband?"

"Stop it, James. I would rather wait for him forever than to marry you. You can cease pestering Father. Find someone else, I beg you."

"I ought to share with you what I found about your betrothed, El," James drawled, linking his hands behind his head.

Elara tensed but refused to react overtly.

"I can see that you are dying of anticipation. I shall tell you. Absolutely naught."

She frowned.

"It is as if he did not exist until four years ago. Where did he study? Where did he come from? Which bank did he use? How can a grown man have no record of his past save four years?"

This was no surprise to Elara. Preston had said he had changed his identity twice to elude his parents.

"I don't care about his past. I just want him here." She hated how her voice shook.

For over two weeks, she had searched for a reason to wake up in the morning. If she had not needed to nurse her father, she may not have got out of bed at all.

It hurt. It hurt so much not knowing if he was safe, if he missed her as much as she missed him. She swallowed the tears that threatened to pour.

"Oh, darling." James placed a hand on her shoulder. In a blink, Smith was hauling him up by his cravat.

"Mr Smith! Unhand him, now!" Elara shouted. Smith dropped him like an obedient dog and glowered.

"He was only trying to comfort me. You do know the difference between comforting and assaulting, do you not?"

"Forgive me, my lady," Smith said evenly. "I overreacted. Safer that way. I did not want to take a chance."

Elara sighed and softened her voice. "Thank you, Mr Smith, for your protection. James, I think it would be better if you went home now."

James straightened out his cravat and ran his fingers through the tousled hair. "I shall see you in a few days for the festivities at Lullingstone."

"You are going?"

"Of course, I am. I'm your chaperone."

Elara laughed. "That is absurd. I have guards protecting me from you!"

The earl did not appear amused. "It is not that ridiculous," James spat.

"I would rather have Mr Smith be my chaperone."

"Don't be daft. He's a stranger, untitled, a bachelor, I gather. Are you a bachelor, Smith?" James asked.

Smith did not respond.

"Whether you like it or not, they have accepted my request to accompany you. I will pick you up early in the morning so we can make it by supper."

"Must I go, Father? They will understand that you are unwell. They would not insist that you send a representative. Please. Let me stay."

The earl shook his head. Elara sighed and rested her head on his chest. The earl's trembling hand stroked her hair. Her eyes became moist, remembering how strong and charismatic her father used to be. Then her thoughts drifted to Preston. She needed him, his soothing whispers and secure embrace. He would have known exactly what to do or say to appease her frayed nerves.

## Chapter Thirty-Two

# *1 April 1833 – half past six in the evening*

The carriage bounced down the long gravel driveway to Lullingstone Castle for the week-long festivities. James grumbled over the noise about women taking too long to dress. Smith stared at the viscount stoically, causing James to grow uncomfortable and eventually quiet.

Elara sat in the corner, shrinking by the hour, wanting to vanish. She would have preferred to be unconscious than to feign good cheer. Her mind was full of concern for Preston. Was he hurt or kidnapped? Were his parents keeping him captive or did he choose a fate that excluded her?

She stifled the tears that threatened to flow. *Blast it. Not again.*

She dug through her reticule for a kerchief, but one appeared in front of her. She took it from Smith and thanked him. By now, Smith read her movements so well that he responded to her needs before they were spoken.

"You will not go anywhere unescorted by me, El," James' declaration cut through the heavy silence like jagged edges.

"James, not only is that impractical, it's impossible," she said weakly.

"Apart from the obvious, I do not see why not."

"I have Mr Smith for protection. You do not need to be concerned for my safety," she said, knowing full well that he was guarding his prised possession.

"Now that it's obvious Preston has abandoned you, I intend to protect you from everyone including Smith. On that note, I forbid you from dancing with any bachelors."

Elara sensed Smith stiffen ever so slightly.

"What? James, I do not have control over who asks me to dance. It would be rude to refuse. I do not wish to gain a reputation as a difficult spinster."

"All the better for my purpose, El," James said with a shrug.

"You are maddening, James. No matter how desperately you guard me, I shall not agree to marry you!"

"You will because you have no choice. If you decide to do anything foolish like propose to the first bachelor you encounter, I shall ruin you on the dance floor."

Elara's gasp was muted by Smith's threatening timbre.

"I think not, Lord Frances. Even if I must smother the last breath out of you, I will not allow that to happen."

"No one asked for your opinion, Smith. Do shut up."

"Mr Preston is my employer and Lady Elara my client. I do not take orders from the likes of you, sir."

James opened his mouth to say more, but Elara interrupted.

"We are here, gentlemen. Please tuck in your feathers and pretend to be civilised."

Elara refused James' arm to his chagrin and took Smith's instead. Aware how foolish he would appear if he wrestled Smith, James fumed silently. Elara walked into the ballroom on Smith's arm with James and four footmen trailing behind.

"Viscount Frances, Lady Elara of Stamford!" the major-domo announced.

Alone in the boisterous crowd, Elara wished desperately to disappear from the judgments raining down on her as the poor spinster who was at her cousin's mercy. But she had appearances to maintain as an earl's daughter, however unbearable.

Mustering poise was its own quiet torment. She felt emotions cracking her polite facade, threatening to expose just how vulnerable she stood without her father's protection. Still, she forced a taut smile and scanned for familiar faces. One friend... she needed just one anchor in this room.

"Lady Elara!" a crisp voice called out blessedly like the horn of a ship. The Duchess of Somerset's radiant smile approached with her husband glowing golden beside her.

"Your Graces," Elara curtsied.

"It is wonderful to see you. I've been wanting to speak with you, see how you and your father are."

"Thank you, Your Grace. He is much improved. He still has no speech, but his appetite has improved, and his mind is still sharp."

"Thank heavens, I am so glad. I–"

The duke cleared his throat. "Do stop talking for one breath, my dear, and introduce me to this charming lady," the duke said, smiling devilishly at Elara.

Elara blushed at His Grace's seemingly inappropriate demeanour towards a single lady in his wife's presence.

"You are making the poor lady blush, darling. Remember, not all women are accustomed to your roguishness. You must behave," the duchess swatted his shoulder playfully. "Husband, may I introduce you to Lady Elara? She is the daughter of the Earl of Stamford."

Elara curtsied and searched the duke's head for a halo, for he was magnificent. She shrank when she felt the duchess' eyes on her.

"I beg your pardon, Your Grace. I, um..." she floundered.

To her relief, the duchess laughed. "Do not worry. He has that effect on all women except for me, and he uses it to his advantage. You shall become immune to him as I have."

"Using trickery, I might add," His Grace said accusingly but gazed at his wife with so much admiration that Elara's heart squeezed with envy.

"Lord Frances, do you mind if I take her away for a moment? I'd like you to meet Lady Salisbury. She is—"

"His Majesty King Ludwig, Her Majesty Queen Beata, Prince Maximilian, and Princess Julia of Bavaria!" the major-domo announced.

"Come. Let us go to the front." The duchess took Elara's hand and pulled her along, with James and the duke trailing behind. They watched as the crowd parted for the royal family. Elara straightened her gown and looked up to find a handsome elderly couple making their way down, nodding and smiling at the crowd.

Then... everything slowed, and the noise faded. She blinked twice as her mind reeled at what she was seeing. He was nodding and shaking hands, his gaze now traversing the onlookers, bearing steadily towards Elara's wing. Elara clasped her hands over her mouth tightly as comprehension dawned. Her pulse quickening, she desperately searched for a place to fasten her stare. Somewhere in the distance, James mumbled, "Curse Hades!" and the duke drawled, "I'll be damned."

There was scarcely a moment left for Elara to wonder if he would acknowledge her before the prince moved on in the receiving line. Was he indeed the same man she had been pining for?

After smiling and nodding to a few people, his intensity glided over her like the gaze of a stranger, aloof and already distant, his eyes alighting elsewhere. She followed their aim towards...

A beautiful, exotic, and regal woman who had her hand on his arm. She, a lone glistening beauty among the gathered court. She, who smiled up at the prince with a seducer's knowing air and met searching eyes that beheld her in kind.

Nicholas Preston, a prince... A prince!

He was clean-shaven, clad in black and white, and hair trimmed short. Two diamonds from his shirt cuffs and a large ruby on his cravat sparkled... Feeling her scarcely drawn breath halt, Elara stepped back into the crowd as though physical retreat could save her heart from a freefall. She clenched the duchess' hand lest her own shaking limbs betray her.

Heat flooded Elara's cheeks as she watched the man she loved bestow his smiling gaze upon another, his wife—a woman who had more right to him than she. That Nicholas Preston, the solicitor and barrister who once promised her the world, should stand by his wife's side while she was rendered invisible, tore her apart.

"Are you unwell, Lady Elara?" the duchess asked, supporting her elbow.

"My lady." Smith approached and took her arm from the duchess.

Unable to unclench her throat, she shook her head, one hand raised to stifle the sob pushing against her mouth's grim line.

"Would you like a moment of privacy?" he asked.

Head spinning, she nodded, allowing Smith to steer her leaden feet from the threats of further public dissolution. Feeling awash with gratitude for Smith's tact, she followed him without hesitation. He parted the crowd for her and discreetly opened a door. He slipped inside with her and locked the door.

She began to sob, sharp breaths jarring as the room tilted dangerously.

"Who is he? Mr Smith, that was Nicholas, was it not?" Elara clutched the wall as her vision swam. "Am I imagining the likeness?"

Smith moved closer. His hand hovered by her shoulder, unsure whether a breach of decorum might bring her comfort. "No imagined mirage, my lady. His Royal Highness is indeed Mr Nicholas Preston."

At this Elara covered her mouth lest a shriek escape. After a long silence, she mastered herself enough to rasp, "You don't seem surprised."

"I've known His Royal Highness these six years in royal service." Smith shifted his stance, blurry in Elara's peripheral vision against the blinding pain in her heart.

As her head spun and stomach churned, she asked the stoic protection officer to escort her to the bedchamber. Smith obliged with the efficiency and discretion that Elara had come to appreciate.

Smith confirmed her chamber was clear of danger and promised to guard outside the room. Elara entered and fell into Shelley's soothing embrace.

---

It was the most difficult feat of self-denial he had ever been called to commit—feigning indifference upon catching a first glimpse of Elara's vibrant mane across the crowded ballroom floor. His gaze had honed on her like a compass to pole despite the merriment swirling about them. How he had yearned to push through the sea of silks, take her hands, and confess all the truths left unspoken–to smooth the anguished frown into joy anew.

For the space of a heartbeat, Preston tasted longing so acute that he found himself biting the flesh inside his mouth until blood trickled down his throat. The sensation of Julia's jewelled grip upon his arm aided him to stay the course.

Duty waved its gilded flag once more, and he exiled Elara back to the realm of forbidden things. The struggle carved furrows beneath his polished veneer that none around him marked. Only she who knew him best of all would have understood his misery—and she alone he had broken.

His body as hard as marble with torment and impatient energy, Preston tried to appear interested in King Ferdinand's droning about his country's foreign policy. Across the circle of the crowd, he spied Somerset and Carlisle glowering at him. Former friends, he supposed. Salisbury seemed to be finding the situation amusing and thoroughly enjoying himself. The rascal was whispering to his wife, who then nudged him sensibly with her elbow. Good on her. He should thank her later for the jab.

His momentary diversion was interrupted by the viper's breath. Julia stood on her toes and leaned heavily against him, squeezing his biceps.

"The woman with red hair, is she the one you wish to marry?"

Preston remained silent.

"She was as pale as a ghost. Had you not revealed to her who you were?"

Despite his lack of response, Julia continued cheerfully, "That was foolish. Whyever not?"

He cleared his throat. A glass of champagne appeared out of nowhere, and he gladly drained the glass. He ought to respond, or people may begin to notice.

"It did not seem relevant at the time. She had chosen me already. I was estranged from my family with no plans to return."

Julia *tsked*. "You know it would have mattered to the woman you wish to wed whether you came from a family of bandits or royalty. The truth is, my darling, you did not trust her. You thought she would clamber for the prince's attention. And perhaps she would have."

"I never doubted the authenticity of our connection, not for a second. And women appreciate me enough without my title."

"Except for me, of course."

"Come now. Don't you think I know the real reason behind your betrayal?"

"Truly? Enlighten me, Your Royal Highness. I thought I simply missed my lover."

"You went to him because you felt unloved by me. Perhaps you wished to make me jealous. Either way, your plan was ineffective."

"Nonsense. If you were not jealous, why were you so angry?"

He met her eyes steadily. "Just this morning, I was angry with my secretary. Not because I loved him but because he broke his promise. My dear, I was angry that you broke your vow and displayed such disrespect for me and my family."

He returned to staring straight ahead when he was met with Somerset and Carlisle's glares. *Blast it.*

He leaned towards Julia and continued, "I thought I would try to love you, the poor woman who was forced into an unwanted marriage just as I was. I soon realised I never would."

Julia waved her hand as if his words were flies. "Nevertheless, you belong to me, and your true love has disappeared into a private room with a man."

Smith's attentiveness to Elara had not escaped his notice.

"That is Smith whom I tasked with her protection," he said casually.

"I think there is affection between them."

"Do not presume to know anything, Julia. You do not."

"Neither do you. You left her vulnerable for two weeks without a word of assurance, available for any man to seduce. A woman will go to any man for comfort when she feels undesired."

Preston schooled his features into an affectionate gaze. He swallowed the insults he wished to unleash on the woman. He took a deep breath, his skin crawling with restlessness and frustration.

"Do not even think about going to her now or later. You will not humiliate me by seeking out that wench while playing my doting husband."

He smiled at her warmly. "I recall now why I found you so distasteful."

"Because my personality is too strong. I am too opinionated. I intimidate men."

"Yes, but none of those are the main reason."

"What is?"

He regarded her. "You are ugly inside, Julia. You are the shite in a golden chamber pot."

Julia looked away, smiling. "As long as it's gold, Husband, it matters not."

---

"You knew all this time, and you failed to tell us?" Carlisle barked at Salisbury.

"Aye."

"How could you not trust us to keep our mouths shut?" Carlisle shouted.

"I trusted Somerset's. Just not yours."

"You bastard!" Carlisle roared as the others broke out in laughter.

"When I first met Preston, he had recently been assigned as an infiltrator in France and was hiding in a mutual friend's home. It was Westminster's, was it not?" Salisbury asked.

"Aye, it was," Preston replied.

"He could not hide his princely speech and haughty manners to save his life. He also had a slight German accent despite having spent half of his life in England. I believe you partook in some training before you left for France."

"Aye, I did."

"Even last month, you were evading your family. Why are you revealing yourself, now?" Somerset asked.

Salisbury knowingly poured a glass of brandy and handed it to Preston, who gratefully accepted it.

"It is one of the terms the King required in exchange for annulling my marriage. I am to present a unified front with Julia to avoid embarrassing her brother, King Ferdinand of Spain."

"For how long? I heard Lady Elara's heart shatter when she saw you. It reminded me of my own heartache before winning Asilia over," Somerset said with a grimace.

"Have your bollocks dropped yet, Somerset?" Carlisle cackled.

"Do shut it, Carlisle. Do not speak to me about bollocks until you've been driven to madness by love," Somerset snapped.

"Hm, now that the good folks of this nation are aware I am not just a pretty face but a prince to boot, do you think Miss Morton would be interested in getting better acquainted with yours truly?" Preston drawled haughtily.

The three men's heads rotated towards Carlisle and waited expectantly.

"He looks to be losing circulation to his brain," Salisbury observed.

"Too much blood in his cock, you think?" Preston asked.

"Nay, too much blood in his fists," Somerset said, pointing his chin downwards to Carlisle's clenched hands.

"I do not give a rat's arse if you are God the creator, Preston. Do not ever utter that name again!" Carlisle shouted.

"Gentlemen, what do you call it when a man loses all sense over a woman?" Somerset asked.

"Love," the three men echoed and howled.

"Let us be serious for a moment," Somerset interrupted the merriment. "Will you explain to Lady Elara what is happening? My wife is quite distraught about her distress. The lady has not quit her room since your arrival."

Preston's ribcage seemed to be closing in on his heart. He felt a pang of longing and sorrow. She had looked thin and haunted. "I shall find the opportunity when I can. I must be cautious now to avoid drawing suspicion from the *ton* or the monarch. It does not bode well that there are more guards and spies in this castle than guests."

"Yes, I've noticed," Salisbury said. "We've had to scramble to purchase more food to feed the sheer number of guards. I believe Alexandra is prying food away from the villagers' babes as we speak."

"I must leave before Julia descends down on me, the suspicious chit." Preston stood, placing his glass down on a table.

"Are you, um, having relations with that exotic woman of yours?" Carlisle asked.

Preston glowered at Carlisle.

"What? What did I say? I was only curious."

"It is none of your business, but I'm not," Preston replied.

"How tragic," Carlisle mumbled.

"Feel free to use Salisbury's quarters for amorous congress, Preston. He does not mind one bit," Somerset said.

"I do not mind as long as you do not sully any surfaces," Salisbury corrected.

Preston scanned the group of imbeciles. "Do you mean to say horizontal surface or any surface?"

Carlisle spoke. "She may be horizontal already with that guard of yours. He's a handsome fellow. Very mas–"

A cushion flew to his head.

## Chapter Thirty-Three

# *2 April 1833 – eight in the morning*

"My lady, you are still as pale as new bed linens. Mayhap I ought to slap your face. Pinching is not doing anything," Shelley lamented.

"At least I don't look like unwashed linen. My eyes are less puffy, too. Compared to yesterday, I look stunning," Elara said weakly.

"You are always stunning, but if you plan to meet your future husband... What is his name? Lord Hugh?"

"I... I don't think I will stay, Shelley. I shall apologize to Lord and Lady Salisbury and depart for home this afternoon."

"My lady, what about your match?"

"Perhaps I can ask Mr Frankland for his assistance. I would rather be home with Father."

"Very well, my lady. When would you like to depart?"

"After the midday tea. That should give me enough time to speak to the marchioness."

Donning her blue walking dress and a matching blue bonnet, Elara walked out of her room and smirked at the guard dosing outside her door. After nodding to the kindly butler at the front door, she strode quickly towards the hill, needing space to breathe. It was cold and damp. Grey clouds loomed overhead, but she didn't mind. The chilly slap of the wind felt good against her mottled head.

*Don't be a baby because he abandoned you. Isn't it better to have loved than not have loved at all?*

Once she reached the top of the hill with a deep exhale, Elara turned around. "Ah!" she yelped upon seeing Smith, who had been following closely.

"What are you about, Mr Smith? You startled me!"

"I saw you leave. You are not supposed to be alone, my lady."

"I can be alone for one bloody minute! And your employer isn't even here!"

"I still must do my job, my lady."

"Perchance you may be good enough to follow me at a distance! Surely, you would see fiends coming from miles away atop this hill!"

"Good morning!" a feminine voice rang through the howling wind. Elara turned and found herself face to face with two magnificent stallions. "We must interrupt your lively conversation as I wish to look in the eyes of the woman who tried to steal my husband," the woman said.

Shocked by the accusation, Elara met the eyes of the intruders. Doubt crossed her mind. Had Preston lied to her about their estrangement?

The exotic beauty and the familiar stranger, the prince, stared down at her from their mounts. A few uniformed horsemen stood guard.

Sneering down her haughty nose, the jagged edges of the princess' gaze scraped over Elara from top to bottom. Preston was unmoving and silent as if he had turned into a stone.

Elara wanted to run, dig into the ground, and disappear. Instead, she belatedly curtsied in their general direction.

Smith, too, stood stoically.

"You are Lady Elara, are you not?"

"Yes, Your Royal Highness," she said weakly, feeling she might turn into ashes as Preston's unyielding gaze seared her.

"I suppose you couldn't wait to spread your legs–"

"Princess, let us not be common," his low voice said with breathtaking gentleness.

The tenderness rocked Elara's core more violently than if an earthquake had swallowed her whole. It was the tone he had used to sooth and love her...the tenderness she thought he had reserved only for her. How could that same voice say something so distasteful? She had not known his gift for trickery, only his skill in seduction. She understood now he could convince anyone he was made entirely of ice or fire.

Elara shrank further into herself, wishing bodily death as her soul tore and stretched into oblivion.

"I was only telling Maximilian yesterday that your gentleman seemed quite taken with you, Lady Elara. I see now that the feeling is mutual."

Elara's body stiffened, and she could not make a sound. She glanced at Preston whose eyes were peering at Smith as impassively as a piece of marble. She was tempted to disagree with the princess but changed her mind. Perhaps the misunderstanding would preserve a modicum of her pride.

"Mr Smith, is it?" the princess addressed the guard with a bright smile. "I've been watching you protect your lady with the utmost devotion. Likewise, my husband would give his life for me without hesitation. I am very fortunate to have him. Precisely the reason we are able to live separately and still be loyal to each other. But when we see each other"–she glanced at her husband seductively–"Well..." The woman left the words unsaid, stirring unwanted images in Elara's head.

"I must advise you, Mr Smith. This harlot–"

"Darling, this is beneath you. Let us be off. We have much to accomplish," Preston intoned in that manner that had left Elara senseless and wanting.

"Very well. Whatever did you see in her, Max?" the princess asked before throwing a contemptuous look at Elara.

Elara hung on to her composure with everything she had.

"I no longer recall," he replied. Preston turned his horse around without a glance towards Elara as the princess followed.

She stared at the couple, only his cold eyes floating around her vision. Tears poured, and she sought solace on Smith's shoulder. After the initial hesitation, he wrapped his arms around her and held her tight.

At a safe distance, Preston looked over his shoulder and instantly regretted doing so. Smith's arm around Elara and her welcome reception confirmed their mutual affection better than if she had spoken the words. Panic engulfed his chest, but he steadied himself. He had a viper to deal with.

"You are losing your touch, Julia. There is no elegance to your attacks anymore. You were as clumsy as a foal."

"Why should I be subtle? I only made an observation."

"Did you enjoy yourself?" he asked evenly.

"I did. Did you?"

He halted his horse and smiled at her. "Not as much as I will when I pluck your children away from you one by one."

Julia's face paled.

He spoke tenderly as if reciting a love sonnet. "Legally, I am their guardian. I can do anything I want with them. Next time you insult Lady Elara, I will make good on my threats."

"You wouldn't."

He smiled kindly like a benevolent ruler. "Why would I not?"

---

Elara gazed woefully at her reflection as dusk's golden light gently filled the room. The pale blue silks she had loved once now hung limply on her thinning frame. Her lady's maid briskly pinned and tucked around her shoulders while she stood resignedly.

"If I tighten the bodice any more, it will bunch in the back, my lady," Shelley said with a sigh.

"I would prefer that over the bodice falling down to my waist."

Shelley then determinedly spun practical solutions under layers of fabric to shore up the deficiencies. More padding was placed under her breasts, pushing her mounds up prominently.

In the end, Elara thought the paddings bestowed her figure all the charms of pig snouts on a stick. Still, she supposed a buxom figure might better entice noble suitors, save admirers like James whose gazes she hoped to avoid at all costs.

Recalling the princess' extraordinarily well-endowed figure, she wondered if Preston preferred the large breasts of his wife. She felt the claws of jealousy gripping her chest. Trying to banish the images of Preston worshipping those considerable assets, Elara swept her eyes down the grand staircase.

Peels of merry laughter floated up seemingly in blithe mockery of her dread. Below, ladies in lustrous silks spun giddy in their gay ministrations beneath the glittering chandelier while she awaited her captor above in grim solitude. Ten minutes passed, then twenty… Elara clung to each delayed moment from James' company, daring to hope she may be free from his grasp for at least one night.

Elara descended with the support of Smith's sturdy arm, scalp prickling from acute sensation of unseen gazes tracing her every step. She wondered if her locks flung open floodgates for rampant scrutiny yet again. Or did her elaborate efforts prove successful to some?

Her gloved fingers stroked her hair nervously, only heightening her self-conscious blush. No doubt her cheeks were ripening to scarlet. Still Elara tilted her chin high against hidden judgment, a lesson hard learned to combat whispers of disapproval.

Relief stirred at sighting one of her allies amidst the sea of strangers. As Lord Hugh threaded closer through the human gallery, muted disappointment tangled strangely in Elara's heartbeat. She must stop searching for him and leash her ardent sentiments towards Preston now and forever.

"May I escort you to the refreshment table?" the elder man asked kindly, offering her his arm.

Releasing Smith's arm, she placed a hand on Lord Hugh's soft blue velvet.

"I have been meaning to send you a missive, congratulating you on your betrothal," Lord Hugh said. Frowning at her obvious confusion, he continued, "I heard you were betrothed to Lord Frances."

"No, my lord. There must have been a misunderstanding. If I were to be betrothed, you would have been the first to know." Elara surprised herself with this bold statement. It was indicative of how desperate and angry she was.

Lord Hugh's eyes flickered with understanding, but he did not say as much. "I see. That explains why the viscount left in a hurry without you this morning."

"Do you mean to say you saw Lord Frances quit the castle?" Elara's heart leapt with joy.

"Aye. Were you not aware?"

"No. He said not a word to me."

"He looked as though he was fleeing. Does this mean you are in need of an escort, my lady?"

In that moment, Preston appeared at a distance and she saw no one else. He was orbiting splendidly across the dance floor, shining brightly while shadows fell on everything else around him.

Then all light in the room seemed to converge upon the radiant couple, displaying every detail as if she was gliding between them. His long fingers that had once soothed her now rested upon his wife's back. The enchanting smile upon his lips now curved to speak his wife's name, his eyes twinkling upon her radiance.

The music soared around the handsome couple, joyful and bright, unaware of one woman's happiness unravelling along the strands of the melody. They moved with such grace and ease in each other's arms, like partners fated.

She observed how the princess glowed under Preston's attention. The adoring gaze they shared left little doubt. He was as entranced by his wife as she was by her dashing husband. With sorrow wrenching her heart out, Elara realised Preston had found a deeper connection with another. As the waltz stretched on, that truth trampled on her fragile hopes heavier than their dancing feet possibly could.

"My lord, I am feeling faint suddenly. Would you mind terribly fetching a refreshment?" Elara asked weakly, disentangling herself to rest against a column as her complexion blanched.

"Of course, my lady." Lord Hugh briskly embarked on his quest.

Smith stepped closer. "Is it the royal couple's presence upsetting you?" he murmured.

Nodding, she replied, "I am being ridiculous. I knew all along he was married. Is it so inconceivable he would recommit to the most beautiful woman I've met?"

"Lady Elara!" The Duchess of Somerset cut briskly through the assembly, providing much needed distraction.

"Your Grace." Her attempt at decorous curtsy was arrested by Her Grace's hand reaching for hers.

"None of that now, Lady Elara. All this formality is trying my sailor-bred patience."

Elara laughed, showing sincere appreciation for such easy confidence.

"Come, there are friends I would like you to meet." Linking their arms close, the duchess guided her nearer a small coterie of gentlefolk. "The Marquess and Marchioness of Salisbury," the duchess heralded as they drew within earshot. All turned, keen speculation in their eyes assessing the stranger between them.

Lord and Lady Salisbury held court most strikingly, both tall and dark-haired with strong features. It seemed that these lovely ladies had attracted the handsomest men. The thought of Preston crossed her mind, and a pang dug deep into her heart. She was grateful to stand with her back to him.

"Lord and Lady Salisbury, may I introduce Lady Elara from Stamford?" the duchess said.

"Lady Elara, how fares the earl?" Lord Salisbury inquired.

"He has much improved. Thank you for your concern."

"I am very glad. I'd hate to be burdened with his work," his lordship jested, receiving a chiding glance from his wife.

"Please allow me to introduce my father and sister, Lady Elara," her ladyship said. Professor Brown's spine was twisted, and his arms rested limply, but his eyes were bright, and his voice was strong. Her ladyship's sister, Miss Brown, was akin to finding a stick only to realize it was made of iron. She was tall and delicate in appearance but with a sharp tongue and clever wit to break anyone's spirit should she choose.

"I don't blame the prince one bit for leaving his home country," Emma said to the group. "The King is fanatical about control, hence the reason why Bavaria's relationship with France is so precarious. He makes decisions based on whether he can control the situation rather than merits. And he has got worse since the assassination of his heirs."

"His brothers were assassinated?" Elara blurted in surprise.

"Yes, by a political rival who opposed the country's alliance with France. They were on a boat together when a bomb exploded."

"How awful," Elara said, her heart breaking for the parents.

"The biggest surprise is Prince Maximilian's reunion with Princess Julia."

"Why do you say that?" the professor asked.

"She betrayed and humiliated him terribly early in their marriage. Now, she seems to be infatuated with him. Watch how she looks at him. That cannot be a mere pretence. And for him to accept her after all these years, one can only assume their bond was unbreakable at the start."

Elara touched her throat, feeling she might swoon.

"Let us change the subject, shall we?" Lady Salisbury coaxed thoughtfully.

The duchess gestured to a chaise where Elara and the ladies arranged themselves elegantly. Her gaze wandered the glittering ballroom, seeking a glimpse of Preston but also terrified that she may witness more of the couple's affection.

Elara dropped her head to settle her rattling thoughts when she realised a goblet waited in her hand. Smith apparently had anticipated her needs before she voiced them. Sipping gratefully, Elara watched the bemused glances from her companions aimed upon her guardian. Save Miss Brown, whose gaze marked a less reserved appraisal.

"May I present Mr Smith, my protection officer, assigned by Nic..." She faltered, not knowing how much Preston had revealed of their relationship.

Lady Salisbury gently prodded. "The prince seems extraordinarily concerned about your welfare, Lady Elara."

The duchess arched a brow. "Pray, did any amongst us know Mr Preston's royal status before now?" At Elara's head shake, she leaned closer, voice dropped to a clandestine hush. "Certainly, His Royal Highness nurtures as many intriguing secrets as my husband once did."

Elara opened her mouth to query about the duke's secrets when she heard Lord Salisbury address Lord Hugh. She raised her eyes to see the earl shaking hands with the marquess and the professor. He held two glasses of champagne, and she dipped her head towards him in thanks. After exchanging a few words with Lord Salisbury and the professor, Lord Hugh came to her side. The two ladies fell away with Emma while Smith stepped aside, granting them more privacy.

"Lady Elara, it seems I am too late," the earl said, raising the extra glass of champagne.

"I am certain you can manage two glasses of champagne, my lord, considering the battlefield you just traversed."

Although the topic of discussion was chaste, Lord Hugh did not seem able to look away from her bosom. He had been the epitome of reserve, but this evening, he reminded her that he was a man after all. Feeling self-conscious, Elara got to her feet, stepping away slightly as she did so. Eventually, they were several feet away from the group, the ever so dedicated Mr Smith drifting with them.

"My lady, my lord," a low voice intoned. She was relieved to find Lord Salisbury by their side. "I'd like to introduce you to Prince Maximilian if you will oblige me."

Lord Hugh smiled tightly and followed while Lord Salisbury escorted Elara on his arm. With her legs trembling and her heart ricocheting in her ribcage, Elara vowed not to crumble. She dared herself to look Preston in the eye and found the same chilliness as the morning air.

How he was the same man who had been inside her, had professed his love for her, she did not know. He was a rare breed that could deceive and slaughter with a tender smile on his face.

"Your Royal Highness, I believe you are already acquainted with Lady Elara," Lord Salisbury said. Elara curtsied on her shaky legs. He bowed gracefully, ignorant of turmoil capsizing in his wake. She clung to the minor mercy that the princess was not with him. She could not bear another occasion of Preston watching uncaringly while his wife attacked her.

Elara allowed her eyes to drift away from him. He seemed to want her to meet his eyes again, but she refused. He had not shown her kindness when his wife was near. He had naught she wanted now.

---

He had kept her in his sight from the moment she entered the room. He had fought back the urge to take her from Hugh's grasp and hide her somewhere no other man could reach. Then he noticed the old man's greedy gaze and could not stand around as an ornament any longer. That man would not undress her with his eyes, and she was not going to propose a marriage to him.

Excusing himself from Julia and her friends, he marched over to Salisbury who read his meaning immediately. Unfortunately, Elara was intent on not meeting his gaze. While Salisbury worked to distract Hugh, he inched closer to Elara. Giving Smith a stern look for privacy, Preston kept his eyes straight ahead and a mask of neutral expression on his face.

"This is not what it looks like," he said. "I am only doing my part to appease Father."

He wondered if she heard him at all when no acknowledgement came from her. He looked down at her and found her staring into the distance, her brows furrowed.

"Did you hear me? I wish I could tell you everything, but there are too many people surrounding me at all times of the day."

"I did not receive a single letter since your departure. Like a fool, I waited and hoped."

"Elara–"

"You may address me as Lady Elara. I cannot discuss this with you for fear I may break into sobs or claw at your face. All I know is that you look at her as you once looked at me. I'm uncertain if you lied to me or are lying to her." Turning towards him, she curtsied briskly and walked away. Glancing at his employer disapprovingly, Smith followed.

# Chapter Thirty-Four

## *3 April 1833 – quarter of eleven in the morning*

Preston was a bundle of nerves. He had hardly slept last night despite feeling exhausted. Waking up during the night to banish Julia out of his bed was not the only reason. Although he had no desire for the woman, her wandering hand to his groin had made his need for Elara more acute. He went riding, took a bath, wrote to his secretary, ate breakfast, and was now staring at the clock for the hundredth time.

It was still awhile until one o'clock, which was when Salisbury promised him his wife would bring Elara to their private quarters. He would finally be alone with her. Preston was pondering if he ought to write a romantic sonnet when Julia walked in through the connecting door.

"Good morning," she said sleepily.

"Knock next time," he said grumpily.

"Whatever for?" she plopped down beside him, pouting.

She was too close. Her thigh was pressing against his which irritated him. He moved to a chair.

"Why are you here?" he asked.

"We are husband and wife. We should do what husband and wife ought to do," she said.

He sighed as he rubbed his face with both hands. "I have no interest in being your husband. I would rather sleep, Julia, so don't ever come into my room again with the intention of seducing me."

"So, the red-haired woman is the only one you want? Or is it that I am the only one you don't want?"

"I only want one woman. You are not her."

"If she does not accept you, will you be celibate for the rest of your life?"

"Yes. Why are you here?"

"You could be nicer to me, and perhaps I will let you touch me when you become tired of her or your hand."

"I am leaving," he said and stood.

"Very well. Here. You are so dull," she griped, tossing a newspaper on the table. He reached for it and scanned the headlines on the folded page.

"Bloody hell," he spat when he saw the article titled, *Mr Nicholas Preston, a Member of the Inner Temple and a Bigamist.*

> *Mr Preston has been earning the respect of his peers and nobilities for his seamless manoeuvres in the courtroom. He has been climbing the social ladder at an exponential rate, dining with dukes, befriending fashionable ladies, and defending his enemies. Everyone who has met him fall under his spell, entangling themselves as his client, friend, or both. That is why we are shocked to learn from an anonymous source that he is a bigamist. He has a wife and children he abandoned years ago yet married a farmer's daughter. We do not know the identity of his new bride, but we intend to discover who she is. Has Mr Preston, the defender of the poor, turned wicked or was he a wolf disguised as a knight all along? We shall follow him closely.*

"Do you know who the source might be?" Julia asked.

"Aye," he said. "I suspected he might be running from something when I didn't see him after the first night."

"What will you do?"

"Hang him."

"That seems harsh," she said.

"Is it? He might single-handedly ruin my reputation and credibility as the officer of the law. Not only that, Elara and my marriage might be tainted even before we've begun." Preston stood and stomped towards the door.

"You should surrender to your present circumstance," Julia said.

"Like hell I will!"

"Where are you going?"

"To kill someone since it can't be you!"

Preston marched over to Salisbury's living quarters and banged on the door. He stomped past the surprised valet and found his lordship lounging on a chaise in his house robe. Preston shoved the newspaper before Salisbury's eyes.

Salisbury looked up at his friend's pacing form. "Unless you are my wife wanting an amorous encounter, I suggest you return at a later hour," his friend said.

"Do you know where Frances is?" Preston asked impatiently.

"Left on the first night. He's likely hiding somewhere to save his neck."

"As he should be. When I get my hands on that rascal–"

"The lie is easily proved. He obviously bribed a farmer's daughter. This is not dire. Now, sit down before I throw you out for ruining my peaceful morning," Salisbury said.

Preston plopped into the nearest chair and ran his fingers through his hair.

"What has you antsy?"

"Elara... Did you talk to her?"

"Alexandra spoke to her." Salisbury languidly sipped on his coffee.

"Well?" Preston made a rolling motion with his wrist.

"She left."

Preston shot up from his chair. "What? When? Why?"

"During the ball, immediately after you two spoke. As to why, it is my understanding she believes you have reunited with the princess."

"Ah!" Preston screamed, at which point his guards immediately came running into the room.

"False alarm!" Salisbury shouted. "Back to your stations, gentlemen."

"Why did you not inform me as soon as you heard?" Preston demanded to know.

"What for? There is naught you can do. You are stuck here. Telling you is like throwing a baby to a drowning man."

"That stubborn woman! I told her it was an act."

"In that case, perhaps act a little less. You even had my sister-in-law convinced you were in love with the princess, and she is as perceptive as they come."

Preston sat on the chair and began rocking with his head buried in his lap. "Did she take Smith with her?" he asked in a muffled voice.

"Smith? Is that her dog?"

"No, Smith the guard."

"Ah, yes. Smith and the others accompanied her."

"What if she falls in love with him? They spend all their time together," he said in a stifled voice.

"Then I wish them the best. He's a good fellow, is he not? They seemed to have developed a friendship of sorts."

Preston raised his head and glowered at his friend. "You are a bloody traitor."

Salisbury chuckled and rose to his feet. Patting his friend on the shoulder, he said, "Would your time not be spent more wisely unearthing that scoundrel, Frances?"

Without a word, Preston stood and hastened out of the room.

---

It was not difficult to find a nobleman when one had palace guards at his disposal. After a few hours of search, James was located at an exclusive brothel known to harbour aristocratic fugitives. Understanding he had committed a grave mistake in falsely accusing a prince, James had hidden in the bosoms of upscale prostitutes.

When the palace guards entered to apprehend him, he was in the midst of wailing like a babe and getting his nappies changed.

Preston glared at the man who was kneeling at his feet while his parents and King Ferdinand looked on. He wished he could pummel the bastard for harassing Elara, but he had to leash his temper to achieve a greater goal.

"Are you still wearing your nappies?" he asked the whorepipe.

His eyeballs shifting from one monarch to another, James replied, "No, Your Royal Highness."

"That is unfortunate. This proceeding may take awhile."

"Maximilian, hasten what it is you wish to achieve," his mother said.

"It seems that Lord Frances has falsely accused me of bigamy and has sold his lies to a publication. I mean to pack him in a trunk and send him to the gallows in Bavaria."

James dropped his head, looking wretched.

"You've also been threatening your cousin, Lady Elara, with bodily harm."

"Please, I beg you for your mercy," James touched his forehead to the floor.

"What punishment do you believe would be just to fit your crime, Lord Frances? A lion's den? An elephant on each limb? A rope or a blade?" Preston asked, his volume increasing with anger.

"Please forgive me, Your Royal Highness," James shrunk before his wrath.

"You are a fortunate man, Frances. Despite my wish to see you suffer, I have decided on a fate much better than death or prison. You shall marry the Princess of Spain."

James lifted his head with a frown. "Did you just say I would wed a princess, Your Royal Highness?"

"I did."

"And that's to be my punishment?"

"Aye."

"What is amiss with Her Royal Highness?"

"Not a thing."

"I don't understand," James said.

"You do not need to understand to marry the princess. Stand up."

Once James was on his feet and his clothes straightened, Preston ordered the guards to bring Julia in. The princess strolled in donning a white silk gown, the skirt flowing around her like a cloud.

"What is all this?" she asked irritably. "If this is about the annulment, I have nothing further to say," she said, standing with one hip cocked and her arms crossed.

"Julia, meet Viscount Frances of Stamford. Viscount, Princess Julia of Spain," Preston said.

James did not make a move for a moment, entranced by the beauty before him. Ferdinand cleared his throat impatiently. Startled, James bowed deferentially.

Julia studied the man before her, not returning his greeting. "Why should I care about this man?" she asked, grimacing at his crumpled attire.

"He is young, handsome enough, wealthy, and an English viscount."

She narrowed her eyes. "And why are you telling me this?"

"You shall marry him," Preston said.

"Marry him? This man?" She pointed at James with a frown. "Why would I agree to that when I have you?"

"Because he will make your children legitimate. They shall become his heirs," Preston said.

"I beg your pardon?" James exclaimed.

"The princess has three children. You will treat them like your own. We shall have legal documents to make it so. They shall be your heirs."

She tilted her head with intrigue.

"How would he make my children legitimate?"

"His Majesty shall decree it." Preston turned to his father who nodded. "He shall become a citizen of Bavaria, marry you, and bring you and your children back to England as a happy family."

"You expect me to make another man's children my heirs? Why, that is ludicrous!"

"I was hoping you'd say that because I'd rather see you hang," Preston said casually.

James groaned.

"What has he done?" Julia asked, raking her gaze over the viscount.

"He has defamed my reputation," Preston said.

"He is not fond of you, then?" Julia asked, circling James who was now gawking at her. She twirled a strand of her long hair around her fingers, reminding Preston of how his fingers had twirled Elara's hair, how he had lathered her with soap... He felt a powerful need to breathe her in, watch her flaming tresses spread across her back while he kissed her perfect arse. His heart and cock stirred ferociously.

At his mother's subtle throat clearing, he hastily replied, "You two have that in common."

Julia approached James and stood within reach. Without a word, she patted his chest and abdomen. She walked around him twice, studying his form.

"Show me your teeth, my lord," she coaxed gently.

James swiftly obeyed.

"Your hands."

James spread his hands out in front of him.

"Acceptable. Do you have any troubles in bed?"

"No, Your Royal Highness," he said with a smirk.

"Very well. I will take him," she said.

## Chapter Thirty-Five

# 6 April 1833 – midnight

The sky was as dark as ink with not a star in sight. This made the sleepless night even more intolerable. There would be no reprieve from her heartache tonight, and there were no moon or stars to gaze upon. She would go mad tonight, she was certain. Elara Frances, age twenty-seven, not a virgin, not a wife, not a mother, not a muse, would go madder than a plucked chicken.

She smiled despite herself. She always did when thinking about chicken ever since the night in Preston's kitchen. She quite liked turnip and purple broccoli, too. She chuckled at the memory, and then her chest squeezed from the same memory. She needed to get out. A walk in the garden with the chilly night air on her skin might help expand her lungs.

Donning her velvet housecoat over the night rail, Elara retrieved a lantern and approached the bedroom door carefully to avoid waking up Shelley. Her lady's maid had been sleeping on the chaise since they returned. Sometimes she stroked Elara's hair to entice sleep or held her while she cried. Currently, she was snoring away, occasionally mumbling nonsensically.

Just as Elara reached for the door handle, she heard a creak from the water closet. Creaks in the old house were common enough. It was likely a rodent or the house settling into a deep slumber. She hesitated, debating if she should call the guard stationed outside her room. But she did not wish to disturb them or Shelley without just cause. She would investigate first. Surely, she could make some kind of noise if there was an intruder.

She walked towards the water closet on her tiptoes, grabbed the fireplace poker, and approached the doorway. She placed the lantern on a table nearby and used the end of the poker to swing the door wide open. The room was empty, but there was an opening the size of a chair in the wall. Gasping, she stepped back when a looming figure appeared in her periphery. Her cry was muffled by the heel of a large hand over her mouth. A strong arm wrapped around both of her arms, rendering her immobile. She dropped the poker to make noise, but the intruder broke the fall with his foot. She felt his hot breath on her cheek.

"Elara, it is I, Nicholas. Do not scream."

His familiar voice made her body limp with relief. She nodded eagerly, and he slowly released her but not before his fingers stroked her lips.

As soon as she was free, she spun around and pounded on his chest with her small fists. He pushed her inside the water closet and closed the door.

"You scared me to death, Nicholas Preston, Max or whatever your name is! A prince? A bloody prince! And not a word about it to me!" she screamed in a hushed tone.

"I am sorry. I've lived as Nicholas Preston for so long, even I would forget sometimes. I did not believe it had any relevance to our present or future." He laid gentle hands on her shoulders and spoke softly. "While I may be Nicholas or Maximilian or Prince, I shall always remain as your servant."

Elara's ragged breaths subsided a little and her tone gentled. "Mayhap, but you seem like a stranger to me, and I must make peace with this new reality. At present, you are more someone else's prince than my servant."

"Elara..." His thumb brushed her bottom lip. She recoiled.

"What on earth are you doing in my chamber in the middle of the night?" she asked.

"I had to see you but could not be spotted by the guards. I am forbidden from contacting you at the moment."

"Of course you are prohibited! Any wife would not allow her husband such liberties, especially a princess who has a reputation to guard!"

The infuriating man grinned.

"What is so amusing?" she shouted in a whisper.

"Come. Let us talk somewhere more private," he said.

"I am going nowhere with you! Go back to your princess!"

"Sweetheart, you have every right to be angry with me, but listen to me for five minutes. What have you got to lose?"

"I have my dignity to lose, what little I have left! And I will not follow a perfect stranger into a private room!"

His eyes grazed over her body greedily. "My sweet Blossom. You are so beautiful."

"Did you come for a tumble because your wife is too elegant for a rough rutting? Excuse me, but you cannot have me. This body is for my husband!"

Elara saw a flash of his hungry eyes before he picked her up and carried her to the opening in the wall. Taking advantage of her disoriented state, he put her down and pushed her through the opening, closing the door after him.

The neatly built tunnel with wood panelling on all four sides was lit with a lantern. It was wide and tall enough for them to crawl through but not for straightening their backs.

"Move forward if you will," he urged from behind her.

"How did you find this tunnel? No one knows about it except me," she said.

"The usual. Inspection."

"Where are we going?"

"Somewhere we can talk."

"I am not lying with you," she said.

"Yes, you are."

She glared over her shoulder incredulously. "You ought to be ashamed of yourself!"

"Can we argue where it's safer?"

Facing forward, she grudgingly crawled, stopping often to free her night rail from beneath her knees. Then suddenly, she felt firm hands grip her hips and pull her underneath his hovering body. In a blink, she was on her stomach with his erection pressed against her rear. With wide eyes, she turned her head to look at him.

"It is torturous to have your arse in my face," he rasped, wrapping one arm around her waist. Her body purred begrudgingly at his touch.

Preston cupped her cheek in one hand and moved his lips around her mouth almost painfully tenderly, his breath and lips barely touching hers. Every trace of his breath and touch felt like an expression of his longing. Wondering if she was being fooled yet again, she moved to lie on her back. He eased the pressure on her backside and allowed her to settle beneath him. She gasped when he pushed his hard length against her crotch. She was already wet, her night rail sticking to her thigh.

"God, I missed you," he whispered before lowering his mouth. She turned her head and avoided the kiss. She needed answers first.

"Why did you not come back after your meeting with your father? Why did you not write?" she asked.

As if he couldn't stop touching her, Preston slid his lips lightly behind her ear, then down her neck. To her annoyance, another moan escaped her lips.

"I was forbidden by Father from contacting you," he said, his lips skimming over her collarbone. "It was important not to insult the King of Spain, Julia's brother."

"Are you reunited with your wife?"

"No," he said while he untied the belt of her housecoat. "It is all a pretence," he said, sliding the sleeve of her night rail down and exposing her breast. He cupped her heated flesh in his hand and squeezed with an appreciative groan. "Christ, I missed this," he rasped and placed his hot mouth over her nipple.

A long and airy sound escaped Elara's throat as she thrust her hips against his cock. Her body tingled with joy as he grunted and moved to caress and lick the other breast.

"Did you tell her about us?"

"I told her you were the woman I wished to marry. I have nothing to hide."

Despite the piercing joy, she cautioned herself from hoping too much too fast until all was uncovered.

"Why... Why would you pretend to love her if you mean to stay estranged?"

"Must we... talk... now?" he asked as he pulled the hem of her night rail to her hips. He moved down her body and pushed her thighs open. He groaned as his eyes feasted on her pussy.

"So beautiful," he said before he cupped her sex with his mouth. With his tongue, he traced the outline of her folds, then the outline of her opening.

"Nicholas... Mm..." She was distracted by his wicked tongue and the fingers that were squeezing her nipple.

"Tell me," she forced out. He slipped his fingers inside her. "Yes... yes..." she moaned.

"To present a united front," he said, his fingers caressing her inner flesh. "The prodigal son returns, love reunites all, anything is possible when full of hope, etcetera," he finished impatiently. His tongue licked her from her entrance all the way to the clitoris in one long stroke.

She pushed against his fingers, needing him to possess her, anchor her. "Nicholas, take me, please…" she pleaded, aching to have him deep in her core, filling and stretching.

Crawling over her writhing body, Preston encircled his arms around her waist and kissed her hard on the mouth. Elara's fingers dug into his hair.

While his tongue breached her mouth deeply and sucked on her tongue, he unbuttoned his falls and nudged his cockhead at her entrance. "God, Elara. You're so swollen…"

Sucking on her tongue again, he plunged into her with a satisfying grunt as she thrust up her hips to bury him deeper.

"Ah…" he moaned. "Take more," he whispered hoarsely. His hand moved to her arse and raised her hips. He seemed to grow bigger inside her, reaching the apex she didn't know existed.

"Why… are you… here… tonight?" she asked between her moans.

"Fuck… can't talk…"

Kissing her deeply, he kept his cock mostly buried while he moved inside her furiously. As his shaft stroked her clitoris with each thrust, tension built in her core. She had craved this feeling of wholeness so very much.

"Bloody hell, Elara… You're incredible to fuck… so tight…"

"Ah, Nicholas, I'm so close…"

Rapture cascaded through Elara as though the heavens sundered wide, spilling forth between gasps transmuting to sharp cries. Some primal energy awakened beyond her physical being, arching her against discarded velvet and silk, now tangled like wild flowering vines. Her ecstasy clutching fiercely at Preston's strong frame, his culmination nearing until, at last, his sturdy protection gave way to convulsing euphoria in her trembling embrace.

In the afterglow, he lay enraptured in her arms, two made one. Elara cradled his head to her heart's drum, the heat of shared intimacy warding all outside perils at bay—two souls privately exultant before civility befitted them once more for the world.

Elara dared not dream of what futures lie ahead. Still, the memory of his passion whispered all was not lost. His all-consuming ardour could warm the most frozen bonds and thaw the coldest silence between two lovers. So, she kindled fragile hopes as Preston raised his gaze to hers once more.

"My only sun, I thought I would wither away without you." His solemn whisper soothed chambers of her heart long starved for such sincerity since his silence. Elara's levee broke, and tears flooded anew.

"You, infuriating man... You left me without a word, with no explanation..." Her outpouring of past pain came fiercely, seeking release at last.

"I am sorry. I am so sorry." With gentle hands, he soothed away the storms of questioning, gathering her close now as before. And in togetherness, wounded pasts started to mend.

---

Once Elara's cries became soft sniffles, Preston relaxed his arms around her. He gazed at her lovely face glowing in the lantern light.

"Shall we go down to the cellar where we can talk more? My aging body is complaining about the hard surface," he said.

"It wasn't complaining while we were... busy," she teased.

"Are you offering again as a remedy? By all means, I would not decline such a thoughtful proposition."

With a smile, she pushed at his chest. He rolled off her and gestured for her to go in front of him so he could enjoy the lovely view of her bottom once more. It had been too bloody long without her.

They made their way towards the below ground staircase. Once inside the soundproof cellar, Preston lit the other lantern he'd left there earlier. Elara looked around the room and gaped at the blankets and pillows he left behind.

"You made preparations," she said. "How presumptuous of you."

"Not presumptuous. Aspirational," he replied smoothly. "I did hope for a harem, but you'll do." His chuckles at her glare dispelled any lingering unease between them. Unfolding a blanket, he enveloped her narrow frame within it and pierced her eyes as if to shield her from memory's bitter winds. After several moments, Preston got on one knee.

"Already? Nicholas, could we wait a little?"

A wide grin split his face. "We certainly could, but what to do in the meantime..." He tapped a finger on his chin pensively. "I know."

Digging into his pocket, he took out a small, ornate box glinting in the light and raised it up to her. She stared at it in stunned silence and remained impressively motionless.

As he studied her beautiful face, Preston's heart clenched and expanded with apprehension and unspeakable joy. He cleared his throat.

"I am a free man now, Cherry Blossom. And I do not wish to spend another day, another hour, without making you my betrothed. Will you be my wife, Elara?"

Preston's pocket watch ticked deafeningly as lifetimes breezed past rather than mere moments. A hundred agonising futures played out as he searched his mind to prepare for her refusal rather than consent.

"Just to clarify, you refer to the freedom of ending your marriage, not your status as a prince?" Elara searched his expression with schooled composure.

Clasping her chilled hands, Preston met her eyes, unwavering. "The former binds us no more. I stand before you untethered... to take new vows if you would have me."

The box trembled faintly in his grip, her muted gaze building years' worth of tension and uncertainty in mere moments.

When finally she gave a slow nod, elation's deluge fell like spring rain to parched earth, gently nourishing barren ground where only sorrow took root before. They hugged, kissed, and hugged some more, finding bliss in each passing moment.

## Chapter Thirty-Six

# 7 April 1833 – half of ten in the morning

There was nothing more delicious than waking up with Preston's arm around her waist and his hardness naked against her naked bottom. Stretching a little, Elara burrowed deeper into his embrace as the mattress dipped. Following the proposal, they talked for hours then returned to her bedchamber at dawn, scaring Shelley to death. Immediately after Shelley's flight, Preston took her against the bedpost before allowing her to sleep.

In the morning sun, the blood-red ruby on her finger was the hue of pomegranate seeds, large and iridescently translucent. The stone held court in an intricately embellished setting of woven yellow gold, as though the metal itself had been stitched. Flanking the weighty centrepiece, four smaller rubies smouldered like lit embers about to erupt into open flame. Elara stretched out her hand, entranced by the glitters that danced and changed hue.

"Do you like it?" Preston's gravelly voice reverberated against her neck.

"I do. It is the most beautiful piece of jewellery I've seen."

"Fitting for the most striking woman," he murmured.

She turned around in his arms to face him. He cupped her buttocks and pulled her crotch against his erection.

"Mm..." His voice rumbled low and seductive.

She looked up at his chiselled jaw, wondering if it was safe to think of him as hers forever or if fate would snatch him away from her again.

"I don't know what to give you for an engagement present," she said.

"I have my present right here," he said huskily, kissing her neck and slowly trailing down. "And here." He rubbed his hard length against her wet heat. "Hold my cock tighter with your thighs, love," he said, his hoarse voice causing flutters inside her.

"Mm..." he made a guttural sound as he kneaded her bottom. With his other hand, he gently tilted her chin up. "You are the most incredible present ever."

"Truly?"

"Yes."

"I could make it better."

"Impossible," he said while moving his cock slowly between her thighs.

"I should still like to try. Show me what you want me to do."

He drenched his thick girth in her juice, then rose onto his knees with her between them. He dragged the heavy weight along her body towards her breasts. Positioning his throbbing cock between the mounds, he squeezed the flesh together to form a gorge. Stroking her nipples gently with his thumbs, Preston moaned as he slid his shaft in the slippery crevice. He then edged closer to her mouth and brushed her lips with his tip.

"Open your mouth," he ordered.

When she did as told, his eyes lost focus with delirium.

"Taste my cock, sweetheart."

Her tongue darted out and gave his cockhead a shy lick. His lips parted with a slow exhale. He moved his rigid rod over her lips, his eyes rivetted on the vision.

One hand braced on the headboard, he rumbled low and commanding, "Suck it."

Holding his shaft with one hesitant hand, she swirled her tongue around his cockhead. He grunted. "That is not what I told you to do."

"Take me in your mouth now."

She opened her mouth wider and sheathed his length as much as she could. She surprised him with a suck and swirl of her tongue. When he groaned, she did it again and again.

"You make it impossible for me to be a gentleman. Release your hand. Take what I give you."

He cursed under his breath when her innocent eyes looked up at him, her red lips stretched tightly around his girth, his cock filling her mouth until she couldn't take any more of him.

"Christ, you're such a good girl," he said breathlessly.

Preston slowly thrust his thick length into her mouth. She maintained friction against his shaft with her tongue.

"Fuck... yes, darling. That's it... so damn good, my little Blossom."

With each plunge, his movements became more rigorous until his tip was pounding against her throat. She tried to become accustomed to breathing while he filled her mouth completely.

"Touch yourself," he ordered.

She opened her eyes wide in reply.

"Come for me."

Hesitantly, she parted her folds pooled with moisture. She spread her nectar over the labia and clitoris, increasing the pressure and moaning with pleasure.

"Sweet Lucifer, that feels good. When you moan... Bloody hell..."

He looked over his shoulder and watched her rub her pussy. He cursed, taking pleasure from her mouth and the incredible vision.

While she gazed at his hungry eyes with her mouth full of his cock, Elara's orgasm broke and shattered through her body. As her scream reverberated through his cock, rapture seemed to crest within him.

With his remaining palm slamming against the headboard, he rode his peak with a violent jerk of his entire body. His thighs squeezed her shoulders tightly, then his head fell forward.

She swallowed the warm liquid.

Immediately after, Preston inserted his half erect cock in her heat and gathered her in his arms.

Elara leaned against his chest with his soft member still inside her. His arms came around her back and stroked her sensitive skin. Every fibre of her being sang with wordless bliss, the heady strains of destiny and desire entwining harmoniously, buoyant into the future with Preston by her side. Basking in his cherished embrace, feeling his chest rise and fall slowly, Elara wondered how she had not evaporated into the sky, so ethereal was this joy.

"I must leave for London today." His words jolted her out of her bliss, and she lingered uncertainly in the space unknown.

"Will you come back?" she asked despite realising how ridiculous she must sound.

A deep crease appeared between his brows. "Of course, I will. I will always come back to you."

She looked into his vibrant blue eyes, no longer cold, no longer the colour of glacier. "I... I trust you. It's just that I am afraid someone might take you away from me."

Preston stroked her hair lovingly. "My parents are ecstatic that I want to marry you and try to sire an heir."

"They are? They don't even know me."

Preston frowned. "About that... They seem to know you well enough."

Elara tilted her head in confusion.

He exhaled deeply, looking extremely guilty and hesitant.

"What is it?"

"They are the ones who orchestrated our capture."

"What?" Elara opened her mouth against the vacuum of disbelief, willing words to form. Yet only a muted squeak emerged before she clamped her jaw shut.

"They chose you specifically because you had been considered a candidate for my eldest brother."

"What?"

"They chose you as one of the potential brides for him."

"I did not know I was being considered."

"They have a bad habit of deciding without consent and forcing their objectives. Unfortunately, you have experienced that first hand."

"Unbelievable..." she murmured with a shake of her head.

"Yes." Preston tilted her head to meet his eyes. "I am sorry for your suffering. Is it wrong that I'm glad it was you and not someone else?"

She grinned, happiness bubbling up inside her. "Not even Martha?"

He smiled. "Not even dear Martha."

He pulled her close for a deep tender kiss which became needier and hungrier. She felt his member grow inside her. The sensation of him swelling in her cunny was incredibly arousing.

---

In a flash, Preston had her on her hands and knees. She looked over her shoulder to watch what he was doing. His eyes were dark and glazed as he pressed his thick girth in her butt crack. He rubbed his cock against her virgin hole while she turned crimson.

"Mm, one day I will claim this part of you as mine," he murmured hoarsely as he increased friction against her bottom.

"H-how?"

"With lots of patience and gentle nudging," he replied. Bending over her back, he dragged his finger against her pussy and soaked it in her nectar.

"I shall breach you with my finger now," he whispered in her ear.

Elara turned her head and watched over her shoulder. They held each other's gaze as he gently squeezed his finger through the crack of her arse and caressed the rosebud flesh. Slowly, he entered her hole, stretching it gently and coaxing it to open for him. Then her body welcomed the intrusion and sucked in his finger. She gasped and bit on her bottom lip.

"There is no part of your body, mind, and soul I don't wish to explore, but Lord knows how much I love your pussy."

With his finger inside her most private hole, Preston slid his cock into her innermost depth, grunting as he did so. He synchronised the thrusts of his finger as he withdrew and lunged back into her pussy. Elara yelped in surprise at the deeper intrusion.

"I'll be gentle. This can be—"

With a loud bang, Smith burst through the door with Davies who appeared to have just woken up. Preston reacted astonishingly quickly, throwing the counterpane over Elara's body.

Elara peeked through a gap and watched the two men gaping back at them. Preston continued to move inside her in tiny increments, wholly unaffected.

"Took you long enough. I was about to send a rescue party after you," he grumbled. "Turn around!" he barked when the men stayed motionless. "Get out and wait for my order," Preston said.

As soon as the men closed the door, Preston moved more urgently. Taking pleasure from her forbidden flesh, he threw his head back in euphoria when she squeezed her pussy and arsehole.

"Bloody hell, that's it. Squeeze my cock. I can't wait to fuck you in the arse."

Her backside quivered with each thrust into her cunny, and her forbidden hole tightened deliciously.

"Good girl, such a good girl…"

One devastating stroke after another, he knew he was at the mercy of his own pleasure, the climax likely more powerful than any he had experienced. He rose higher and higher even when he thought he could not rise anymore. Then finally, dazzling sensation exploded, each pulse of his orgasm carrying euphoria through every fibre of his body.

Utterly spent, Preston gently pulled out of her and collapsed next to her. He moaned from the remnants of the pleasure until he could muster the strength to rise and clean himself up.

Tending to her afterwards with a clean cloth, he said, "I must go to London, see to it that my clients are in good hands before we leave."

"We?"

"Yes. In a month or so, we shall leave for Bavaria. In the meantime, my mother will oversee the wedding plans. We shall be wed shortly after our arrival."

Overwhelmed, Elara wrapped her arms around his neck. Preston held her and spoke into her hair. "Invite your family and friends while you are here. Mother's lady in waiting shall take your measurements for the wedding dress and such."

"I cannot believe this is happening. Are you certain you won't regret this?" she asked, releasing him so she could bear witness to the truth of his words.

"I've never been so sure in my life."

"This means giving up your law practice and your autonomy, does it not?"

He held her hand to his chest. "It is much preferable to having my heart ripped out, Blossom," he whispered.

Then he kissed her mouth, full of tender passion, conveying volumes beyond words. His touch worshipped her courage over all adversity.

She was guiding him towards renewed purpose now. Her resilient heart had breathed air back into lungs once choking on despair. So he held Elara close, pouring endless gratitude into each gesture of affection. For she was breath, she was life, she was sunrise exalting over the night's surrender.

# *Epilogue*

## 25 JULY 1833 — NINE IN THE MORNING

"*Du siehst wunderschön aus!*" exclaimed the ladies surrounding Elara.

"*Danke,*" she replied as the ladies fussed over her.

"*Gib ihr Raum zum Atmen!*" Her Majesty's voice echoed in the spacious room as she clapped sharply twice. The ladies dispersed, and her mother-in-law guided her towards the mirror.

Elara's eyes opened wide at seeing the bride she did not recognise. The woman in the reflection had regained her weight and was happy with a rosy complexion. The off-the-shoulder neckline of the dress revealed much of her alabaster skin, glistening with sparkly dust. The pale green dress was tight around the bodice and flared out into a wide skirt. The beads on the bodice and the skirt gleamed in the morning sun.

"It is time, dear," Her Majesty said softly as she draped the veil over her face.

Elara's heart began to thump wildly in her chest as the organ started to play. She smiled brightly at her father who was waiting outside, leaning on his cane. The eight cousins of Preston lined up, side by side, and began walking down the aisle to the music. Elara was restless with excitement, wanting to run to Preston and hurry along the ceremony.

As she marched, supporting her father more than being supported by him, she saw Preston's silhouette through the veil. He was tall and distinguished in a white suit with golden coiled ropes and a ruby brooch adorning it. The brooch was identical to hers on her decolletage but larger.

Preston's gaze followed her all the way down the aisle, his humble smile turning into a devilish grin as she approached. She narrowed her eyes suspiciously, and he laughed silently. After her father shook Preston's hand, and they faced each other, he leaned forward to whisper, "The veil is an improvement from the burlap sack."

She tried to glare at him, but a smile broke on her face instead. After what felt like hours of the archbishop droning on, Preston was allowed to lift her veil and kiss her. Rather than the soft kiss expected from the groom, he planted an enthusiastic kiss like a young lad. Laughter and gasps spread through the church.

"I can't wait for tonight," he muttered before releasing her.

"I can if you plan to kiss like that," she chided.

As the wedding party filed out of the church amidst the angelic voices of the choir, Preston stopped Elara and kissed her tenderly. They had abstained from physical intimacy for almost two months since their arrival to Bavaria. This had not been planned but forced upon them by the Monarchs. It had not been too difficult since they had been exhausted after a long day of Preston's princely duties and her bridal activities. Besides, they both had an entourage of servants following them at all hours.

"Are you ready?" Preston asked, grinning at her with warm eyes.

"What are you referring to?"

He did not need to respond. The large crowd of people and their shouts were deafening. There were hundreds of thousands of people filling the streets to watch the newlywed couple making their way to the palace. The guards parted the way for them, but some still managed to touch her arm and grab her dress. She was glad to finally board the phaeton pulled by a pair of white horses.

Elara waved her hand as taught, albeit awkwardly, looking both ways and keeping a pleasant but reserved smile on her face. Preston was doing an expert job of looking modest, personable, and confident.

"You don't look like you've been a commoner for a decade," she said.

"That's because I've spent most of my decade deceiving people."

Once they entered the palace and waved to the people who had gathered, they were quickly ushered to change their clothes and escorted through the garden entrance. They embarked the unmarked carriage to board the Ludwig for their honeymoon to the Greek Islands.

As soon as the carriage started moving, Preston pulled Elara onto his lap and kissed her with urgency. "I missed you. I thought I'd go mad," he said over her open mouth during a long and amorous kiss.

"I didn't," she replied.

"Minx, your wifely duty includes feeding my pride."

Just as he swallowed her chuckle, the carriage abruptly stopped. Alarmed, Preston placed her on the seat and called out to the driver and footmen. Upon looking out the window, they both noticed the absence of the equerries. The door opened, and they were thrown into the darkness.

"Blast it!" Preston exclaimed in a voice muffled by the foul sack over his head. Then, "Ouch," following a sharp slapping sound.

"Are you all right?" Elara asked, choking from the stench of the sack. Rough hands bound her hands behind her back.

"Who are you? What do you want?" Preston asked impatiently. There was no reply.

Elara heard Preston sigh next to her as the door closed shut and the carriage began to move again.

"Are your hands bound?" she asked.

"Aye. I have a knife in my boot. I can cut the rope when it suits."

"You may not have a chance later," she said. "You ought to do something now."

"One kidnapping and you're already an expert," he said grumpily.

"It seems fairly straightforward," she said.

"If I cut the rope now and they happen to see, I have no fighting chance in this confined space. Better to wait until we have assessed the situation."

"You could pretend your hands are still bound. Then you go out of the carriage and pull your blade out to fight."

"And what will happen to you while I'm fighting the knaves?"

"I can handle myself using my feminine wiles."

"Is that so? It was merely four months ago when you swore you didn't have any."

"I had to learn to hook myself a prince."

"Do not be overconfident. These blackguards see you as their way to wealth. God forbid they see you as entertainment," he hissed.

# ABDUCTED

"The knaves likely want you, anyway. A prince is more valuable than a princess by marriage. All I need to do is wait and saunter out of the cell while your parents haggle for your life."

"That is true. Unless this is their doing," he grumbled.

When the carriage eventually stopped after an hour or so, they were pulled out roughly. A man guided Elara by the arm. Next to her, she could hear Preston negotiating with the captor.

"We will be an immense trouble and bother, I assure you, especially the missus. Release us and we'll give you all the money you want."

At the prolonged silence, Preston gave up. "Are you still here?" he whispered.

"Yes."

"Good. Do not worry. I shall get us out of here."

"Strangely, I am not too worried. I have faith in you."

"Wonderful. I was hoping for more pressure," he grumbled.

The blackguards took them into a building of sorts and pushed a chair to the back of their knees, making the joints buckle. They collapsed onto their seats. To their surprise, they immediately pulled the sack off their heads albeit roughly.

"Surprise!" voices thundered.

"What the hell!" Preston bellowed.

"Sorry for the rough treatment, old chap," Salisbury said. "Your Royal Highness," he bowed to Elara.

"You are resorting to kidnapping now? Are you low on funds, Salisbury?" Preston hollered.

"We thought it would be more entertaining this way," Somerset replied.

"For whom?" Preston barked.

"I have to admit your composure was admirable," Carlisle said.

"Are you the one who smacked me around?" Preston asked.

"Aye," Carlisle replied with a chuckle.

"You imbeciles! Do you have any idea how much you scared my wife?" Preston roared.

"No, they didn't," she said calmly. Preston turned and glared at her.

"You knew about this?" he asked.

She nodded slowly while he gawked at her. "Please don't hurt them after they cut our ropes," she said.

"You had me captured by these idiots, and you are worried about their well-being? You ought to worry about how you will get home once I annul our marriage!"

"I am sorry, but I could not go against your parents, could I?"

"My"—Preston looked to the sky and sighed—"parents? So the guards knew?"

"Of course, they did. We were not about to be killed for a prank," Somerset said.

Once they were unbound, Preston continued to glower at his friends.

"We wished to present you with our wedding gift before you left. I assure you. You will be much cheered up once you see them," Salisbury said.

Somerset opened an ornate wooden box and presented it to Elara. She looked inside and gasped, her hands flying to her mouth. Preston peered into the box, then punched Somerset in the arm. All his friends and the guards in the room howled. Preston removed the gold handcuffs from the box and dangled them in front of his eyes.

"These better be solid gold," he said.

"Of course, they are. There is a gold pin in there as well. Better not lose it," Carlisle said, still laughing.

"Bastards," Preston griped. "Too parsimonious for a gold key?"

"That would not be challenging enough for you," Carlisle said.

"We wanted to intercept you before you left. These could be useful during your honeymoon," Somerset said.

"I fear for England that you fools are allowed in Parliament," Preston said. "How did you convince my parents to go along?"

"They saw the value of vexing you. We thought they might gift wrap you before handing you over," Salisbury said.

"Off you go, then," Carlisle said. "You must be dying for some privacy."

"That is understandable," Somerset said, "precisely the reason we are joining you on your honeymoon."

"What?" Preston shouted. "Don't you dare!"

"Our wives are on the ship already. You are surrounded by subordinates all hours of the day. A few friends will not hurt," Salisbury said.

"So you didn't need to kidnap me," Preston pointed out.

"It appears that way," Carlisle replied, heading towards the door.

Preston looked at Elara's smiling face and narrowed his eyes. "Perhaps you ought to go with them, and I will stay here where it is peaceful and quiet."

# ABDUCTED

Elara linked her arm through his. "I will let you shackle me to bed," she whispered. Preston's eyes opened wide.

"On second thought," he said, "what a marvellous idea. More the merrier, as they say."

With that, they headed towards the waiting ship with the men singing, "*There once was a barmaid with large...*"

*The End*

Join Mihwa's Den of TMI on FB for exclusive content: https://www.facebook.com/groups/2110002726016346/

IG: https://www.instagram.com/mihwawrites

Newsletter: www.mihwawrites.com

# More Spicy Stories by Mihwa Lee

**Saving the Marquess**
Book 1 of Rogues Worth Saving Series
https://www.amazon.com/dp/B0CLKZBX2T
**In Regency England, scandal binds them, but passion ignites them.**

Arthur Redesdale, the Marquess of Salisbury, hides a dark secret behind his charms. When he meets Alexandra, she stirs a deep yearning in him like no other. Despite her resistance to his seductions, he's determined to make her his marchioness.

Alexandra, governess to the Salisbury children, is torn between duty and temptation, propriety, and passion. But just as she gives in to desire, deception threatens to destroy them both. She must decide whether to trust the marquess or flee from his threats and lies.

Will she surrender to the darkness with the man she's grown to love? Or will buried secrets keep them apart?

Saving the Marquess weaves a steamy, sweeping tale of romance, danger, and forbidden love in Regency England.

# ABDUCTED

## **Lady Asilia's Gamble**
Book 2 of Rogues Worth Saving Series

https://www.amazon.com/dp/B0CTG4XS7C

**He vowed revenge against her world. She would change his world with love.**

Fiery passion ignites between a trailblazing lady and a mysterious fugitive in this steamy historical romance.Rebellious aristocrat Asilia flees the scandal of high society, finding bliss instead in the thrilling world of competitive horse racing. When she meets the clever inventor Cameron, she sees the perfect partner for an epic Arabian race. Little does she know he harbours a secret vendetta years in the making.

Cameron Pembroke is presumed dead, set on avenging his murdered family. He views the high-stakes race as the ideal chance to enact justice undetected. But working closely with the audacious Asilia soon ignites an irresistible passion within him.

As their magnetic attraction grows, will Cameron sacrifice Asilia's happiness for the sake of vengeance?

Can Asilia forgive the deception once she learns Cameron's true motivations?

Or will revelations about their intertwined pasts force the star-crossed lovers apart when they need each other most?

Join Mihwa's Den of TMI on FB for exclusive content:
https://www.facebook.com/groups/2110002726016346/

IG:
https://www.instagram.com/mihwawrites

Newsletter:
www.mihwawrites.com

Made in the USA
Monee, IL
19 May 2024